Fearless

Erin O'Reilly

Affinity E-Book Press NZ LTD

Fearless

Copyright © Erin O'Reilly 2011

Affinity E-Book Press NZ Ltd.
Canterbury, New Zealand

All rights reserved.

ISBN: 978-0-9876517-1-6

This is a work of fiction. Names, character, places, and incidents are the product of the author's imagination or are used fictitiously and any resemblance to actual persons living or dead, businesses, companies, events, or locales is entirely coincidental.

Other than actual historical persons, who are portrayed according to my interpretation and understanding, all other characters appearing in this work are fictitious. Any dialogue attributed to a deceased historical person(s) is fiction and not an actual conversation.

Executive Editor: Gail Robinson
Associate Editor: Nancy Kaufmann
Cover Design: Valerie Hayken

Visit our website at http://affinityebooks.com
Visit cover design artist at: http://www.valeriehayken.com/

Acknowledgments

This book would never have made it to this stage if it weren't for the support and encouragement of those who kept prodding me to continue writing.

Julie, as always, you were there when I couldn't find my way in this story. You listened and let me discuss my sometimes bizarre ideas until there was a vision of where to go next. Thank you.

Nancy, how incredibly fortunate I am that you cared enough about *Fearless* to tell me where the story needed a bit of a rewrite to make the storyline flow without the *HUH?* factor. Thank you.

For the women of the Sapphic Reading Group book club of Austin, Texas, who have always graciously given me their support. Thank you.

Gail, Wendy, Ann, and Yvette thank you for your support, input, and generosity for it kept me going when I wasn't certain that *Fearless* would see the light of day.

Thank you my friend S. Anne Gardner for helping me with the French translations.

Henriette, I appreciate you taking time to help me with the German translations. Thank you.

Valerie Hayken, thank you for the fabulous cover that brought *Fearless* to life..

Finally, thank you to my publisher, Affinity E-Book Press NZ LTD, for believing in *Fearless* and taking a chance on it in both eBook and printed versions.

Dedication

For the women who were the brave pioneers that loved to fly and became magnificent role models for generations of girls who discovered that there is no boundary to what they can do.

Any venture into the unknown, although fraught with doubt, will always succeed when you have love and encouragement as your guide.

Preface

As the German Army cut a swath through Europe, they captured all the countries they invaded, except the United Kingdom. The British came to the aid of the French when the Germans began their invasion of that country. Unable to stop the Germans in 1939, the government and military knew that an invasion of Britain was inevitable.

Factories went into full swing in the manufacturing of airplanes and war armaments for the coming battle. It became evident early on that the Royal Air Force was wasting resources by having their pilots ferry planes from the factories to various air fields. As the need for more pilots and planes escalated, the Air Transport Auxiliary was formed hiring pilots, who could not meet the strict standards of the RAF. The pilots of the ATA were highly qualified to fly planes, but were, in some instances, too old to fly or too infirmed. Some were missing limbs and several only had one eye. This led to the ATA pilots being referred to as *Ancient and Tattered Airmen*. As the need for more planes grew, the number of pilots in the ATA grew, including eight women, who joined in January of 1940.

Often the pilots would have to fly in wet, changeable weather without radios or instrument training in what became a war zone. They also faced danger from the UK— barrage balloons flown over main cities as a deterrent to enemy aircraft—anti-aircraft batteries with over anxious troops that would occasionally fire on the UK planes.

The role of the women pilots was to expediently deliver airplanes, return to their command as rapidly as possible, and then do it all over again. Initially, the women pilots were instructed to fly as close to land as possible so that the troops would recognize them and not fire. They flew only Tiger Moths, biplanes with open cockpits requiring them to take blankets to stay warm in the frigid temperatures of altitude. Most of the aircraft they flew had no instrument capability and more often than not, they had to fly *by the seat of their pants* since there was little time to familiarize themselves with the aircraft that they flew. ATA pilots had small notebooks or index cards that they strapped to their legs that contained notes about the planes they flew and would share that information with each other. Often the only way they gained knowledge about an aircraft they had not seen or flown before was through those notes.

The women pilots had to fly in all weather conditions, often relying on landmarks to find their way to an airfield. They were required to fly with a parachute and would have dingy drills to acquaint them with emergency procedures over water.

Eventually, these pilots graduated from the Tiger Moths to Spitfires and by the end of the war, most were certified to fly all types of aircraft.

It was the brave women fliers of the ATA that helped the Allied Forces eventually defeat the Germans in their quest to conquer all of Europe.

The following *fictional* story is about the women of the ATA, who fearlessly took to the skies over the United Kingdom during World War II.

Prologue

January 1941
Hatfield Ferry Pool No. 5
Southampton, England

The sound of clacking heels on the linoleum floor made all those in the briefing room look up as Dorothy Clarke, who was the Commanding Officer of the Hatfield Ferry Pool No. 5 of the Air Transport Auxiliary, made her way to the lectern. Her appearance—dainty, one might say—belied her tougher than nails attitude about her job and the women who served under her. As she stood at the lectern, her eyes gazed at her *girls*; the women who ferried aircraft between factories and airfields, freeing up male pilots so they could fight the Germans. With lips firmly set in a grim expression, her gray eyes stared at the paper in front of her before she cleared her throat to speak.

"Ladies, can we please have quiet?" she said in a strong yet soft voice. With all eyes riveted on her, she continued. "Last night we lost two of our fellow pilots…" Her voice caught and she briefly closed her eyes to regain her composure. "While on a routine flight to deliver Vickers Wellingtons to Plymouth Air Station, Jo Laughlin and Sarah Faulkner apparently encountered dense fog that suddenly rolled in from the Channel. It is speculated that they lost their bearings and found themselves somewhere over the Channel. Spotters on the Isle of Wight reported seeing an aircraft slam into the water at great speed," Dorothy swallowed hard then continued, "rescue efforts failed to recover a body or the aircraft. As for the second aircraft, there were no sightings of it…at least from our side."

As Dorothy spoke, the room was deathly quiet as all the women sat in stunned silence—their division had never lost a single plane or pilot. One woman, Meg O'Brien, began sobbing with deep gulps of despair. Soon the sounds of soft crying prevailed as the group of closely knit women digested the news.

"Ladies," Dorothy said in a louder, more forceful voice than she intended. "We still have a mission and neither Jo nor Sarah would want us to forget our goals." Holding up a piece of paper she said, "Here are your assignments for today."

In stilted motions, the pilots stood and walked toward their commander, each seemingly bewildered by what they had just heard. As they received their assignments for the day, they left the briefing room with a cloud of sorrow following them.

Meg, with moisture filled eyes, was the last woman to get her assignment. "Are you sure?" her shaky voice asked.

With compassion, Dorothy touched Meg's arm—the striking twenty-three year old woman towered over her slight five foot four frame. Meg had a trim body with red hair, green eyes, and a deep rich Irish accent. "Yes, dear, I'm afraid so."

"It's not right," sobbed Meg, "I should have been flyin', not Jo…or Sarah."

"That was my decision, Meg. I picked both Miss Laughlin and Miss Faulkner for that specific mission."

"Damn," Meg cursed. "It's not fair."

"Neither is war, Meg. Just like you, both Jo and Sarah knew the risks and just like you, they were willing to accept the danger because they loved flying." Dorothy drew in a deep breath. "They were lost doing what they loved."

Meg nodded. "Will you let us know if you get any more information?"

"Of course." Dorothy watched the woman leave before she allowed the grief she'd been holding in to take hold. After a few minutes, she composed herself and headed for her office—the war was still raging.

Just as she stepped outside the door, Dorothy saw the ATA commander and momentarily froze in place before glancing at her watch. *Commander Gower must have left headquarters before dawn to be there now.*

"Have you heard anything more?"

Commander Gower lightly rested a hand on Dorothy's shoulder. "Let's go inside."

With the sound of the door closing behind her, Dorothy turned and looked at the woman who had been instrumental in ensuring women pilots would have a role in the war effort by ferrying planes throughout Britain. "It is bad news, isn't it?"

In the softest of voices, Commander Gower said, "Except for the report of seeing something go down in the Channel—we are not even sure that it was a plane—we have no concrete information on either Laughlin or Faulkner." The commander's eyes kept steady on Dorothy's face for any sign she might know something about the crash—she saw none. "At the moment I am considering them as missing and nothing more." She gathered her thoughts and continued. "I chose both women because of their experience and flying abilities. Laughlin has a good head on her shoulders, as does Faulkner. Until we have information that tells us otherwise, I am keeping them both on active status." Commander Gower shrugged slightly. "The more likely possibility, they were shot down

Dorothy closed her eyes. "Yes, I thought that too." Dorothy said. "If any of my pilots could survive a crash, it is those two women."

Commander Gower nodded. "I cannot justify using resources that are stretched tight to search for them…I would like your group to do a search while they are on their missions today. I would also like to speak to them before I go."

"Of course. Thank you for your time, Commander Gower."

*

The barrack's rest room, which was what the RAF called the large room where the women pilots gathered, was abuzz with soft voices, all discussing the same topic— the loss of two of their ranks. The entire group, save Meg O'Brien, from the briefing stood in a loose cluster, none in a hurry to take on the day's assignment.

Bess Potter, a good looking, slight woman with light brown hair from Essington, England, wiped an errant tear away before she said, "I can't believe it. Just yesterday Sarah was telling me about how much she loved flying."

With her thick Chilean accent Camila Calvo, who had just returned from a flight, added, "She told me how happy she was. Her fiancé was coming back from the war."

Brenda Hiller, one of two Australian pilots at Hatfield, nodded as a grim look crossed her face. "No doubt about it, mates, they were both bonzer women," her strained voice said. "Sarah is the reason I'm here," she added with great sadness.

Midge Reister, a lanky blonde, who looked more like a fashion model than a pilot, added, "I remember barnstorming with Jo all around Texas and Oklahoma." Her eyes scanned the group. "Of course, you already know that.

When Meg O'Brien came through the door and joined the periphery of the group, everyone looked in her direction.

Beverly Maddox, an American standing next to Meg, softly asked, "How's it going?"

Meg nodded before she lifted her head to reveal red rimmed eyes. "Right shattered," she whispered in her rich Irish brogue. "I can't believe she's gone."

Midge let out a sarcastic chuckle. "Save the sentiment, Meg. No one cares about your tears."

Meg balled her fingers as her green eyes narrowed and she moved aggressively toward the woman.

Not allowing Meg to intimidate her, Midge growled. "Jo is *my* friend, not *yours*. You were only a convenient bedmate for her. She loved *me* and wanted to be with *me*."

Meg let her Irish temper surface. "She couldn't get far enough away from you, Midge," she cried as her open hand met the blonde's cheek."

Holding her cheek, Midge advanced on Meg with a scowl.

Millicent Smyth-Armstrong, who was married to a lowly member of British royalty, stepped in between the women. "I have no love for the Irish but the brashness of you Yanks is too much. Jo and Meg shared a room. If something else was going on, it is none of *our* business," she said in a soft tone. "We all care about both Jo and Sarah." She focused her soft brown eyes on Midge. "Your remarks are uncalled for, Miss Reister." Millicent lifted her arm and pulled Meg close. "Just ignore her, my dear...."

At that moment, the door opened and Dorothy Clarke, along with Commander Gower, entered the room and all went quiet.

"Ladies, Commander Gower has requested that you take some time today as you start your missions and fly over the area where Sarah and Jo flew last night. Keep your eyes open for wreckage, debris or any other signs of a plane crash."

A low rumble of voices filled the room.

Commander Gower held up her hand. "Right now our resources are running thin and I, along with the RAF, can't justify an intensive search. It is up to you to look for your fellow pilots." Her eyes scanned their faces. "Can you do that?" When everyone nodded, she said, "Right, now it is time to get busy. Fly safe, ladies."

Once the two women left, the senior pilot, Shannon Brannigan from Galway, Ireland, cleared her throat. "I can remember when you all first got here and how quiet and scared you were. You have turned into first rate pilots and now we must do our part in findin' our lost pilots and friends."

"By Jove, we will." Bess Potter commented as she ran her fingers through her light brown hair. "I couldn't believe I was actually accepted into the program and when I got here and saw all of you speaking so many different languages, I didn't know if I'd fit in." A slow smile filtered onto Bess's face illuminating her hazel eyes. "It was Jo who first spoke to me. I had never heard an American accent before that," With a self-effacing chuckle she added, "Except in the cinema. I remember thinking how great her voice sounded in real life."

"She was a fair dinkum woman to me, too." Brenda looked around at the blank looks. "Blimey, mates, you've been around me long enough to catch onto my slang. It means *excellent*." For a brief moment, a smile curved her lips.

A ripple of laughter flowed through the group.

"Sarah always understood me," Brenda said with a somber expression.

"Aye, lassie, that's because you are roommates and she didn't have a choice," Mara Nasmith said in her distinctive brogue. "She came ta me one day and asked if I understood what you meant. I remember laughing and saying *no*." Mara's lips formed a tight line. "She can't be gone."

It wasn't long before everyone added their memories of their two fallen comrades.

When the door opened again, a bald Reginald Applewhite, the senior group leader, entered and everyone went silent. "Ladies, you have missions to perform," his tone slightly pompous, though he was nothing of the sort. "You accomplish nothing with tears." He then turned and left the building.

Meg broke the silence when she said, "Too bad the door didn't hit him in the arse." Everyone laughed as she pulled out a small notebook from her jacket. "I'm flying a Hawker Typhoon today. Anything I should look out for?"

"Be careful not to dive…I had a hard time controlling it," Bess offered. "I've even heard of the tail section falling off in a dive."

Meg nodded and left the group—she didn't want them to see how devastating Jo's absence was to her. No one could ever know what Jo meant to her.

That day as each of the pilots flew, they kept their eyes peeled on the ground, hoping against all odds to find their friends and bring them back home.

Chapter One

September, 2, 1939
Near the Cliffs of Moher, Ireland

Meg O'Brien's hair looked like a wind sock as it flew in the stiff breeze as she stood in rich, green grass near the edge of the Cliffs of Moher. With her hand shading her eyes, she scanned the morning sky for the first glint of the sun pinging off the body of the plane flown by her uncle, Shamus O'Malley. When her uncle first took her into the skies years earlier, she began begging him to teach her how to fly. Once Shamus convinced Meg's mother that her daughter would be safe, she became airborne.

She caught sight of the yellow wings of the Avro 621 Tutor bi-plane, turned and began running through the calf high grass toward the sod and grass landing strip. As the plane glided past her, she waved madly and picked up the pace. Soon she was standing next to the plane, waiting for Shamus to climb out of the pilot's seat.

When Meg saw a leg slide out of the plane and step on the wing, she gave the man her brightest smile. "Did you get it?" she asked eagerly.

Shaking his head and chuckling softly, Shamus said, "Hold on now, Lass, let me get me feet on the ground."

Shamus O'Malley, a flight instructor for the Royal Air Force of the United Kingdom, was a big man and Meg was always amazed that he could fit in the crammed cockpit. She watched as his bulk finally made it to the ground and her heart soared with love for him. He had taken her under his wing after the tragic death of her father. Her eyes focused on the hand that reached inside of his leather jacket and pulled out a folded magazine.

"It's six months old," he said as he handed her a copy of *The Sportsman Pilot*. "The Yank I got it off of also gave me this," he said plucking another folded paper from his inside pocket.

Meg's face filled with more excitement, if that was at all possible. "It's about barnstormin'," Meg said with her eyes wide and round like an owl's. She quickly flipped through the pages and stopped when she saw a plane flying upside down only inches from the ground. "Look" she exclaimed. "Can this really be done?"

Shamus let out a hearty laugh. "Of course it can, Lass, can't ya see it bein' done?" He grinned. "When you read about that particular pilot, you will find it's a woman flyin' that plane."

Meg looked back at the picture again. "Flyin' upside down so close to the ground. Oh, the wonder of it all." She looked at her uncle and moved close so she could embrace him before they started toward her mother's pub. As they walked, she smiled, remembering the same twinkle in his light blue eyes two years earlier…

"What?" Meg asked as she looked at the man she dearly loved.

"Well," he said reaching inside his jacket, "Don't ya remember askin' me about the form for a pilot's license?"His eyes twinkled.

"That I did," answered Meg.

"Well, Margaret Mary O'Brien, here it is."

"But I haven't soloed yet," Meg said softly. "Besides, me mum will never let me…it's way too modern for her likin'. She told me yesterday that I had ta get my head out of the clouds and think about marriage, with a husband and babies ta look after."

Shamus slung his arm around Meg's broad shoulder. "First you solo…then we'll tackle your mum."

"When?"

"What about right now?"

Meg clutched at her heart. "Really? Are you sure I'm ready?"

Shamus looked at her and cocked his head. "It should be you, Lass, who knows if you're ready or not."

Squaring her shoulders, Meg said, "I'm ready."

Nodding, Shamus pulled out a white silk scarf and handed it to her. "Then get your goggles and helmet and I'll speak ta your mum and let her know where you are."

With her hand going to her mouth, Meg gasped. "If you tell her I'm going up alone, she won't allow it."

Shamus patted her on the shoulder. "You get your things and I will take care of your mum. Is she in the pub?"

Meg nodded. "The last time I saw her she was tendin' bar." She watched as her uncle strode between the buildings and disappeared. Her family owned "O'Malley's," the small town's only pub—she had worked there ever since she was old enough to sweep the floors.

Thirty minutes later, Meg was sitting in the cockpit with her leather helmet and goggles in place over her eyes. With a flip of her white silk scarf, she started the engine and gave her uncle a little wave. Pulling the stick toward her, she maneuvered the plane out onto the grass runway. She swallowed nervously as she pushed the stick and the plane began its run. Then she pulled back and the plane began its ascent into the sky.

"I'm doin' it!" she thought as she and the plane became one, suspended in the air above houses, trees, and livestock. As she flew, she saw the pattern of stone walls that marked the boundaries to parcels of land. The lush green of the land—her Ireland—made her heart swell as she pulled the stick backwards and the plane shot upwards into the blue sky. This was where she had wanted to be ever since she saw a plane soaring above her when she was ten. She remembered that day vividly—April sixteenth, the eighth anniversary of her father's death. When she saw the bi-plane in the skies, she wondered if her father could talk to the person inside. "I'm here, Da, can you see me?" she asked as a tear trickled down her cheek. "I'm flyin'."

Once Meg had landed and watched as her uncle signed the pilot's application as her instructor, she floated back to her home to help her mum with supper—flying always made her euphoric. That feeling kept her smiling, all through the preparations for the evening meal.

"How I'd love ta go out and join a flyin' circus and do all those fancy loops and things," Meg enthused as she leafed through the magazine. Meg stopped her forward motion. "Have you ever seen such a thing, Uncle Shamus?"

A low chuckle emanated from deep within the older man. "Well now, I have." He laughed. "Even done a few of 'em meself."

"You have?" Meg squealed. "Will you teach me?"

Shamus, with a serious look shook his head. "I can just hear your mum if I taught you how to do loop-d-loops. You're twenty years old, Lass, and it is time for you ta think about settlin' down and not thinkin' of doing such dangerous things." He shrugged. "Ah, but 'tis a glorious thing ta be flyin' upside down."

Meg saw the familiar twinkle fill his eyes. "I think it would be splendid."

*

The kitchen was large, with a massive fireplace that at one time Meg's ancestors used for cooking. Above, a mantel held various pans and kettles. Now there was a large cast iron cook stove located across the room. Opposite the fireplace was a large hutch that held all the plates and serving dishes. In the center of the kitchen was a large wooden table covered with a blue checked tablecloth, along with two benches and chairs at the ends.

Meg's four brothers and uncle sat talking around the table, as she and her sister-in-law, Matthew's wife, Mary Kate, helped her mother place the food and drinks in front of them. When she put a bowl of potatoes on the table, her older brother, Matthew, said, "Sean Sullivan is askin' if he can court you." He eyed his sister. "I told him he'd be a welcome addition ta our family.

Meg glared at her brother. "You're not Da and you have no business tellin' him that. It's me who will decide who I'll marry," she said slamming a bowl of vegetables on the table hard.

Her other three brothers, Mark, Patrick and John, along with her mother, uncle and Mary Kate, quickly tucked into their food—when Meg was on a tear, no one was safe.

"Don't be such a gack."

"Matthew," his mother cautioned while glaring at him. "You don't use that kind of language in my house!"

"Sorry, Mum," Matthew said softly before he turned back to his sister.

Meg looked at him and smirked.

Matthew's eyes narrowed. "As the oldest man in this family, it was my responsibility ta take up for Da when he passed. I need ta see that you are married," he said in a tight voice. "You're almost twenty-one, well past the age when you should have wed. You should count your blessin's that Sean has taken notice of you. You have your head up in the clouds and it's time you came down ta earth and marry. You need ta have children and a husband ta look after you. Look at Mary Kate, she is seventeen, and about ta have my baby…that is her role and it is yours, too."

Green eyes tinged with anger fixed on Matthew's equally green eyes. "What about Uncle Shamus? As far as I'm concerned, he's the head of this family."

"He's an O'Malley, not an O'Brien," Matthew said sharply. "I *am* the one who decides who courts you. Sean is a good man and will provide well for you."

"You will *not* tell me what ta do. I'm not ready ta marry…I might never be!" She tried to suck in a calming breath—it didn't help. "I want ta fly and maybe go ta Glasgow and get a job."

"That's the most ridiculous thing I've ever heard." Matthew laughed as he speared a potato with his fork. "Have you not been listenin' now, Margaret? You are not going anywhere. You are marryin' Sean Sullivan." He began chewing and turned his attention to his uncle. "Are those Brits you're training any good?"

"You just keep talkin' like that Matthew and the O'Brien family might be havin' a lovely wake come tamorrow." Meg stomped back to the cook stove knowing that she would never marry Sean Sullivan and no one was ever going to make her. Matthew would not change his mind and Sean Sullivan would come around as her suitor. Meg's eyes captured Shamus's blue ones and they blinked, then he shrugged and nodded toward his jacket on a hook by the door.

We'll see about that she thought before she picked up a platter of mutton.

"Those Tan's talk funny…not ta mention the Yanks," Shamus said laughing, hoping to alleviate the tension around the table. He opened his mouth to share the latest rumor he heard but then opted to tell his niece in private. If he were to mention the women's auxiliary, he was certain another contentious discussion would take place.

John, at sixteen, was the youngest sibling and just the right age to want to flex his male prowess. "Is it true that Chamberlain is talkin' about war against Germany?"

"Chamberlain gave the Germans an ultimatum ta get out of Poland in two days. Now it's up ta them and it doesn't look like they'll leave. Sadly, war is inevitable. I expect any day now ta hear we are at war." He shook his head and shrugged. "The flow of young men lookin' ta fly is non-stop and the factories have geared up ta get more aircraft ta the pilots."

"I'm goin' ta join," John said with the exuberance of youth."

Meg's mother, Alannah, put her hand over her mouth and gasped. "No…you are too young ta go ta war," she whispered.

"Your Mum is right," said Shamus. "They won't even talk ta you unless you're older. Besides, de Valera said we'd be neutral."

Alannah crossed herself and softly said, "Thanks be ta God and our president."

John's face scrunched in disappointment, with a touch of anger that added to the look. "It's not fair."

"Life's not fair," Shamus said as he ruffled his nephew's hair. "Take your time; you'll be old before you know it."

"Oh, dear Lord." Alannah quickly crossed herself again and looking at her son. "Thank you, Mary, for your blessings."

*

Once supper was over and the dishes cleared, Meg and her mother stood silently side by side doing the dishes. Not able to stand it any longer, Meg said, "I don't want ta marry."

Alannah dropped the dishrag into the soapy water and looked at her daughter. "Of course you do, child. That is what women do. What else is there but church, a husband, and children?"

Meg wiped a plate hard. "Surely there is more ta life than gettin' married and havin' babies. I want ta see the world and be free ta laugh…having a husband…well, I haven't seen too many women who marry laugh much."

"Are you daft, child?" Alannah asked as she dipped her hand into the water. "No self respectin' woman doesn't want a family," she said as she began scrubbing a pot. "It's that flyin' that's got you thinkin' crazy things."

"No, flyin' has nothing ta do with it, Mum," Meg said harsher than she wanted. "Why do I have ta be like everyone else? Can't I just be me?"

"Margaret, you will do exactly as you're expected ta do. Now go and get yourself in a pretty dress before Sean gets here!"

Meg scrunched up her face and opened her mouth.

Alannah held up her finger and narrowed her eyes. "No more."

With her teeth gritted, green eyes darkened to emerald and her hair flying behind her, Meg stomped out of the room. "It's not fair," she grumbled as she climbed the stairs. "I don't even like Sean Sullivan. He stinks like the pigs he raises and slaughters. Matthew's probably marryin' me off ta him so we don't have ta eat mutton all the time."

When she got to the top of the staircase, she saw her uncle coming out of his room and she ran to him as the tears she was holding back finally broke through.

"What's this? Tears?" Shamus wrapped his big arms around his niece. "Why the tears, Lass?"

"I don't want ta marry Sean Sullivan or anyone else," sobbed Meg. "Why do I have ta marry anyone?"

Shamus patted Meg's shoulders. "There now, Lass, all is not lost. Bide your time. I'm sure somethin' else will come along."

"Just go along pretendin' I will marry that man? Matthew won't stop until he marries me off ta that pig farmer."

With a step backward, Shamus let go of Meg and smiled softly. "Once the war breaks out everything will change."

"Not for me," Meg said belligerently. "I'll still have ta marry that man and have babies…that won't change. That's the life me brother has chosen for me."

"Ah, but it will, Lass. It happened during the last war and it will happen now." He pulled Meg close. "Give it time. I need ta go back first thing in the mornin'…but when I come back we will talk more about what your choices are."

Meg squeezed him close then let go when she hear her mum calling her.

"Meg, are you ready? Sean is here."

"I'll be right there," Meg said as she opened her bedroom door. "I don't want ta marry anyone," she whispered as she closed the door.

Shamus shook his head as he continued toward the stairs.

*

The next day after waving goodbye to her uncle, Meg opened the newspaper and read: *Great Britain Declares War On Germany*. A cold shiver ran down her spine as she recalled her uncle's words just before he left. *"War changes the whole scenery of life for everyone involved. Stay close to home, Lass,"* he told her in an ominous voice.

Clearing the tables at the pub from the night before, Meg looked at her mother, who was wiping down the big oak bar. "Great Britain declared war on Germany."

Alannah looked up from her task. "Makes no difference ta us. You heard Shamus, Ireland is neutral."

"I read that many of our lads are going ta sign up with the Brits."

With a grim expression, Alannah said, "None of me boys will be goin' off ta fight for them Tans. They are needed right here, helpin' me."

"Mum, have you read about what the Germans did ta Poland? How can we just sit by and do nothin'?"

"Hush, Margaret. I'll have none of that talkin'. You sound like those *pissheads* that come in here at night…it's the Guinness doin' all the' loud talking about nothin'." Her eyes narrowed as she looked at her daughter. "No decent man will want you if you talk like that."

Meg covered her mouth to hide the grin that threatened with her mother's slang for drunks. "It doesn't matter, since I don't want a man."

Alannah sucked in a deep breath. "You better tame your ways, daughter…marriage, a home, and wee ones is what the church teaches." She glared at Meg. "Why were you so rude ta Sean last night? He's you're only hope, child."

Meg's back stiffened. "He is not me only hope! He stinks like pigs."

"That's the smell of an honest day's work."

With her hands resting on her hips, Meg pulled a face of disgust. "Still smells like pig. I don't care what Matthew says, I'll not be marryin' the man."

Green eyes, the same as Meg's, fixed on her. "You'll marry Sean Sullivan and I'll say no other word ta you. Now, get busy and finish. There's work ta be done."

Meg looked at her mother and was about to retort when a man walked into the pub. Meg studied the woman behind the bar—her mother—life had not been kind to her. Widowed shortly after her last child, John, she bore the brunt of taking care of the pub that had been in her family for three generations. Her brother, Shamus O'Malley, had helped the best he could—he lost his wife and two children to influenza and it was difficult for him to cope with his sister's raucous children.

Although she was only forty-five, Alannah's face, etched with the deep grooves that spoke volumes about her hard life, never seemed to smile. She was a sturdy woman who went through her daily life with the mechanics of a routine that varied little. Her green eyes had lost their luster and her lips were, more often than not, in a tight line of resolve.

Meg had always thought that her mother's lack of affection was because she did not love her children. A conversation she had with her uncle earlier in the year made her understand that it was far more than lack of love. The death of her husband, followed closely by her brother losing his entire family, made Alannah pull away not only from her children, but also from any kind of personal relationship. *Tis easier ta close your heart than risk losin' all that is dear ta you,* her uncle told her. *Your mum loves you deeply. She just cannot show it.*

As she looked around the dark pub and listened to her mother's lackluster conversation with a regular, she bit on the inside of her cheek. She could not comprehend how her mum could shut her heart off from the children she bore. *I'd never do that.* She wanted desperately to distance herself from the restrictive life that she feared she was destined to live.

*

The quiet of the parlor was broken only by the ticking grandfather clock. Meg sat in one chair while Sean Sullivan sat in another. It had been several months since the Commonwealth declared war and in that time, Sean became a fixture around the dinner table and in Meg's life. The variety of meats Sean provided ingratiated him to all family members except Meg. It wasn't that she didn't like the man. He was kind and generous to her and her family. She simply was not interested in marrying any man, especially one who always bore the stench of the animals he tended.

"It's turnin' colder," Sean said as he lifted his eyes from his hands to take in Meg.

With her eyebrows knitting, Meg couldn't help her retort. "It's October, Mr. Sullivan, what did you expect?"

Sean's face went red and his brown eyes looked past the woman he was courting to the window behind her. "Did ya hear that Will Byrne and Patty Donohue left ta go fight with the Brits?" he asked.

"I don't understand why Ireland has ta be neutral," Meg said in a flat voice.

"Why shouldn't we?" Sean said with conviction. "We fought hard ta rid ourselves of British rule. Why would we want ta invite them back in?"

Meg looked at the man curiously with her head tilted and her forehead deeply furrowed before she fixed him with a stern gaze. "The Brits are not our enemy, Mr. Sullivan," she stated in anger. "Who will defend us if the Germans decide ta invade Ireland? Northern Ireland has British protection…what do we have?"

"I didn't mean…," Sean stammered before Meg interrupted.

"Do you know how ta read, Mr. Sullivan, or do you pick up most of your information from your pigs?"

Indignant, Sean said, "Of course I know how ta read."

"Have you read a newspaper lately, Mr. Sullivan?"

Sean's sheepish look answered the question.

Meg stood up and Sean immediately followed her.

"I'm tired, Mr. Sullivan, so I'll be sayin' good night." With that, she turned, walked toward the staircase, and disappeared up the steps.

*

It wasn't until late December that Shamus finally returned to his home town. His slouched shoulders and grim expression reflected the toll taken by months of training pilots.

Meg was the first to hear the drone of the airplane engine and ran out into the cold winter snow to greet him. She waited impatiently as the plane touched down and skidded slightly on the snow covered landing area. When he finally climbed out of the aircraft, Meg ran to him and hugged him close.

Speaking loud enough for her uncle to hear through his leather helmet, she cried, "You're home. I've missed you so much."

"As I have you, Lass." The tiredness and strain in his voice was unmistakable. He looked at her and shook his head. "Where's your coat?"

Meg laughed. "When I heard the engines, I had ta run out ta see you."

Shamus took off his flight jacket and offered it to Meg.

"No, you keep it. I know how cold it is up there."

As they walked toward the pub, Meg clung to his arm. "Will you be here tamorrow for Christmas?"

"That I will," he said with a happier note to his voice. "Once I'm settled, I have some news for you."

Meg stopped dead in her tracks, stopping Shamus's forward progress too. "Tell me now. Please. I know that once inside we won't have much of a chance ta talk…especially about flying."

"I've been transferred ta an airbase closer ta London," Shamus said as he rubbed his big hand over his face.

Meg's eyes widened. "Isn't that more dangerous?"

Shamus smiled. "Not for an old rascal like me." He winked then continued, "Have you heard of the ATA?"

"Sure, the Air Transport Auxiliary in England. I read an article about it…run by a woman, right?"

"Aye, Pauline Gower…but there is a man in charge of her. Do you know what they do?"

Meg frowned. "Yeah, they transport mail and medical supplies."

With a twinkle in his otherwise lackluster eyes, Shamus said, "Not any more. Commander Gower has opened a new branch—the Women's Section of the ATA. She just hired eight women pilots to transport airplanes ta bases throughout the British Isles."

With disappointment, Meg said, "Guess I missed out on that one."

Shamus wrapped his arm around his niece and began walking toward the pub. "You're shivering. We need ta get you inside where it is warm."

Meg just shrugged. "I'm ok."

Again, the twinkle entered Shamus's eyes. "Word is she'll be hiring more."

Meg's eyes widened into saucers. "Do I qualify?"

"Everyone who applies has ta prove their ability as a pilot, Lass." He reached out and opened the door to the kitchen. "I don't think that will be a problem for you."

With a bright smile, Meg said, "I'm so glad you are here for Christmas…" Her words cut off as her mother and brothers rushed to the door to welcome the returning man.

That evening after they ate, Meg and her mother cleared the table and did the dishes before they placed a loaf of bread filled with caraway seeds and raisins, along with a pitcher of milk, on the table. Then they added a candle, which they lit before unlatching the door so that Mary and Joseph, along with weary travelers, knew they were welcome.

*

Christmas morning brought the news of the Irish Republican Army's actions of the night before when they raided the Regular Irish Army's ammunition magazine fort in Dublin's Phoenix Park. "Why are we fightin' two wars?" Shamus asked. "I know we are neutral but many of our young lads are out there fightin' for the Brits."

"Maybe they took the ammunition so they could go and fight," Matthew offered.

"Enough of war talk," Alannah said as she smoothed her skirt. "It is time for church."

After the Christmas Mass, the entire family trudged to the cemetery to visit the graves of those who had passed. They tidied the grave area and they laid fresh holly on the headstones. Once they neared their home, they saw the candle in the window that greeted their return.

The Christmas feast consisted of rich meats and vegetables, along with cakes and puddings. For the family, the Christmas celebration lasted until the sixth of January— the Epiphany—by daily visits to church and remembering that it was Christ's birthday they were celebrating.

The day after Christmas, Shamus and his niece left the house for a walk.

Shamus put an arm around his niece's shoulders. "I've talked ta my superiors and they approved your working with me in training pilots. If you are going ta get into the

ATA, you need ta increase your flying hours." He lifted one shoulder. "That, along with aiding me in instructing new pilots, will also give you an advantage when you apply."

Meg considered his words as she kept walking. Once they had gone about a mile in quiet reflection, she asked, "Do you think Mum will let me go?"

Shamus shook his head. "I doubt she will be happy but I think she will let you go."

"What about Matthew?"

After a few more steps, Shamus stopped and turned toward his niece. "It is best you not tell him…let your mum do that. I will talk ta her when we get back and then it will be up ta you ta talk with her. It will not be easy for her ta let you go, so you must convince her that you will be safe and out of harm's way." He began walking back toward the house with Meg by his side. "Now that there is a grandchild, it will be easier for her ta let go. I've seen how she dotes on that little baby…it will lessen the sting of your leavin'."

*

Alannah sat quietly as she digested her daughter's words. To Meg she looked weary and much older than her years. "I need ta do this, Mum."

"What about Sean?"

"The only one who thinks I will marry him is Matthew. I told Sean I'm not interested in marriage and he needs ta find a woman who cares for him—I don't—not even a wee bit." She couldn't recall ever seeing her mother cry but now she saw moisture surround and fill her eyes. "I will come back often and Shamus will be there if I need help." She touched her mother's hand. "Shamus fixed it so I can work with him…I won't be anywhere near the fightin'."

With tears streaming down her cheeks, Alannah reached out to her daughter. "What will I do without you?"

"You have Mary Kate… three in the kitchen is too much. She needs ta feel like she's a part of the family, especially now with little Gabrielle."

The child in question picked that moment to convey that she was upset. Meg went to the nearby cradle and picked up the small girl with bright red hair. "She even has me hair, Mum, it will be like havin' me as a baby all over again."

Alannah lifted a hand to wave away the comment. "You were a handful from the moment you were born. Head full of red hair and a bellowin' cry I was sure they could hear a mile away. You'll not be wishin' that on me granddaughter, will you?"

Once Meg changed the baby's nappy, she walked to her mother and handed her Gabrielle. "She does have me coloring, Mum, but luckily not the bellow."

Alannah reached out and took Meg's hand. "You promise ta write regularly?"

Meg nodded.

"When will you leave?"

"When Shamus comes back for me at the end of January."

"Why not take the train? It has served people well long before that flyin' contraption came along."

Meg bent down and kissed her mother's forehead. "I love you, Mum," she said, surprised at her words. Her mother was not one for words of affection but now seemed the time for Meg to let her know how she felt. "I will come back."

With a push of her feet, Alannah began to rock her granddaughter. "Make sure you do then.

*

As the training bi-plane circled the runway before lining up to land at Attlebridge Station, Meg couldn't believe her eyes. Never had she seen so many aircraft in one place. Truth was that she had only seen one parked plane in all the flights she made. Now, looking down on the massive air station with all the planes lined neatly along the runway, she felt intimidated for the first time in her life. The first time she got in a plane didn't faze her—it felt right—as did the first time she flew.

The wheels touched down and the plane rolled along as her uncle guided it to a stop. "Well, here you are, Lass."

"This is it…really it?"

"Aye," Shamus said as she began to climb out of the plane. "Get your things together now and I'll show you where you will be stayin'."

A momentary panic filled Meg. "Won't I be livin' with you?"

The man shook his head. "No, Lass, it wouldn't look right."

"But…"

"It'll be all right. You'll be stayin' with the women who work on the planes." He smiled. "They're nice women, nothin' ta be afraid of."

"But…"

Shamus laughed and picked up Meg's satchel. "Come along now and I'll introduce you."

With hesitant steps, Meg followed her uncle, unsure of what the future would hold for her. *But it's a lot better than bein' married ta Sean Sullivan.* She smiled and skipped to catch up to her uncle. "Yes," she said as she strolled by Shamus's side, "it's goin' ta be quite the adventure."

Shamus stopped outside a hangar and held his hand up. "You stay put. I'll be right back."

Meg was too excited to stand still so she turned completely around while taking in all the sights and sounds of the airfield. She noted the tarmac, which was, for her, the first landing on something other than grass and dirt. Her eyes took in all the different airplanes lined up in neat rows at the side of the runway—she could only hope that someday she'd fly one of them.

The sound of an airplane engine starting made her turn and watch as the sleek silver plane taxied in a path that put it right in front of her. With unwavering eyes, she watched as it sat at the end of the runway before running full throttle down the tarmac and lifting into the sky. Meg could feel her heart flutter as she watched until she could no longer see the craft.

"Quite a marvel ta behold, isn't it, Lass," Shamus said from behind Meg.

"Aye, it is." Meg turned to her uncle and saw a woman, dressed in coveralls. She was slightly shorter than Meg was, with pale blonde hair and eyes that were so clear blue that they were mesmerizing. Holding out her hand, she said, "Hello, I'm Margaret O'Brien…my friends call me Meg."

"So you're the girl this man keeps talking about," the woman said with a smile. "I'm Penelope Burns-Jones."

"Lass, Penny here is the best engine mechanic, bar none."

Meg cocked one eyebrow and clutched at her heart. "You mean I'm not? I'm shattered." An impish smile crossed her face. "It is good ta put a face to the name."

"Likewise," Penny said. "You will be sharing a room with me and two others over there," she pointed to a long two story building, "We are all a friendly group and have been looking forward to your arrival." She nodded at Shamus. "He tells me you're one hell of a pilot and we need to get you more hours before you apply to the ATA."

Meg nodded before a broad smile crossed her face. "I can't believe I'm really here."

"We'd best get you settled so you can write your mum that you are safe," Shamus said as he picked up her bag. "Then I'll introduce you to the commander and the other pilots."

"Are you scared," Penny asked as they walked toward the barracks."

With a laugh of delight, Meg said, "I've been dreamin' of this all my life…there's nothin' ta be scared of."

*

Meg followed her uncle around like a puppy for three weeks, taking notes and observing his interactions with the recruits. She often smiled when she listened to Shamus's rich accent as he instructed the men, for he said the exact same thing to her on many occasions. For the most part, the other flying officers tolerated her presence and some even smiled when they saw her. She was acutely aware of the whispers concerning her trying to do *a man's job*. But with the war intensifying and the steady influx of male trainees, they begrudgingly began accepting her as someone who helped lighten the load of their heavy responsibility.

In March, when the Germans bombed the Royal Navy's base at Scapa Flow, the demand for the training of new pilots intensified. It was at that point that Meg became the first instructional person new recruits listened to. This relieved the flying instructors, such as her uncle, to concentrate solely on hands-on training. She would outline what was expected of each potential pilot, instruct them in the basics of flying, and then show them the cockpit while explaining what all the instruments were for.

As everyone else assigned to the air field, Meg found she only had time to eat and sleep when she was not with the new recruits. Occasionally she and her three roommates would have time to chat or share a meal but that was the limit of their interaction. In May, Meg excitedly opened a letter from the ATA—an acceptance letter. It was then that she left Attlebridge Station for White Waltham, where she would begin her training as a ferry pilot.

Chapter Two

Spring, 1939
West Texas, USA

Jo Laughlin saw the ground approaching and leveled the Curtiss JN-4D before she flipped a switch to let the pesticide spray on the cotton field below her. As she let the plane skim just over the field, her blue eyes sighted a landmark so she would know where she sprayed. Unlike other crop dusting businesses, Jo didn't have a person on the ground marking where she'd been so she had to rely on her landmarks. She was paid by the job, not the spray, and she was on a shoestring budget and couldn't afford to waste insecticide or gas. Boll weevils were a major threat to cotton and that gave Jo a steady income she hadn't experienced since she took over the crop dusting business from her father. Coming to the end of the field, she pulled back on the Curtis Jenny's stick. The bi-plane climbed straight up before it leveled out and Jo maneuvered it back into position for the next pass. Once the plane made the final pass, Jo pulled up on the lever that stopped the insecticide flow. She made the plane climb before she banked left and headed home.

The wheels of the Jenny touched the dirt runway behind the house that she and her two sisters shared. Her father, Richard, was a pilot in World War I. An injury in 1917 sent him home to his wife, Elizabeth, who lived with his parents on a cotton farm in West Texas. Josephine, his first born, came into the world in 1918, followed by Amy Sue two years later and Bonnie Mae in 1922. Elizabeth died in childbirth, along with a son, early in 1923. Richard's father passed three months later. He found himself responsible for three daughters and his mother, on a farm that just eked out a living to support them. His war injury left him with a severe limp that made farming all that much more difficult. Fed up with the daily rigors of farming, Richard came up with a plan to start a crop dusting business. In 1928, he found out he could buy a rebuilt Curtiss JN-4D, the plane he trained on, for the ridiculously low price of two hundred dollars.

Jo showed an interest in not only the plane but also flying when she was twelve and her father encouraged her interest by teaching her to fly. She took to it as a duck takes to water and by the time she was fifteen, she had her pilot's license. With a depression that seemed to have no end, Richard's crop dusting business dwindled until only those farmers who had cash crops that paid well could afford the luxury.

The Laughlin family was luckier than most during the Great Depression, for they had land that sustained them, making the family more or less self-sufficient. Every so often, a crop dusting job would come along and that would help the family to survive longer. Richard went back to farming, changing the cotton crop to soybeans, which always had the higher bids at auctions. When Richard's mother died in 1933, he fell into a deep depression and it was up to Jo to make sure there was food on the table, wood in the fireplace, and a roof over their heads. At the tender age of seventeen, Jo tried and failed to nurse her father back to health after he developed pneumonia. Once he passed away, she became the head of the household, trapped in an existence she neither wanted nor needed.

For two years, Jo struggled to keep her sisters and herself afloat. When the economy started to improve and more farmers returned to growing cash crops, the demand for crop dusting increased. Her income grew but it still wasn't enough to feel comfortable, so Jo supplemented that income with an aerial show and by offering rides in her airplane.

*

Jo scrambled out of the plane onto the wing then jumped down to the ground. She walked quickly to a small nearby shed, procured a step ladder, and returned to the plane before setting up the ladder near the plane's engine. She noticed a rumbling sound from the engine on her last pass over the cotton field—not a good sign. Cautious of the scorching exhaust pipes, her initial observation of the still hot engine yielded nothing significant but she knew by the sound that she'd have to investigate further once the engine cooled. With her eyes turning to the sun, she estimated that there was about two more hours of sunlight—not enough time to do a thorough inspection of the engine. She climbed down from the ladder and headed for the house.

As she put her hand on the doorknob, she cringed, knowing what awaited her inside. Her foot stepped onto the worn linoleum, as her eyes scanned the large kitchen—it was just as she left it. A black skillet still rested on the old cook stove, other pans cluttered the counter between the stove and the sink, which was full of dishes. A low growl escaped Jo's mouth as she moved further into the kitchen and saw the water collected on the floor around and under the old wooden icebox—the linoleum buckled more than it previously had.

"Amy Sue. Bonnie Mae. Get in here right now," she yelled. Her ears listened to the silence and her anger grew. "Now!"

A few minutes later, both her sisters appeared in the doorway to the kitchen.

With eyes blazing, she gritted her teeth together as she tried to calm her raging emotions. "I thought I told you to clean up the kitchen and start supper," she growled.

Amy Sue shrugged and Bonnie Mae looked at her feet.

Jo pointed to the sink. "Get over there and get busy." She stomped on the puddle of water causing droplets of water to fall on her sisters' bare legs. "And clean this up!"

The two girls, with blonde hair and blue eyes, had such an uncanny resemblance to each other that people often thought they were twins. They skulked to the sink and began their task.

"I don't know why we have to do this," Bonnie Mae whined.

In an instant, Jo was hovering at the young girl's shoulder. "Because I work all day so you don't have to," Jo said in a tight voice. "Maybe you'd like to go work and hoe cotton fields all day. I can arrange that," Jo offered. "I hear old man McCurdy is hiring field hands."

"That's not fair," Bonnie Mae cried. "We work in our fields already."

Jo rose to her full five foot eight inches and took a step closer to her sister. "Only when the weeds need hoeing and most of the time I have to come behind you and do it again."

"That's not fair," Amy Sue said from where she was wiping up the water around the icebox.

"Daddy never made us do that," Bonnie Sue added.

Jo moved so close to Bonnie Mae that her shoulder was touching the girl. "Well, Daddy isn't here and I'm in charge, so you best get this cleaned up and make supper." She let out a deep sigh. "I can't do it all," she whispered. "One day I might not be here. Then what would you do? I doubt either of you would survive."

"Aunt Gloria told us we could live with her any time we want," Amy Sue interjected.

Tired of the same old argument, Jo shook her head. "Is that what you want?" When neither sister answered, she said, "Fine. I'll arrange it. Until then, you still live under this roof and I expect you to carry your weight around here." With that, she moved away from her younger sister, walked past the kneeling Amy Sue and went into the sitting room, which was in disarray, too. "Sending them to live with Aunt Gloria is the best solution all around," she muttered as she went down the hall to her bedroom.

*

It had taken a week of going back and forth, but Jo had eventually moved all her sisters' belongings into the large farm house owned by their Aunt Gloria. The woman, considered a spinster by the community, lived alone and worked the land by herself. Occasionally, she would hire day laborers to help her out but for the most part, she kept to a solitary life. Her large home certainly was big enough for both Amy Sue and Bonnie Mae.

Jo had carried the final load into the house and deposited it in the hallway next to Amy Sue's bedroom. Her aunt, who stood leaning against a wall, gave her a curious look.

"You sure you don't want to stay here, too," the older woman asked.

Jo shook her head. "No, I've got to overhaul the plane's engine before I can work again. I won't have money coming in if I don't do it now."

"You could still live here and not out there all by your lonesome," Gloria said as she moved closer to her niece. "I'll worry about you."

"I'll be fine. Besides, you've lived here by yourself and done ok."

Gloria laughed. "I've got better coping skills with loneliness than you do, Jo."

Jo straightened her shoulders and brushed past the older woman. "I'll do just fine." She stopped and looked at Gloria. "You know they're lazy and you won't get a lick of work out of them."

This time Gloria's laugh was rich and full. "Come with me," Gloria said as she walked past Jo and entered the kitchen. Once Jo caught up and was standing next to her aunt, Gloria pointed out the window. "They just needed a little prodding."

As her eyes tracked outside, Jo saw both girls hanging clothes on a line. "How'd you get them to do that? I usually have to stand watch over them or they go off and do something else."

"Two nights ago after they ignored me and what I told them to do, I made supper—just enough for me—and ate it while they watched. I told them unless they got off their lazy asses and started to help, I wouldn't feed them." She winked at Jo. "Told 'em you and I had an agreement and you weren't going to take 'em back."

"Amazing," was all Jo could think of to say. She stuffed her hands into her jeans pockets and turned away. "I need to get going…that engine isn't going to fix itself."

"You always have a home here," Gloria said as she touched Jo's shoulder. "I could use the support when Rebecca comes for a visit next month."

It was common knowledge among the family and community that Gloria wasn't what they called *normal* in her relationships with women. But, most everyone genuinely liked Gloria—her *affliction* ignored.

"If you want, I can let them come back and live with me while she's here."

"That won't be necessary," Gloria said as she walked her niece to the door. "I asked them the first night they were here if it would be a problem for either of them." She laughed. "They looked at me like I had two heads and said *it wasn't a problem.* I suspect they don't know who Rebecca is or what she means to me."

Jo nodded as she tucked an errant strand of ebony hair behind an ear. "You're probably right but I think when they do realize, it won't make a difference." She studied her aunt's face. "Daddy taught us to be tolerant and accepting of all walks of life...and his love for you was always evident."

"Some days I miss him so much," Gloria mused. "He was so sad at the end, like life had taken all his happiness away." She sucked in a deep breath. "I wish I could have helped him."

"He's where he wanted to be...with mom and granddad and grandma," Jo said trying to hide the resentment in her voice.

Gloria slipped her arm around her niece's shoulders. "He loved you very much," she said. "What he did was out of love for you and your mom. A week before he passed he told me that he didn't want to burden you anymore."

Jo shrugged and moved away. "Yeah, I guess." She had heard it before and this time was no different—she doubted her father's sincerity. She gave her aunt one last quick look and put her hand on the doorknob. "It looks like it's fixin' to rain. I gotta get going so I can cover the plane."

Moving closer, Gloria engulfed Jo in a hug. "You've always got a home here," she whispered before letting go.

Jo nodded and went through the door.

*

It was a cold December as Jo stood leaning against a large stack of hay bales. The crowd milling around the field of a farm in southwest Oklahoma was larger than most Jo had encountered lately while barnstorming through Texas and Oklahoma. She and two other pilots would spend their weekends landing in the pasture of a farm with the requisite barn, and negotiating with the owner to use their field for an air show. Once taken care of, they'd take to the skies again. Handbills were dropped over the surrounding area, alerting everyone that there would be daring and death defying aerial stunts in the area, along with offering plane rides for anywhere from a nickel to twenty-five cents. Her group was small compared to some of the larger flying circuses but Jo preferred the smaller, close knit group.

Most residents of the small towns they visited over the last three years had never seen an airplane up close, much less ridden in one, so their appearance was a big event. Many times the towns would virtually close down so everyone could go to the *air show*. But now, in 1939, the novelty of what they did was not as acute.

Pilots had their own specialties, ranging from daring spins and dives to what Jo did—flying upside down only a few feet from the ground then going upwards in a tight spiral until she peeled off and plunged straight down. One of the other pilots, Dave Russell, walked the wing of his plane while it flew through the air. Another pilot, Midge Reister, along with Dave, would perform a stunt where Jo and Midge flew in a tight formation while Dave transferred from one plane to the other.

Jo loved the thrill of defying gravity and doing daring stunts and would have happily done that for the rest of her life. But, as there was talk of Britain going to war against the Germans, the crowds for their shows seemed to dwindle. The depression was finally showing signs of ending for good. With the government offering a federally funded pilot training program, the attraction for barnstormers and spectators alike began to diminish. This day, however, was different, for there was a good sized crowd that was eager to watch and ride.

As the last plane with a paying passenger landed, Jo pushed off the bales of hay and headed toward her friend Midge. "Hey, what was the take?"

Midge sorted through the bills. "Looks like we each get thirty-six dollars. Not bad for such a cold day."

"It's gas money," Jo said as she took the money. "With all the war talk going on, I wonder how much longer we can keep doing this."

With a friendly smile, Midge winked at Jo. "Well, there is an alternative."

Jo felt herself pulling away and taking a step backwards. She and Midge had one hot night of sex and ever since, the woman kept after her for more. There was no doubt that Midge was cute in a movie star sort of way, but for Jo there was no connection—not even sexual attraction. "Midge, listen I…"

"Not what you think, although I'd welcome it." The woman gave Jo a once over. "Have you heard about the ATA?"

Jo shook her head.

"Well, the British have set up a program for women in the Air Transport Auxiliary. They are hiring women pilots to ferry planes between the manufacturing factories and the airfields. They are paying them almost as much as the male pilots." Midge searched Jo's face. "What do you say…let's go and join."

Jo mulled the information over in her mind, tasting it and trying it on for size before she said, "How would we get there?"

"Tramp steamer," was the simple reply.

For a moment, Jo remained silent. "I'll need some time. I've got responsibilities." She fixed Midge with an inquisitive look. "How do we know we'd qualify?"

Midge reached inside her leather jacket and pulled out what looked like a folded newspaper clipping. "Here. I picked this up when I was in Dallas last week." When she saw Jo's hesitation she added, "You can keep it. They had several of the magazines I got it out of...took one for you just in case you might want to go." She rattled on. "I'm not afraid to go by myself but it would be more fun if someone was along to share the fun with me."

Jo took the piece of paper, opened it, and began to read all about the woman's Air Transport Auxiliary in England. When she finally looked up, she saw the expectant look on Midge's face. "Can you give me a few days?"

With a smile Midge said, "Sure. I've got some business in Amarillo. What do you say I swing by your place and we can talk about it more?"

A wary look crossed Jo's face. "Midge, you know there can never be anything between us...other than friendship, that is."

Midge winked. "Sure, kid, I know that."

"I might not be there, so call before you come." Jo felt her face redden as she waited for the reply she knew would come.

With sure steps, Midge closed in on Jo. "You know I'll always call your name before I come."

"I gotta go," Jo said as she hurried steps took her to her plane and away from Midge. *Why do I always let her do that to me?*

*

The logs burning in her aunt's fireplace helped warm Jo's bones, frozen by the frigid air that enveloped the open cockpit of her bi-plane. In her haste to get away from Midge, she disregarded the cold air factor and didn't wear a warmer jacket. Once she returned home, she immediately jumped into her old pickup and made the fifteen minute drive to Gloria's house. The heater in the ten year old vehicle offered no comfort for her cold body.

Jo sighed, "I don't know what to do."

"How would you get there?"

"The friend that told me about it said we'd take a tramp steamer," Jo said as she looked away.

Seeing something in her niece's face that told her there was more to the story, Gloria asked, "Do you want to go to England?"

Jo hedged, "I do, and I don't."

"Why's that?"

With a shrug, Jo studied the fire as she tried to collect her thoughts. "It sounds like a dream job, especially for women pilots." She turned her gaze to her aunt. "I'm just not sure it is the right move...with Amy Sue getting married this spring and all."

Not being someone who minced words, Gloria responded with, "I got the impression you didn't think much of the wedding or Amy Sue's choice of Bo Meeks."

Jo's eyes widened before her face flushed. "She's marryin' him, not me...she'll have to live with that decision. Nevertheless, I will be at her wedding."

Unconvinced, Gloria raised a dark eyebrow and frowned. "Ok, if you say so. Will the job in England go away if you wait to go until after the wedding?"

Jo's blue eyes regarded the fire again. "Probably not...from what I've read and heard, the war isn't going to stop any time soon."

When Jo looked up, eyes the same color of hers were looking at her with such an intense gaze that she couldn't look away.

"What's really going on?" Gloria asked softly. "There's more to this than a wedding or a dream job."

Jo squirmed in the chair and finally stood up and looked down on her aunt. "The woman, Midge, who told me about the ATA, wants more than friendship," she whispered.

Gloria tried to hide the surprise she felt as she looked at Jo. She had often speculated that her niece could be a lesbian but Jo's words now made her wonder if she was wrong. "And you don't want that?"

Walking to a window, Jo looked out to the dry dusty land that held the only home and family she'd known. "Not with her. We were stuck in some backwater town in east Texas, waiting for fuel to arrive and ended up spending the night…*together*."

Not wanting to lose the tentative bond she and Jo had, Gloria asked "Together?

Jo turned around and looked squarely in her aunt's face. "Yes."

"First time for you?"

"No, first time with her." Jo's eyes remained fixed on Gloria. "She does nothing for me."

With a nod, Gloria got up, moved toward Jo, and engulfed her in a hug before she took a step back. "Early on in my life I realized that I could either go with the flow or take a path that was not *normal*. I tried to conform. I even had a fella that wanted to marry me. It didn't take long for me to realize he wasn't what I wanted and I really didn't want to be like everyone else. So, I hid who I was until I couldn't stand it anymore and moved away, hoping I would find what was lacking in my life."

"Did you?" Jo asked.

With a breathless voice, Gloria answered, "Yes. Her name was Gretchen. She was ten years older than me…" Her eyes softened. "I loved her more than she cared about me but that was ok because I learned why my life seemed so empty."

"Why did you come back here? It certainly couldn't have been easy for you."

Gloria smiled. "This is my home. It's where my people are."

With a frown, Jo asked, "But you couldn't be yourself here, could you?"

"I went to a bank in Dallas to take some money out of my account and that's where I met Rebecca. We clicked right away and soon we were sharing not only a bed but also our lives. She was the one that encouraged me to move back home."

"She didn't love you?"

With a soft laugh, Gloria said, "Oh, she loved me and came back here with me. I wanted everyone to meet the love of my life."

Jo frowned. "I don't remember that."

"You wouldn't, Jo. I quickly realized that if I wanted to have a relationship with Becca, I couldn't speak of our love." She sighed. "The only one who supported me was your father. He told me I couldn't chose who I fell in love with, and that love is love no matter who it was. Your mother and father welcomed us into their home and we lived together for several years before Becca's mother took ill and she had to return to Dallas."

"Is that why she only visits you now?"

Gloria shook her head. "Little did we know her mother would hang on for another twelve years and, by that time, an aunt had moved in and Becca was stuck being her caregiver, too." She looked at her niece and smiled. "Her aunt passed away a month ago and once she has all the affairs settled from the estate, she is moving here permanently."

Jo digested the information and the sudden fact that she would not be able to go to England for years to come, assaulted her. "Then you won't want Bonnie Mae under foot." She sighed in resignation but she knew it was a sigh of relief—she couldn't go with Midge.

"Don't be ridiculous," Gloria chastised. "Rebecca and Bonnie Mae get along famously. Your sister doesn't have a problem with my lifestyle. If you don't want to go to England, just say so and not latch onto any excuse not to go."

Again, Jo's face reddened. "I want to go but I don't know what to do about Midge."

"Have you told her that you're not interested?"

"Yes, repeatedly. She's coming here in a week to show me all the information she's gathered about the Air Transport Auxiliary."

"Good."

Jo's forehead creased. "Good?"

"Yes, good. As matriarch of this family, it is my duty to see that you are not intimidated by this woman." She winked at Jo. "Trust me…she won't come on to you anymore once I'm done with her."

A smile of gratitude crossed Jo's face. "Thank you."

"Don't thank me yet. It's time you learned to stand up for yourself. Once you get to England you'll need a strong will and a backbone."

"But all I want to do is fly."

"The world out there, Jo, is not a friendly place. Except for the weekends barnstorming, you haven't a clue as to what lies ahead for you if you go to England. Flying will be no problem for you but you'll find that, if you don't grow a backbone, the others will walk all over you. You have three months to learn how not to let that happen." She moved closer to Jo, put her arms around her shoulders and hugged her close. "I think going to England is a wonderful opportunity for you, Jo."

*

Midge Reister's bi-plane rolled across the makeshift landing strip that Jo had behind her house. A big smile crossed her face as she saw Jo Laughlin standing next to the house. She was determined to make Jo her lover and the fact that Jo had agreed to her visiting gave her hope that that would happen. She knew she would have to play it close to the vest and act as though her only thoughts of the woman were friendship based. She chuckled as she climbed on to the wing of the plane. *She'll never see it coming.*

With her feet firmly on the ground, Midge waved at Jo, who was approaching her. Every nerve ending in her body was responding to the black haired beauty. The object of her affections was tall—probably an inch or so taller than her five six—with a firm, trim body that exuded sensuality when she moved. As Jo drew nearer, Midge swallowed back her arousal. *Now isn't the time...not yet anyway.*

"Hi, how was the flight?" Jo asked, stopping several feet from where Midge stood.

"Not bad but it was cold up there. At one point I had to come down to where I was barely above the trees to warm myself up." Unable to stop eyes that seemed to have a mind of their own, they raked over Jo's body as a lascivious smile curled her lips. *I'd let you warm me up any time you want.*

Jo scowled and gritted her teeth as she let out a slight growl. "You can put your stuff in the house before we go to my aunt's house." Without looking at Midge, Jo began toward the house.

With a slight skip to her steps, Midge hurried to catch up with her *friend*. "I hope it's warm inside," she said. "I'm still freezing."

When she opened the door, Jo stood to one side to allow Midge to go inside first. "Follow me and I'll show you where you can put your things. My aunt expects us there in fifteen minutes."

"Do we have time for me to go to the bathroom and freshen up some?"

Jo nodded before she opened the bedroom door that used to be Bonnie Mae's room.

"Good," Midge said before she took in the room. "Nicer than some places I've slept in." She raised her eyebrows then smiled. "Which room is yours?"

"We leave in five minutes," Jo bit out. "I'll wait in the kitchen for you."

Midge laughed and went into the room, sat down on the bed and bounced slightly. "I'm up to the challenge, my friend. You will be mine. That, I guarantee."

*

Jo had been squeezing her fingers into fists as she waited for Midge to get ready. Her aunt had been right. She wasn't prepared for the sharks of the world—her guest was certainly in that category. Over the last week, she and Gloria had talked about strategies to prevent people like Midge from getting the upper hand. She shrugged. "I didn't handle that well at all."

Her mind traveled to the conversation they had about stopping unwanted advances…

"Keep your distance and don't allow the other person to get into your space if you don't want them to. The way you stand and what you say will convey your feelings. If you're open, like this," she let her arms dangle at her sides, "Then the person will think you are receptive to their advances." She crossed her arms over her chest. "What does this tell you?"

Jo thought for a moment. "Keep away."

"Exactly." She kept her arms crossed and smiled. "Now what do you think?"

"Maybe you'd let me close."

"Good girl." Gloria crossed her arms again, lost all the expression on her face, and fixed Jo with a cold glare. "What about now."

Jo nodded her head in understanding. "I'd better back away and maybe find somewhere else to go."

Her attention turned to the sound of footsteps heading toward the kitchen. She looked at the doorway and saw Midge standing there, dressed in a skirt and blouse with a big grin on her face. Jo refused to let the smile that she usually would make in response to another person's smile curve her lips. Instead, she schooled her features and gave the smiling woman a bland expression.

Midge held up an envelope. "I've got all the information we'll need." She put the envelope on the table. "We can look it over when we get back."

"Bring it along," Jo said in a clipped tone. "I want my aunt to know what's involved." She turned to the door and over her shoulder said, "Let's get going…we're already late."

*

Gloria Laughlin looked up when she heard the door open and saw her niece and a blonde walk in. Jo's friend, dressed in a too tight blouse that accentuated ample breasts and a scandalously short skirt that was almost to her knees, looked like she belonged in a brothel instead of her kitchen. *No one has hair that blonde naturally—she looks like a two bit whore.*

Once the introductions were over, she shooed the two women out of the kitchen and resumed finishing dinner preparations. It wasn't long before Bonnie Mae and Amy Jo were by her side at the cook stove.

"Did you see how red her lips were?" Bonnie Mae asked with a note of awe in her voice.

Amy Sue scooped potatoes into a bowl. "Where did Jo find her?" She started for the table then turned back. "She isn't coming to my wedding! I don't care what Jo says."

Gloria laughed. "I doubt she'll be at your wedding, Amy Sue. I can't imagine Jo would want her there.

"I think she's beautiful," gushed Bonnie Mae.

Amy Sue came back to her sister and felt her forehead. "Nope, she doesn't have a fever."

Bonnie Mae shoved the hand away. "What do you know about anything," she hissed, "all you know about is some dirt poor farmer who hasn't got a lick of ambition."

"Take that back," Amy Sue said in a loud voice. "Bo is a good man who works hard and I can't wait to marry him." She eyed her sister. "At least I have a man interested in me…unlike you."

Before the discussion turned into a full blown altercation, Gloria said, "Hush, both of you. That...*woman*… is a guest in my house and we will treat her as such." Gloria grinned. *I'll have a good time putting her in her place.* 'Supper's ready,' she called out.

*

Gloria sat at the head of her kitchen table flanked by her niece, Jo, and her friend, Midge. Next to Jo sat Amy Sue and at the end of the table, Bonnie Mae. While everyone tucked in to the business of eating, Gloria covertly studied Midge Reister. She hadn't liked the woman from the moment she walked in the door and her opinion hadn't changed during supper. The leer in the woman's brown eyes when she looked at Jo was

48

unmistakable. She wanted her niece in more ways than just a friend. In her opinion, the woman was a user, without a sincere bone in her body. Jo didn't need that kind of friend.

"Tell me about this scheme you have to go to England and fly planes, Midge," Gloria said in her sweetest voice. She'd found that the best way to control a user like Midge was to let them think they are in charge.

Midge looked up with a raised eyebrow then smiled. "I have all kinds of information on that," she said scooting her chair back, "let me go get it."

Gloria held up a hand. "We don't bring that sort of thing to the supper table." She fixed the woman with her blue eyes. "Just give me an overview."

With a pout on her lips, Midge moved her chair back to the table and narrowed her eyes at her friend's aunt. "First we take the train to New York City…that should take three days. Then we board a tramp steamer to a little town that I'm sure you don't know about in England named Portsmouth."

With a sweet smile, Gloria interjected, "Portsmouth, yes, I know it." When she saw the flustered look on Midge's face, she smiled inwardly. *Score one for me.*

"How nice," Midge cooed sweetly. "Then we go by bus to a small town, Hatfield, which is north of London."

"Hatfield, I know it well too." Gloria's eyes lit up. "A friend and I spent a week in the area taking in all the historical places. It is quite a wondrous place to visit." Seeing the woman next to her grind her jaw, she turned to her niece and continued. "We stayed at the Eight Bells Inn. Legend says that one of the characters from Charles Dickens's novel *Oliver Twist* resided there."

Midge interjected, "They're fighting a war over there," she said succinctly. "We won't be there to sightsee."

Gloria shrugged. "I know that," she said before she turned to her niece. "Remind me to show you the photographs I took when I was there. It really was a marvelous place to visit."

"Well," Midge countered in a confrontational tone, "since you know so much, you should join us."

Gloria gave the woman her sweetest smile. "If I went along there wouldn't be any need for you, now would there."

Jo looked at Midge then at her aunt. "I hear Wilburn Foster wants to call it quits. You probably could get his land for a good price."

Gloria turned to her niece and winked. "Yeah, I heard that rumor, too. Wonder if it's true." She shrugged. "It's all I can do to keep up with my hundred acres plus the land I rent but, if he does sell, I might give it serious consideration. As with everything, it depends on the price of cotton."

"You don't always have to plant cotton, you know," Jo added.

"Right now it's what sells for the most so I'm gonna keep growin' it." Her eyes surveyed the rest of the occupants around the table. "Who's ready for some peach cobbler?"

*

After they washed and dried the dishes, Gloria, Jo and Midge sat at the kitchen table looking at all the information Midge gathered about the ATA in England.

"What do you say, Jo? You with me?" Midge asked.

Jo looked at her aunt and saw no indication of how she felt about it. From the conversation at dinner and her aunt's actions, she could tell that Gloria did not like Midge—at all. "I can't leave until the second week in April," she said, half hoping that Midge would opt to go it alone, "My sister's wedding…I won't miss that."

Midge nodded. "I wouldn't expect you to, Jo. Besides, that will give us three more months to get in more hours. As I said before, the jobs are given to the most experienced of flyers, so the extra time will only help us."

"I've heard all these words about joining the ATA but what will you both do if you are rejected?"

With a chuckle, Midge fixed her eyes on Gloria. "Won't happen." Her hand slid into the envelope and took out one more piece of folded paper. "I've already been in contact with the head of the ATA, Pauline Gower." She opened the paper. "She said, and I quote, *we are always in need of women pilots who have experience. It sounds to me like you and your friend will do just fine if you choose to join the ATA.*"

Gloria frowned. "That isn't a guarantee that you'll be accepted. I imagine she says that to all the pilots that want to join."

With her voice filled with anger, Midge said, "Well, I disagree. Jo and I are damned good pilots and they'll be lucky to have us! I, for one, have no doubts about my abilities or my acceptance into the ATA."

Jo looked at both women before her eyes rested on Midge. *Therein lies the difference between us. She has confidence and I don't.* "Can I tell you in a few days?" Jo asked. "I need to get things settled with my business. I can't just leave my customers in the lurch."

Midge nodded. "Sure. I have nowhere else to be."

*

After Jo got into the truck, Midge immediately scooted over so their hips were touching and then put her hand on Jo's thigh and began rubbing the fabric.

Jo stiffened, remembering her aunt's words. *If she does anything suggestive and you don't say anything, she'll assume you are interested.* Other than her sisters, Jo was uncomfortable with any type of confrontation, especially when she had to stand her ground—it was far easier to go with the flow. Sucking in a deep breath and gathering courage she wasn't sure she had, she took Midge's hand and moved it off her thigh. "Move over to your side," she said as forcefully as she could.

Midge gave what Jo thought was an odd look but complied with her request, and for a moment Jo was taken aback. The trip back to her house took about fifteen minutes and she hoped Midge wouldn't cause any more trouble.

"I'm pretty sure your aunt doesn't like me," Midge remarked.

Jo remained silent.

"I think she doesn't approve of us," she said in a husky voice.

Jo knew that tone of voice well, for she had heard Midge use it many times in the past when she made sexual overtures. "Us? You have got to be kidding. There isn't an *us*, Midge."

Midge laughed and slid back across the seat, wiggled her hips and put her hand between Jo's thighs. "Of course there is…or are you trembling for some other reason?"

Jo's right foot hit the brake pedal as her left one depressed the clutch and the truck came to a stop. She almost pressed her thighs tight around Midge's exploring fingers but instead grabbed the woman's wrist and yanked it away. There was no doubt that she was sexually charged and woman next to her was a very competent lover. Yet, Jo knew she couldn't let that happen. "Move back to your side now," she ground out. When Midge remained by her side, Jo reached across her and opened the door. "Get out!"

"How will I find my way back to your house?" Midge asked in an indignant voice. "I'm your guest. You can't just throw me out into the dark night."

"You have two choices, Midge. Either move or get out. Either way, you and I are never going to be anything more than acquaintances."

In what appeared to be a conciliatory action, Midge shrugged, returned to her side of the truck, and then chuckled before saying, "We'll see about that," as she closed the passenger door.

Jo collected her almost out of control emotions, shifted into first gear, let out the clutch, and pressed on the gas pedal. *I'd better lock my bedroom door tonight.*

*

Crop dusting during January, February, and March in the panhandle of Texas was nonexistent, so Jo supplemented her income by flying in air shows. She was gone for weeks at a time as she, Midge, and Dave skipped around Oklahoma and Texas, dazzling the crowds with their aerobatics. Midge remained her obnoxious self and was constantly seeking Jo out and making sexual overtones. When the group took on a new pilot, Liz Westcott, and Midge turned her attentions to the petite dark-haired girl, Jo felt a sigh of relief.

In her time off, she prepared for the trip to Britain by concentrating on her flying skills. Often she would fly to larger towns such as Oklahoma City and Dallas where she could readily find information about what was new in aircraft. With the war in full swing in Europe, the manufacture of new and improved models of airplanes exploded. Unlike the Jenny she flew, the new planes had retractable landing gears, along with radios and advanced navigation. If the ATA was going to accept her, she needed to be familiar with all types of aircraft, thereby giving her an edge over other applicants.

Soon preparations for Amy Sue's wedding grew to a fevered pitch. With her sister becoming a banshee, Jo stayed near home in an attempt to quell her sister's anxiety.

"This looks awful," Amy Sue cried. "I look like a stuffed pig," she bemoaned as she looked in the mirror that reflected her wearing her wedding dress.

"No, honey, it's perfect," said Gloria as she smoothed out the white taffeta. "You're beautiful."

Amy Sue raised her arms and scowled. "How can you say that? Bo's going to take one look at this and say *I don't*. Why can't I have a store bought dress instead of this big fluffy thing?"

Gloria looked at Jo and rolled her eyes. "Amy Sue, honey, this was your mama's dress. I thought you wanted to wear it so she would be close to you at your wedding," she said in a soft voice.

Jo gritted her teeth and suck in a deep breath. "Look, your wedding is in ten days. There isn't time or money to get another dress so you'll wear this one and like it," she growled. "So stop the bellyaching."

"You're so mean," Amy Sue cried as she stomped her foot. "No wonder you can't find a man."

"If I wanted a man, I'd have one," Jo retorted. "The way I see it, Amy Sue, you can either wear this dress or be married in the dress you wear to church. It's up to you. Just know that there's no way you're getting a new dress."

*

Two weeks later, Amy Sue walked slowly down the aisle as all eyes gazed on her dressed in her mother's wedding gown. Gloria, Jo, Bonnie Mae, and Gloria's partner, Rebecca, stood in the front pew watching her advance on them—all with tears in their eyes. The reception in Gloria's home that followed was, by the town's standards, better than average. Bonnie Mae called it *classy* after spending nearly ten days polishing and cleaning. The center of attention was the three tier wedding cake that Jo had flown to Dallas to get—it was her wedding gift.

Jo stood by a window watching her sister and new husband dance to music from Gloria's Victrola. Her feelings were conflicted about the marriage, her responsibility for Bonnie Mae, and her leaving to help a foreign country fight a war. Her eyes tracked to her youngest sister, who was smiling as she stood tapping her feet to the music. It wasn't long before two young men, sons of her neighbor, Ben Wallace, approached Bonnie Mae. Jo saw the blush on her sister's face and wondered how long before she, too, would be married.

"Looks like she'll be ok. There's really no reason for me not to go to England," she whispered.

A warm arm wrapped around her shoulders. "We will all be ok while you're away," Gloria said. "Don't use us as an excuse not to go," she added.

Light blue eyes sought out both of her sisters and when she saw them, Jo smiled. "Yeah, I know," she replied. "It's just if Bonnie Mae gets married, I don't know if I could get back for it."

"I'll let you in on a little secret," Gloria whispered, "Bonnie Mae has big plans for her future and they don't include getting married any time soon."

Jo's eyebrows knitted. "What do you mean?"

Gloria laughed. "She doesn't know it yet, but as soon as she can, she'll leave here. You must have seen it, Jo. Your sister will never be content with the life this place offers…she wants more."

Jo mulled the words over in her mind before she shook her head. "Yeah, you're right. If she stays here she won't be happy…ever." Her eyes tracked to Amy Sue, who had her arm wrapped in Bo's as her eyes looked at him adoringly. "The bride is right where she wants to be."

"Yes, she is, Jo, and so should you. Flying is your passion. I've known that since the day your dad first took you in his plane. Follow that dream, Jo, wherever it takes you."

An arm went around Gloria's waist. "Thank you for all you've done for my sisters and me," Jo said pulling her Aunt a bit closer. "I'm going to miss you…" She pointed her chin in the direction of her sisters who were now laughing together. "I think that is what frightens me most, not having the contact with you and them."

Gloria reached over and lightly touched Jo's chest over her heart. "We are in there always, Jo, so you'll never lose us."

Jo leaned her head onto her aunt's and held it there. "Thank you."

*

One week later, Jo, along with Midge, stood on a pier in New York City harbor looking at the SS Sea Spectre, the rust streaked tramp steamer that would take them across the Atlantic Ocean to the United Kingdom. Jo regarded the ship, taking in all the aspects of the antiquated looking cargo vessel. She saw a large man dressed in some sort of uniform spit what she thought was tobacco into the water and shivered.

Her gaze then turned to her traveling companion. Tall, blonde and attractive, Midge was the type of woman that got cat-calls and the attention of a multitude of men. Since they would be two women alone on a boat full of what she thought were *shady* type characters, she wondered how long before Midge would become the object of those men's desires.

"I don't know about this, Midge. This thing looks like it belongs in a ship graveyard and not something that will stay afloat. And did you see the men up there on the deck looking at us? Will we be safe?"

With a raucous laugh that made the few others on the dock turn and look, Midge slapped Jo on the back. "Didn't you see *King Kong*? This is what a tramp steamer is supposed to look like." She continued laughing before her tone turned serious. "It's filled with all kinds of seedy and sinister characters, matched only by the cargo of contraband that they carry. You'll have to lay awake at night worrying if the motley crew of misfits will ravage you."

Jo's face went white. "You're kidding, right?" A laugh, louder than the first, was her answer. Her eyes then focused on a middle aged man and woman who stood near the gangplank of the ship with suitcases resting on the dock. "Looks like we'll have company," she said, pointing in the couple's direction.

Midge finally stopped laughing and looked at the pair. "I think this one has room for six passengers."

"We could have gotten separate rooms then, couldn't we?"

"Not unless you wanted to pay more than a hundred dollars for the trip." Midge eyed her companion and grinned. "Don't worry…I'll be good…unless you decide you want me to be bad."

The blue of Jo's eyes darkened. "We've had this discussion at least a dozen times since we decided to go on this trip. I don't know how many times I have to tell you, Midge, I'm not interested in a romantic relationship with you. Besides, don't you have something going with Liz?"

Midge flicked her hand in the air. "God no, she wanted a home and babies and I'm not ready for that. You, on the other hand, are," she lifted one shoulder, "very desirable. I plan on being like a dog with a bone and persistence does pay off in the long run, Jo."

Jo nodded toward the other couple. "Looks like it's time to board." She picked up her two suitcases and headed toward a long, steep staircase when a man, dressed much like the one she'd seen earlier, approached her.

"Let me help you with those, Miss. You'll need to hold on with at least one hand climbing up those," he said taking her bags.

"Hey, wait for me," Midge said as she dragged a large trunk behind her. It wasn't long before several of the hands from the steamer came running toward Midge to help her with her trunk. "Why, thank you," she cooed as she ran her fingers over the man's well muscled arm. "You're just what I needed; a big strong man."

In no time, both Jo and Midge were standing on the deck of the steamer where a young man, dressed in a blue uniform was greeting the man and woman. Soon after the two women were settling into the room they'd share for the duration of the voyage, they heard a loud horn signal the ship was on its way.

*

The steamer had lumbered along over seemingly calm waters for several days and both Jo and Midge were thankful for that. The cabin they had was small and narrow and Midge's trunk seemed to take up most of the open space. Still, the journey was uneventful. Jo spent her time standing against the five foot solid side of the ship with her arms crossed along the cold metal, gazing out on the water and dreaming of flying through enemy fire and escaping by doing all the aerobatic flying she did while barnstorming. The rest of the time, she found places to hide away from Midge and her constant advances.

Jo had met the woman who boarded with the man. Joyce Valletta and her husband, Jeffery, traveled on tramp steamers often and were on their way to England to witness the war first hand. The woman and Jo walked early each morning and often would stand by the wall of the ship watching the sun come up.

"Each day is a gift," Joyce said one morning. "Life needs to be lived at its fullest. How I envy you and your friend being able to actually participate in the war."

With a frown, Jo said, "We won't actually be fighting in the war. We'll be helping get the planes to the RAF and even that isn't assured."

Joyce grinned. "My friends sometimes call me a witch 'cause I can see what will happen. What I see for you, Jo, is you flying…," she wrapped her arms around her body as she shivered, "you will face peril many times…" Her brown eyes fixed on Jo as she reached into her coat pocket and took something out. She reached for Jo's hand and opened it before she pressed the object into her hand. Keeping her hand over Jo's, she said, "This will keep you safe, even in the darkest of hours. Carry it with you always, Jo." Then she removed her hand and smiled. "I need to get back to my husband."

Jo watched the woman leave before she looked at her opened hand and the object in it. Her fingers began rolling the flat circular stone between them. On one side, a symbol that looked like some sort of Chinese letter and, on the other, there was a different marking "I wonder what it means?" Her eyes traveled to the doorway Joyce went in. "She carried it with her so it must hold some sort of importance." When she looked back at the object, she closed her fingers around it as a cold shiver went up her spine.

*

Uneventful days went by as Jo adjusted to the sensation of being in the steamer and the havoc it was playing on her stomach. Everything she ate caused her stomach to revolt so she stopped eating but the nausea was still present.

On the fifth day, the ocean began churning and Jo not only experienced motion sickness but feared for her life. As what felt to Jo like 20 foot waves rocked the steamer, she grabbed for anything that would steady her. When the large trunk slid the short distance across the cabin floor, Jo clung to Midge. Loud creaking sounds seemed to surround her as she felt the steamer pitch and groan with every wave that crashed into the steamer's side.

In a moment of irrational fear, Jo's terror of dying outweighed all else as she tightened her hold on Midge. She needed to feel alive and the intimate contact of the woman's body with hers helped allay some of her fear. As the storm raged, she began frantically tearing at Midge's clothes until they were both naked.

"What's the matter, lover?" Midge asked with a noticeable levity to her voice.

"Shut up," Jo cried as she pulled Midge to her.

As soon as Midge lowered her naked body over hers, Jo found her mind focusing only on her bourgeoning arousal. The waves incessantly crashing against the side of the rusty vessel added to Jo's anticipation of what was to come.

Soon, Midge's fingers were pounding inside her, challenging her to heights, only to pull away before persistently stroking her center and making her clit grow painful with the need for release.

"Please," Jo cried.

"Please what?" Midge cooed. "What do you want me to do?"

Jo felt tears forming. "Make me come," she pleaded. She felt and heard waves slam viciously against the side of the ship's hull before a loud metallic creaking seemed to fill the room. "I need to feel alive before we die."

Midge leaned in, captured Jo's lips, and kissed her savagely before pulling away. "You only want me because you think you're going to die. Is that it, Jo?"

Jo nodded. "Please, Midge."

"So you decided to use me for one last go around before you go to the briny deep."

"No, it wasn't like that at all," protested Jo until she saw Midge raise an eyebrow. "Yes, I do think we won't last till morning but…what's wrong with finding comfort in your last moments of life?"

Midge only snorted before she stood up and began dressing. "There's no way this ship is going to sink. If you'd done your homework, you'd know that. This is nothing. If it were, you and I wouldn't have been able to lie in that bed." She snickered as she pointed to the floor. "We'd be tossed out onto the floor and rolled all around this room." She looked around her and laughed. "We probably would have rolled back and forth between the beds…but we didn't, Jo, this storm isn't that bad."

"But why are you mad, Midge? Isn't this what you wanted?"

"Believe it or not, Jo, I do have feelings. I want you to want me and not because I'm your last hope before you die."

With that, Midge stormed out of the room, leaving Jo with her mouth agape as another monster wave struck the ship.

"Midge, it's dangerous out there."

Once outside the door, Midge began to chuckle. "Now, I know how to make you mine, Jo," she said as the storm continued to rage. "Fear is always a good motivator."

*

The bright blue skies of the morning gave no hint of the storm of the night before. Jo stood at her usual place at the rusted metal side and looked out on the relatively calm water. The sun was still low in the sky, reflecting what looked like diamonds on water's surface. The gentle sight did not stop the trembling in her body or the embarrassment of her encounter with Midge. If flying had taught her anything, it was to take life by its tail and go with it to the fullest. Instead, she allowed the fear of dying to control to her actions. *Why did I let that to happen to me?*

After a while, Joyce joined her. "That storm was a beaut...but we weren't in any danger. We've sure seen worse."

Jo felt her face heat as she remembered how foolish she was the night before by thinking the ship would sink. She smiled at the woman as she remembered the odd thing Joyce gave her. She reached in her pocket and took it out. "Here," she said holding the object out, "I can't take this."

"Why," Joyce asked.

"You were carrying it, so it obviously means a great deal to you."

Joyce folded Jo's fingers over the stone. "I want you to have it. Please keep it."

Unfolding her fingers, Jo looked at the stone. "What does it mean?"

"This," Joyce pointed to the symbol, "is the Chinese word for life," she turned it over, "and this is for love. Keep it with you always, Jo, and you will be safe from all that falls on your shoulders."

Jo's hand reached up and pulled her collar closed as a sudden cold breeze shot through her—she shivered. "Why are you giving it to me?"

Joyce smiled. "Because I like you." She looked at her wristwatch. "It's breakfast time. I'll see you later, Jo."

Once again, Jo found herself watching the woman go but this time her eyes caught sight of Midge. *I need to talk with her.*

*

Jo cautiously approached Midge, who was standing in front of the water closet waiting for her turn at the bathroom. Using the woman the way she had was wrong on so many levels that she knew she must apologize. Standing behind Midge, Jo saw that she was dressed in dry clothes. She lightly touched her shoulder and Midge turned around.

"Hey, where have you been?"

Midge let out a sarcastic laugh. "Don't tell me you care."

"I do, Midge. I was worried about you out in the storm."

"How touching. Not to worry, I found a bed to sleep in."

The intonation was not lost on Jo. "Well, I'm glad then. I'm going to get some breakfast so I guess I'll see you there or later." Jo turned and began to leave but turned around. "Midge, I'm sorry," she whispered before she turned and left. In the background, she heard Midge laugh.

For the next two days, Jo suffered through Midge taking every opportunity to touch her, squeeze past her, or rake her eyes sensuously over Jo's body. When the steamer finally docked at Portsmouth, England, Jo breathed a sigh of relief—the close quarters with Midge were finally over. Now all she had to do was disembark and find her way to ATA administrative headquarters in White Waltham.

Jo fingered the stone Joyce had given her as she and Midge set out to their new adventure. She knew that luck had nothing to do with earning a job with the ATA. No, it had to do with her flying abilities only and no amount of luck would change that. Still, she kept fingering the object in her pocket, just in case.

Chapter Three

Spring 1940
Essington, England

Lady Millicent Smyth-Armstrong stood in the middle of an elegant room looking at the back of her husband, Philip. Had he been facing her, he would have seen the anger darkening her eyes and her fists clenching. He wasn't handsome by any means—at about five foot eight, he was slightly overweight. Overshadowing his lack of good looks was the way he carried himself—standing straight, his neck always extended with his head held high. He was every bit an aristocrat. The Armstrong family line dated back to the sixteen hundreds with the royalty of many European countries in his blood.

"Millicent, I forbid you to join the ATA."

"You cannot do that, Philip."

The man spun around on his heel and his hazel eyes fixed his wife with an angry stare. "Yes, I can and you had best remember that. I am the one in charge here."

"I have to do this, Philip. I am honor bound to help the empire in any way I can. Aren't you the one that taught me about God, the King, and the Empire, in that order?"

"This war is rubbish. We have no business being in it. It was foolhardy of Chamberlain to send troops to France. The Germans aren't threatening any of the realm's countries, so why declare war?"

"Because they have invaded Norway, Finland, France, Belgium, Luxembourg, and the Netherlands. It doesn't take a *Cambridge scholar* to know we are next."

Philip snorted. "Now that we have this Churchill fellow as Prime Minister, it shan't take long."

"Churchill is a good man and we should give him our support."

"I am not getting into an argument with you about the new prime minister or what is right or wrong with this war. What I am telling you is, I will not allow you to go off and fly planes for them.

"Philip, I am joining the ATA. I will be home everyday…all I will be doing is ferrying planes to different factories."

"What about the children? What about me?"

"Darling, the children are one and three and, at your insistence, they spend more time with the nanny than us. You have me on so many charities and committees that my own children don't know who I am."

"Then we shall fire the nanny and you can take over fulltime care of the children."

"Until when, Philip? When I'm not visible enough in society for your liking? When those snobs you call friends frown that your wife stays home with the children?" She laughed. "My staying home with my children would be looked upon as lower class and I know you would never stand for that."

"You will not join the ATA, Millicent, and that is the end of this discussion.

"I think not, Philip."

"I know you don't like charity work, luncheons, and all the various social events, Millicent," he said softly. "That is why I bought you that bloody plane. Can't you be happy flying for pleasure and not be part of a war that is fated to end miserably for England?"

"If it fails miserably then at least I can say I did all I could for our country." She eyed her husband. "Will you be able to say that, Philip? Will you be able to proudly tell your children that you fought for the greater good?" Millicent moved closer to her husband. "I think you shan't."

"Perhaps that is true," Philip said in resignation. "But neither will you. You will not join the ATA. You will maintain your social standing, Millicent. A Lady of your status does not partake in such foolishness. I have heard that anyone can join…even the working class. I can't tolerate you mixing in those circles and I forbid you from joining that, or any other organization that has to do with this ill-conceived war." He picked up his gloves and hat by the door. "I will be home for tea."

*

Millicent was still fuming by tea time. She had instructed the cook to make foods she knew Philip detested—she'd show him. As she heard the door open, she regretted the choice and went to join her husband in the hallway. "Darling," she said with a sweet tone, "Juliet called earlier and said she and Dennis were going to the club for dinner. Cook has prepared a meal I know you won't like so I thought we could join them."

"Why has the cook prepared foods I dislike?" Philip asked with a frown.

"She got mixed up and thought you'd be gone tonight," Millicent said smoothly. "Besides, it has been ages since we spent any time with Juliet and Dennis."

"Oh, all right, we can go. What time?"

"She said their seating was at seven."

Philip looked at his wife. "You'd better change into something better than that if we are going to the club."

"Yes, of course, dear." Millicent left the hallway quickly and made her way to her suite of rooms. After closing the door, she lifted the receiver from the phone and called Juliet.

While she waited for Juliet's servant to fetch her friend, Millicent thought about what to wear. She looked down at her full length gown and wondered what Philip objected to. "Looks fine to me."

"Millie, darling, tell me you will be joining us for supper."

"Philip has agreed so we will meet you there at seven."

"No, come earlier and we can have drinks."

"I will try. You know how Philip is about drinking."

Juliet laughed. "Right. I will see you soon then. Goodbye."

"Goodbye."

"Who was that?"

Startled by the voice, Millicent looked around and saw her husband glaring at her. "It was Juliet. I called her to say we would be joining them tonight."

Philip nodded. "I gave cook a good tongue lashing for preparing a meal she knew I didn't like."

Millicent groaned inwardly—she'd have to make it up to cook for her husband's harsh words. She was confident that the woman would not defend herself by telling him that his wife had ordered the meal. No, she was loyal to Millicent, as all the staff was. The home had been in her family for generations and the staff had been the same since she was a girl. No, the cook wouldn't sell her out but Millicent would make it up with a few more pounds in her paycheck.

*

Three days later, Millicent sat across from the ATA Commander, Pauline Gower.

"Well, this is a surprise," the commander said. "I heard on the grapevine his Lordship refused to allow you to consider joining us."

"I am my own woman and can make up my own mind," Millicent said with a clipped tone. "I want to be of service to my country and since I am an experienced pilot, I can be of help by ferrying planes for you."

As always, the commander was friendly and warm. "I see," she said softly. "Does this mean the ATA will come between a husband and wife?"

Millicent thought about that for a long moment. "As I see it, Commander, my husband's stance in this matter is wrong. I realize that as a woman, especially from my station in life, I should consider my husband's wishes seriously and I have. My country is at war and my services will help our soldiers win that war. I cannot sit idly by while they die in battles they are fighting for everyone's freedom."

"I see." The commander nodded her head. "I like your passion, Millicent. If I accept you into the program, it will cause quite a stir among the society establishment that you know. There are many who are against women's roles in the ATA. I must weigh all that against the need for qualified pilots. The simple thing to do would be to let you join and allow you to deal with your husband, but more is at stake here and I'm not sure I can justify the risk."

Millicent felt deflated as all her hopes to help her country evaporated. "Is there nothing I can do or say to convince you?" She knew that many of her peers would be shocked to hear her beg but in this matter, she didn't care.

The commander tapped her pen against the ink blotter on her desk before she looked into the woman's soft brown eyes. "I don't suppose you would like to help out in the hospital or roll bandages or anything such as that."

The hair, perfectly coiffed into a bun, nodded. "I abhor that type of busy work. Although I can see the need, I don't think my services would be well utilized there."

A smile crept around the commander's mouth. "I thought that was what you would say." She thought for a moment, then said, "Give me a few days and I will get back to you. In the meantime, work on your husband…his attitude in this matter is all that stands between you and flying for me."

"How sad that my desires cannot be met unless my husband says I can do something."

"I know, but I must think of how the public as a whole views the ATA. If I don't have the support of those who are influential in our funding then my job will be made more difficult." The Commander shrugged. "Unfortunately, politics is the nature of the beast."

"I understand. "Millicent stood and held out her hand. "Thank you for taking the time to meet with me. I will look forward to hearing from you." Once she shook the woman's hand, she left the office with her heart not broken but not soaring either.

*

Daphne Hill-Allen sat watching her long time friend, Millicent Smyth-Armstrong, absently finger a teacup. Millie's appearance was what some would call plain but her soft brown eyes drew people in and made the person feel safe. Today her friend seemed pensive, with pent up energy that transferred to the teacup.

As she reached to cover the fingers stroking the cup, Daphne said, "Tell me what is going on with you, Millie. You look positively dreadful. Has something happened with you and Philip?"

Millicent lifted her eyes and looked at the woman who had been her friend since she was seven. *Daphy* was a dark haired beauty with hazel eyes and a smile that seemed to light up wherever she was. "I love flying," she whispered.

"I know you do," she acknowledged as she withdrew her hand as one of her maids walked into the room.

"Would my Lady care for more tea," the short stocky woman asked Millicent.

With a half smile, Millicent said, "No, thank you, Mildred."

Once the maid left, Millicent looked at her friend and shrugged slightly. "Philip has been very indulgent of my…*hobby*."

"Then what is wrong, Millie?"

For a long while, Millicent stared at the rich texture of the oriental carpet covering the floor. She said, "I don't enjoy all the trappings that people in our class seem to covet."

Daphne smiled. "I've always known that, Millie. Is he pushing you to do more?"

Millicent shook her head. "No. I want to make a difference, Daphy. I don't want to listen to the latest gossip about our circle of friends, nor do I want to participate in all those daft charity meetings. I want to fly." Her brown eyes fixed on her friend. "I want to join the ATA and help the fight for my country."

Daphne sat in stunned silence. She knew that her friend had always shied away from the dictums her social status. The only time she saw Millie truly happy was when she spoke of flying. *But to join the RAF…that is lunacy.*

"You want to join the RAF? Millie, are you crazy? You have children to think of…what would they do without their mother?"

"Not the RAF, Daphy, but the ATA, the Air Transport Auxiliary. The pilots are all civilians who ferry planes from the factories to the RAF bases. The pilots come from all walks of life with one purpose—to relieve the RAF pilots."

"Still," Daphne said holding up a hand, "what about your family, Millie? Are you going to abandon them so you can go do something you think is meaningful?"

Frustrated, Millicent shook her head vigorously. "No, I won't abandon my family, Daphy, and I am hurt that you would think that I could do that. I love my children desperately, but Philip has me so busy with so many committees that I never see them. So what difference does it make if I fly for the ATA or do charity work?"

Daphne could see the hurt and annoyance on her friend's face. "I know you would not do anything to endanger or hurt your children," she said softly. "But how can you both fly and take care of the needs of your family?"

"Take care of the needs of my family? Daphy, I'm not allowed to take care of my children. Philip abhors having the children break his routine. I rather think he wishes I had never insisted we have them in the first place."

Unable to look her friend in the eye, Daphne looked out the window. "You are right, Millie, but can you imagine how you will be perceived by others?"

Frustrated, Millicent stood up. "I don't care about that. I want to do my part for my country. It is as simple as that."

"Where would you serve?"

"There are ferry pools in Hatfield and I hear there will be a new one at White Waltham. Both of those places are within easy driving distance so I could live at home." Millicent's brown eyes beseeched her friend for understanding. Daphne smiled at her friend. "Now to convince Philip."

"Yes."

For a long moment, Daphne contemplated what to say. She thought Millie hadn't given her plan enough consideration but at the same time, she wanted to support her. She recalled the time when Millie had sought out her advice and how much her beliefs had changed…

"Of course you want children," Daphne said. "That is what someone of your social status is expected to do—have an heir so the family line goes forward."

"But, I do not want that, Daphy. I do not like children so why would I want to subject a child to a mother who does not want them?"

Millicent always wanted to be different but on this matter, Daphne knew it wasn't about being diverse. It was about wanting things her way. "You have no choice in this, darling. Philip married you with the understanding that you would bear him children." She saw the resignation in her friend's face and knew the matter was settled

Her friend had taken her advice. After the birth of the first child, a girl, she could see the change in her friend's demeanor toward her daughter. She glowed in the child's presence and doted on her daughter until Philip insisted she leave the child with a nanny. He wanted her to be visible on various committees and charitable organizations. When her second child was born, Millicent welcomed him and was happy to once again be home with her children. After only two months, Philip demanded that both children be with the nanny fulltime so she could reintegrate with their social circle.

Daphne knew her friend needed her support whether she agreed with her or not. "Then we shall come up with something, Millie." The smile on Millicent's face at that moment was worth the world to Daphne.

Little did her friend know that Millicent had an ace up her sleeve and hoped that using it at this time would work to her advantage. She smiled remembering the letter she received describing the steamy love affair Philip was having with a woman named Pricilla Prescott-Knowles. She could almost see her husband's face as she confronted him with his infidelity. Not that anyone within their circle of friends would find his actions reprehensible, but Philip would do anything not to have a public scandal—for him it was all about appearances. Silently she chuckled. *I will be part of the ATA and he won't stop me.*

*

Once again, Millicent sat in Commander Gower's office. In the previous meeting, she noticed the Commander was younger than she originally thought. Light brown wavy hair, pulled back in a small knot, complimented an unlined face, which was unexpected since from all accounts, the woman's days and nights were filled with non-stop work.

"Are you back with good news for me, Lady Armstrong?"

Millicent smiled. "Yes, I'd like to officially be considered for a position as a pilot with the ATA."

"Excellent," the commander said before her attention turned to the paper on her desk. "I see here that you've logged five hundred hours," she looked up, "is that correct?"

"Yes. I have my own plane, a Tiger Moth."

The commander nodded, "The one-twenty-engine?"

"No, the one-thirty."

"Impressive. You do know that the RAF uses that model extensively as a trainer, don't you?"

"Yes. My husband is acquainted with the de Havilland family and had my plane built especially for me."

"For now, the ATA only flies single engine planes. Most of them come out of the de Havilland factory near Hatfield. I fully expect to have additional pools set up near

74

other airplane factories soon." She eyes Millicent. "Will that be a problem?"

Millicent wondered *indeed, will it be a problem*? The answer, *yes*. "Commander, I would appreciate your allowing me to be in the pools closer to my home, at least for the time being. Right now, my husband's support is tenuous and I would like to see my children on a daily basis. Once my husband adjusts to my working for the ATA, I believe he will be accepting of my staying away for short periods of time."

"I am in the process of setting up a new ferry pool at White Waltham, where my main headquarters will be. Are you familiar with the area?"

"Oh, yes, I belong to the aero club there. I've heard the rumors about it becoming ATA headquarters. Will you be ferrying planes from there also?"

The commander smiled at the woman sitting on the other side of her desk. "Yes. I have many applications to go through for the next group of *my* pilots." She looked back at the paper on her desk. "How much time have you spent training others to fly?"

Millicent had the answer. "I would say about two hundred hours."

"Excellent. I can always use someone versed in training." The commander placed her hands flat on the table, stood up, and extended her hand. "Welcome aboard, Lady Armstrong."

Chapter Four

January 1935
Fifty miles north of Brisbane, Australia

Life had never been easy for Brenda Hiller. The Great Depression had forced her to leave school and go to work to help her family put food on the table. Each day she got up and watched as her brothers and sisters went off to school—she growled before pummeling her pillow with her fists. Two of her brothers, Jack and Richard, were older than she was yet they stayed in school while she was the one singled out to work. When she asked her father *why*, he grunted, slapped her across the face and told her keep her mouth shut and do what he told her to do.

Her family's ramshackle house had a rusted metal roof and walls that threatened to fall every time there was a strong gust of wind. It was cold and miserable in the winter—hot and even more miserable in the summer. She and her three sisters shared a small room where a dirty, stained mattress they all slept on rested on the floor. Her three brothers shared a larger room with actual bed frames—they each had their own mattress. Thomas and Barbara Hiller slept in the warmest room in the house near the kitchen.

Six days a week, she begrudgingly walked the three miles toting a milk pail and basket to a local dairy farm where she'd spend her days mucking the barn and cleaning out the chicken coops before she distributed fresh straw in both places. If she was lucky, it wasn't a hot humid day and she could actually breathe while working. Otherwise, she covered her mouth and nose with a bandana but invariably she'd still smelled the stench when she got home. The dairy paid her in milk and eggs but would occasionally give her some beef or chicken if they happened to be slaughtering at the time she was there. It was a hard life and she hated every minute of it.

*

Rain pelted the sides of the run down building all night and when Brenda stepped outside her foot sank into a sea of mud. Shoes were a luxury. Every day, regardless of the weather conditions, her bare feet would walk to work where they would provide her with boots to do her job. A light mist soaked her clothes and when she stepped into the warm barn, she was very conscious of her thin shirt outlining her budding breasts. She could feel the eyes of her employer, Claude McGuire and his son, Harvey, on her and she tried to cover up by crossing her arms over her chest.

"Stop standing there like a bludger and get to work," Claude yelled.

I'm not lazy—Brenda nodded, slipped into the barn boots, and grabbed a pitchfork. Keeping her eyes downcast, she got busy lifting the manure filled straw and carrying it out of the barn. The air was thick and moist making the disgusting odor all the more distasteful. Her arms ached as she deposited the last of the straw into a wagon. Next, she would have to throw buckets of water on the floor before she swept it out of the barn.

"You're too slow," Claude chided as he walked into the barn. "It's already two and you haven't started on the chicken coop." He stood in front of the young girl and sneered before wadding the front of her shirt as he pulled her close. "You want to keep this job you better get busy and work faster. There's plenty out there who'd take this job in a heartbeat." He slapped her face before releasing her shirt and pushing her backward, causing her to fall on her bum.

Harvey laughed at her. "She's got a stinky bum," he said as he walked by her and purposely stomped in a puddle of feces filled water.

Brenda got to her feet, refusing to cry or let either father or son know how much they humiliated her. With determined steps, she walked toward the chicken coop and began the chore of shooing the birds out so she could clean the place. *Someday I'm getting out of here.* Often she would find eggs still in the nests and was tempted to keep them but never did. Her brother told her that the last bloke was caught stealing eggs and Mr. McGuire chopped off his fingers. She was satisfied with whatever Claude McGuire saw fit to give her. Some days it would be one egg, others ten. The milk she received for her work was always one bucket full, which lasted the Hiller family one day.

"I don't know why I have to be the only one who works," she mumbled as she scooped the last of the straw from the chicken coop.

Her father made a meager living by herding sheep for a man who no longer could do it himself. The pay was next to nothing but occasionally he would bring home a dead sheep for his family to eat. *Be glad you have something to put in your belly*; he would say when all they had to eat was some week old mutton.

"I hate mutton," she grumbled as she walked home. "Jack should be here shoveling poop and I should be the one going to school."

Startled by a noise she had never heard before, Brenda looked up into the sky and scowled at what she saw. "Crikey!" She blinked and looked again at the object flying in the sky. The next thing she knew, the giant flying thing was falling through the sky before it landed in the field next to where she was walking. Her eyes quickly looked up and down the road—she was alone.

Brenda wanted to run and hide but didn't—the thing resting on three wheels in the field held her in a grip of fascination. With an intense gaze from her dark blue eyes, she watched as a person climbed out onto the wing of the machine before lightly jumping to the ground. When she heard *hello*, her eyes grew wide. *It's a woman!*

Dumbfounded, Brenda gawked at the woman as she made her way across the field. She was on the tall side—not as tall as Brenda's father was but a good inch or two taller than Brenda—the woman wore trousers, heavy boots, and a worn leather jacket with a fur collar. In all her fourteen years, Brenda had never seen anything like it and her mouth was still open when the woman came up to her.

"Hello," a rich British voice said. "Can you tell me where I am, please?"

With a nod, the girl finally said, "About eighty kilometers north of Brisbane." Brenda shrugged. "You're out here with us bushies."

"Bushies?" the elegant voice inquired.

"Yeah, it's the people who live out here."

The woman nodded, looked around, and then smiled. "Yes, I can see that." She pulled a map out of her pocket and frowned. "Brisbane, you say?" After the young girl nodded she asked, "Can you tell me where I might find some petrol? I seemed to have run out."

"Um," Brenda said, trying to buy time, for the woman's light blue eyes disconcerted her. She could take the woman back to the McGuire place. They would know where to get petrol. It was clear to her that Claude and his son didn't think much of females and figured one who came out of a flying contraption would not receive the kindest of greetings. On the other hand, she could take the woman to her house and hope that her father would know where to get the petrol. She looked at the woman again. *I'd be embarrassed to take such an elegant person there.* "Um, I don't know where you'd get it around here…not many can afford a vehicle."

"Oh, I see." The woman's lips became a thin line, as she seemed to be contemplating what to do. "Eighty kilometers, you say?"

Brenda nodded. "Maybe a little more. It'd be a fair piece to walk to the big smoke."

Light brown eyebrows knitted.

"Brisbane…the big smoke."

The tall woman nodded. "Ah. Yes, I would think so."

The young girl could see the stranger looking around as she tapped a finger against her lips. "Hmm, whatever shall I do?"

When the woman looked at her with kind eyes, Brenda desperately wanted to help her. *But how?* Then she remembered. "Maude Taylor," she blurted out. "Maude Taylor lives about four miles from here and she'd know how to get petrol." Pleased with herself, Brenda smiled at the woman before she put the basket of eggs down. "I'm Brenda Hiller."

With a warm smile the woman said, "Sarah Faulkner and I am pleased to meet you, Brenda."

"Right," the younger girl said. "Let's get crackin'." She picked up the basket and looked at the stranger once again. "I have to drop these at my house…it's along the way."

"Lead on, Brenda."

Neither spoke as they walked down the dirt road. After they had gone about two miles, Brenda stopped. "Down there is where I live," she said nodding down a small dirt road. "I'll be right back," she said nervously as she glanced worriedly down the path.

Sarah smiled at her young companion. "If you don't mind, I'll wait here," she said as she brushed a lock of auburn hair off her forehead. "I need to catch my breath."

Brenda took in the whole of the woman, noting that she seemed fit and there were no outward signs that she was in any kind of distress with her breathing. However, she was glad that the woman opted not to follow her down the path to her house. "I won't be but a mo," she said before she hurried down the path.

*

As the dilapidated house she called home came into view, Brenda quickly looked over her shoulder. The last thing she wanted the elegant woman to see was the squalor she lived in. She pushed open the door and walked quickly to the kitchen, stopping when she spied her mother standing at the sink.

"Here's the milk and eggs," she said as she moved toward the sink. After putting the basket and pail on the table she added, "I'll be back after a bit."

Barbara Hiller turned and looked at her oldest daughter with vacant eyes. She rested a hand on her bulging abdomen and asked, "Where are you going? I'll need your help with supper."

Brenda filled with resentment as her eyes took in the pregnant woman. How hard would it have been for someone else in the family to help? She had spent the day working. *Why is it I always have to be the one to help with supper and the dishes?* "I met someone who is lost and need to show her were Maude Taylor lives."

"Well, you can't go. I need your help here," Barbara said in a flat voice.

Without hesitation, Brenda turned and headed for the door—no one, including her, ever listened to what her mother said. As far as Brenda was concerned, her mother was nothing more than a pathetic woman who stood by doing nothing while her husband abused his children and wife. She had no respect or love for the woman.

Brenda's steps lengthen as she walked quickly back to the waiting Sarah. They needed to be gone before her father came home. The last thing she wanted was to subject the woman to her father.

*

"What was that flying thing you were in?" Brenda asked as they neared Maude's house.

"It's called an airplane. I was going to Sydney," she said dryly. "Someday I will have to give you a ride."

Brenda looked at Sarah and smiled. "Crikey! Me, up in the air in that thing?" Smiles never filled her face and she wondered why it did now. This woman, Sarah Faulkner, had an easy way about her and that made Brenda at ease too. "Sydney is south of here."

Sarah chuckled. "Yes, I know. I was studying my map while you were gone. It seems I am a tad off course." She looked up to see a large white house at the end of the path. "Is this where Maude lives?"

"Yes. Let me go to the door…people around here don't take too kindly to strangers."

"Certainly. I will wait here."

Brenda climbed the steps before knocking on the door. After a minute, the door opened. Maude was a short woman with steel gray hair and dark brown eyes that were staring at the young girl in question. She owned the biggest farm in the area and, at sixty, was still in charge of the day to day activities of the farm.

"You one of those Hiller brats?" the old woman asked. She leaned toward Brenda. "Right, the oldest girl."

"G'day, Miss Taylor," she said before pointing at the waiting Sarah. "She's lost her way and needs petrol."

Maude's eyes took in the woman who was standing at the bottom of the steps before she nodded and said, "You both might as well come in."

Once seated, Maude looked the woman over. From the looks of her, Maude guessed her age to be around maybe eighteen or twenty—far too young to be out in the bush and lost. She was tall with auburn hair cropped shorter than any woman she knew. Her eyes were haunting since they were so light blue that they appeared from a distance to be clear. Maude then turned her attention to the Hiller girl who had done a few odd jobs around her house before she began working at the McGuire farm. *Such a sad girl.* The unruly black curly hair made her want to take a brush to it. *If someone would only take an interest in keeping her clean, she'd be a beauty.* Maude knew that would never happen— the depression took a cruel toll on those that had nothing before it began.

Maude broke the silence. "How much petrol do you need?"

Sarah straightened her back and smiled at the small woman. "Enough to get me to the nearest big town."

"That'd be Brisbane."

"She's in a flying machine," Brenda blurted.

Maude's eyes widened. "Is that true? You have an airplane?"

With a nod, Sarah said, "Yes, I was trying to set a record for the shortest time from Christchurch, New Zealand to Sydney." She lifted her shoulders as her face took on a pink tinge. "Took a wrong turn and ran out of petrol."

"How old are you, child?" Maude asked.

"Eighteen."

"And you fly?"

A nervous smile crossed Sarah's face. "Yes."

Maude looked at the girl with renewed interest. She reasoned that if the girl had one of those flying contraptions and could afford petrol, her family must be well off considering the economic times. *Where is her family? Her accent is definitely British.*

"Do you live in Australia?" the older woman asked.

"No, England. I was trying to set a record for the shortest time from London to New Zealand." Sarah lifted her eyes and smiled. "I didn't do it so now I am trying to do it in reverse."

"There's a small town fifteen kilometers from here," Maude stood up, "it is too late to get there tonight. I'll have to take you there in the morning."

"Oh, I see. Thank you." Sarah too stood up. "I will stay with my airplane tonight and return in the morning then."

"Nonsense, you can stay here. No one will bother your machine." Maude's eyes turned to Brenda. "You best be getting home, child."

Relieved that Maude asked Sarah to stay there, Brenda was also disappointed that she would have to go back to her horrible home. She wanted to stay and listen to the soft cadence of Sarah's cultured voice. "Right," was all she could say.

Sarah looked at the young girl. "Thank you for helping me," she said as she took a piece of paper and pencil from her jacket and jotted something down. "This is my address. Will you write me?" she said hesitantly as she offered Brenda the paper.

With a look of embarrassment, Brenda took the scrap of paper. "I'll try." She got up, walked to the door and said, "Hooroo," before leaving the house.

Once the door closed, Maude gave Sarah a contemplative looks. "You know she probably hasn't the money for paper, much less an envelope and stamp."

"I gathered as much," Sarah said. "She is such a beautiful child, it is too bad…how much does a bar of soap cost? Can't she clean herself up?"

Maude snorted. "I can assure you, Sarah, that soap is the last thing that family would want. When you force your child to quit school to work for milk and eggs, you don't have money for luxuries such as soap."

"That's horrible. I will buy them some then. Surely the town we are going to for petrol will have soap."

"Being poor doesn't mean you're not proud, Sarah. Giving that family anything would not be received the way you'd mean it…and I suspect that child would suffer if you did."

Sarah's eyebrows knitted as a look of horror crossed her face. "Surely not…why would anyone want to hurt her…she's a sweet child."

Maude patted Sarah's arm. "Because he can."

*

Brenda walked on the path leading to her house, filled with apprehension. She was late and supper was probably already over. "I know what that means," she mumbled as she reached the front door and pushed it open. The first person she saw was her father.

"You stupid sheila," he screamed as she moved closer to his daughter.

Brenda took a step back as she braced herself for what she knew was coming.

With his fists clenched, Brenda's father hit her hard in the jaw causing her to fall back into the unsteady door frame. "You think you're so high and mighty that you can just waltz in here when you like?" he bellowed as he picked her up by grabbing the front of her shirt and hit her again.

Brenda hung suspended in air as her father repeatedly hit her body.

"I'll teach you," he growled as he threw her to the floor. He gave Brenda a kick in the stomach and snarled. "You fuckwit. Get the hell out of my sight."

Once her father had walked away, Brenda struggled to her feet and looked at her mother who shrugged. "You got what you deserved. No supper for you tonight."

Brenda swallowed hard knowing if she said anything, he would beat her again. With downcast eyes, she walked slowly to the small room where she slept. All three of her sisters were crowded in the room trying to change their clothes.

"Are you ok?" her youngest sister, Charlotte, asked.

After a swipe of her hand across her bloodied mouth, Brenda nodded. It wouldn't pay to say anything. She was her father's punching bag and if word ever got back to him that she complained, he wouldn't hesitate in beating her again. She gingerly lifted her arms to take her shirt off—it was blood stained—then put it back on before she left the room.

The night air was cold against her bare skin as she dunked her shirt in a trough used for washing. Brenda bunched two parts of the shirt in her hands and vigorously rubbed them together under the water. Once she was satisfied that the blood stains were gone, she splashed her face with the dirty water. Her mind focused on the woman she took to Maude Taylor's house and how elegant and beautiful she was. Never had anyone asked for her help or advice. She tried to think back to a time when she had any type of conversation with someone that didn't relate to her family or her job. She couldn't recall one instance in her fourteen years when anyone cared about what she said. *But Sarah did...didn't she?* Her fingers slid into her pocket and retrieved the scrap of paper. The writing on the paper was neat and precise—Sarah Faulkner, 55 Waverley Place, Kingston upon Thames, England. She fingered the paper and looked at the name again before sighing deeply and stuffing it back into her pocket. *There's no way I will ever be able to write her.*

The next day as she was walking home from the McGuire farm, she spotted Sarah standing by her airplane. Hoping she wasn't spotted, she began to walk faster.

"Hello," the rich British accent called.

Brenda stopped in her tracks and considered running away from the woman before she waved back. "G'day," she called out.

Sarah walked quickly in Brenda's direction before she stopped suddenly then took tentative steps until she was standing in front of the girl. "Wh…what happened to you?"

Hands went immediately to her face as Brenda tired to cover the bruises. "Nothing," she said softly. "I ran into the door when I went home last night…it was dark and I didn't see it." Fingers tugged at her hand then gently touched her bruised cheek.

"Who did this to you?" Sarah asked.

Brenda shied away from the touch. No one ever touched her in anything but anger—the gentleness of the touch disconcerted her. "Don't," she said.

"I'm sorry."

"Did you get the petrol?" Brenda asked, grateful that the woman made no further effort to touch her.

"Yes, I am ready to take off. I was hoping I would see you before I left." Sarah turned to leave then spun back around. "Look, I know we just met, but I want you to know that if you ever need anything…please tell me." She spread her arms and took Brenda into a fierce hug.

Brenda stood and watched as the woman climbed into the airplane and continued to watch as the vehicle rolled down the field before lifting into the late afternoon sky.

"Goodbye," she said as a tear ran down her cheek before it stung her cracked lip.

*

Three years later, Maude Taylor stood waiting by the path leading to the Hiller home for Brenda to appear. When she saw the girl walking toward her, she had to catch her breath. The last time she saw the girl was four months after she had helped Sarah Faulkner obtain petrol for her flying machine. Sarah had sent her a letter and included one for the girl. The girl who stood at her door years earlier was now a much taller and sleeker woman. Her clothes were not new by any measure but they were clean, as was Brenda's face and neck.

"G'day, Brenda," Maude said in a strong voice. "I've been waiting for you."

Brenda smiled. "G'day, Miss Taylor." Her forehead creased as she cautiously asked, "Why have you been waiting for me?"

"I have something for you," Maude said. Her arm lifted and she reached out with an envelope.

With eyes opening wide, Brenda took the envelope. "Is this another letter from Sarah?" she asked as she looked at the envelope before she carefully opened it. With a smile covering her face, she read the letter.

Dear Brenda,

It has been a long time since I have written you a letter and I apologize for that. I have thought of you and your kindness toward me often. I can still see the amazement on your face when you first looked at my airplane and every time I do, I smile.

I have been busy honing my flying skills so I can make another attempt at a record. This time it will be from

London to Sydney. I will be leaving in a week's time and if all goes well, I hope to be spending time in Sydney shortly after that.

If it is at all possible, I'd like to see you when I visit Maude in a few weeks. I remember offering to give you a ride in my airplane and hope to fulfill that promise then.

Looking forward to seeing you again,
Sarah Faulkner

Brenda turned her now bright blue eyes to Maude. "She's coming here?"

The happiness in Brenda's face made Maude smile back at her. "Yes, it would seem so."

"Will you let me know when she arrives?"

"Of course, dear. I suspect once you hear the sound of the engine on that contraption, you will know long before I do."

Brenda tentatively reached out and touched Maude's arm. "Thank you," she said softly. Her eyes then turned to the path. "I'd better get going…my dad doesn't like me being late."

Maude watched her go and shook her head. "What a shame." She had made overtures to the girl's father about his daughter coming to work for her—he offered a different daughter—she declined. *I need her to keep working where she is. We need the milk and eggs* he had told her before slamming the door in her face.

*

Brenda smoothed out her shirt as she stood nervously at Maude Taylor's door.

In secret, she had spent time getting her clothes as clean as possible with the limited resources her mother had. She got up early and washed her body and hair then spent an hour combing the unruly curls with her fingers. She had carried her clean clothes with her and hid them behind a rock on her way to the McGuire farm. Once there, she worked fast and was done by the middle of the afternoon. After collecting the eggs and milk, she hurried down the dirt road, stopping where she stashed her clothes and disappearing behind a rock where she changed. The only problem—she smelled like manure.

"Crikey, what am I going to do about that?" She ventured further into the brush and stopped at a gently running creek. She passed a lemon myrtle on the way and grabbed a handful of the fragrant leaves. She squatted and splashed the cool water over her arms before rubbing the lemon scented leaves over them. She did the same thing to her face and ended by running her wet fingers through her hair.

Fortunately, no one was around when she dropped off the milk and eggs so she didn't have to explain her cleanliness. Now, as she heard the door open, Brenda panicked and had to make her feet stay in place.

"She's here," Maude said as she opened the door wide.

Brenda couldn't mistake the sound of excitement in the older woman's voice—it reflected how she felt. "G'day," she said as she walked past Maude and stopped when she saw Sarah Faulkner standing in the sitting room. Her mouth opened then closed. "G'day, Sarah."

Sarah's long stride had her facing Brenda then wrapping the girl in her arms. Taking a step back but still holding onto the girl's shoulders, she said, "My, my how grown up you look." She sucked in a breath. "And you smell good on top of that."

Brenda felt heat on her cheeks and she wondered if she might be running a fever. "G'day," was the only word she could think to say.

Sarah grinned. "Are you ready to go for a ride in the sky?"

The younger girl's eyes widened.

Maude, standing nearby, chuckled. "Don't be afraid. Sarah took me up this morning and it was ripper!"

Brenda felt light hearted around the two women. It was the kind of life she wanted but with the family she was cursed with, she knew it would never happen. "I'm ready," she whispered.

*

Never in her life had Brenda felt so free or happy. Flying above everything was so thrilling that she had to keep pinching herself to be sure it was real. Her mind turned to the squalor that was her life. *I don't need to live that way.*

Invigorated, Brenda was sad to see the land below getting closer as Sarah landed the airplane. When it came to a stop, she felt the bubble of happiness burst inside her. The reality that was her life came into view in the form of her father standing next to Maude. Then he was walking quickly toward the plane flapping his arms. She could see the still turning propeller that was drowning out the words she was sure were angry. Her eyes looked around for an escape for what she knew would be coming—there was none.

"You fuckwit, get your ass out of there," Thomas Hiller screamed as he began clutching the wing.

"Excuse me, sir," Sarah said in a deep threatening voice. "Get your bloody hands off my airplane."

Thomas stopped and looked up at the auburn haired woman glaring at him. "Stupid shelia," he said as he proceeded to climb onto the wing.

In a much louder voice, Sarah said, "Stop," as she pointed a tiny revolver at the man. When he continued forward, she pulled the trigger and fired a warning shot.

The angry man stopped and looked at the woman whose eyes were glaring at him.

"The next time the bullet will not miss."

The resoluteness in Sarah's voice filtered past the man's anger. "That's my daughter and I have all the say in her life." He glared at Brenda. "Get down here now!" he commanded.

Just then, several of Maude's hired hands were standing by Thomas. The bigger of the two said, "Ratbag, Miss Taylor wants you off her land."

Thomas looked to his left then his right before looking up at the woman with the gun. He spat on the ground. "She'll have to come home eventually," he said in a cocky tone. "I'll deal with her then."

The two men accompanied Thomas to the road then stood watching him walk away.

"You can't go back there," Sarah said to Brenda once they both were on the ground.

"Sure I can."

Brenda's bravado was met with a skeptical look.

"It's nothing that hasn't happened before."

Maude cleared her throat. "Sarah is right. You can't go back there. You can stay here with me until we can figure out what to do."

Brenda nodded her head. "No, I can't."

"Why?" Maude countered. "What do you have there?"

As she chewed on her lip, Brenda tried to think of one compelling reason to go back to the hovel she lived in or back to the job she hated. "Nothing," she said softly.

"Then it is settled," said Maude. "You are coming to live with me and Sarah."

With her head flicking to the woman beside her, Brenda's eyebrows lifted. "You are living with Miss Taylor?"

Sarah laughed. "For a few weeks then I need to get back to London." She cocked her head and looked intently at Brenda. "Say, why don't you come with me? You can start a whole new life in London."

Brenda's eyes widened. "Oh, I don't know."

"Sure, it will be perfect. I will teach you to fly then you can get a job flying."

It all sounded so incredible that Brenda could only stand with her mouth wide open. *Is it possible? Can I really get away from here?* She pulled at her shirt and trousers. "This is all I have to wear." She shrugged. "I doubt people in London would accept me."

"Leave that to me," Maude said as she patted Brenda on the shoulder. "I think you going to London is…bonzer."

The three women walked back to Maude's house— Brenda shook her head as she was still trying to figure out what had just happened. The bubble of excitement returned and she grinned.

*

For someone who had never been more than three miles away from the place she was born, Brenda felt her mouth was in a constant state of an *O*. The trip to London, via countries and cities she never knew existed, was mind boggling. The first stop after leaving Sydney was Java, in the Dutch Indies.

As they were flying over the island, Brenda saw houses with thatched roofs, palm trees that swayed in the breeze, and brown people. Never before had she seen such sights—women walking with baskets on their heads, small horse drawn carriages, multi-tiered pagodas, and a port filled with strange looking boats. She saw people that had brown skin and since she had never seen anything like that before and since her only point of reference was Aborigines, she assumed that was who they were. Sarah laughed and told her that all over the world, there were people with different skin colors and most were not Aborigines.

"I can't believe all that I am seeing," Brenda said as they prepared to take off.

Sarah turned, looked at her companion, and smiled. "Before we land in London you will see more incredible sights, Brenda." She started the engine and over its loud noise, she said, "They will all astound you."

And they did. They made stops for petrol in Singapore, Bangkok, Calcutta, Baghdad, Constantinople, and Vienna. At every stop, Brenda took in the rich sights and sounds she saw, imprinting the images in her mind so she could recall them any time she wanted.

At one point after they left Calcutta, Sarah said, "Do you want to learn how to fly?"

With eyes wide, she looked at the woman. "Crikey…that would be ripper!"

Sarah laughed. "I'll take that as *yes*."

*

As the wheels of the de Havilland DH.88 touched the tarmac of a small airport north of London, Brenda felt like singing. Never had anyone taken the time to care about her yet here Sarah, a relative stranger, had shown her the world asking nothing in return.

"I can't believe I'm here," Brenda said softly as she jumped off the airplane wing, landing next to Sarah.

Sarah patted her arm and smiled. "The best is yet to come.

Brenda stood looking at the woman who took her away from squalor and abuse to give her a chance for a better life. "Only now have I thought of my family…my father actually. I wonder who he has chosen as his next fuckwit."

"What exactly does *fuckwit* mean?" Sarah asked.

With her lips pursed in concentration, Brenda tried to think of the English words that would convey the meaning of the word. "Well, I guess it is something like…stupid."

Sarah's eyebrows lifted. "You are far from stupid, Brenda," she said softly. "No one will ever call you a *fuckwit* again," she lifted the girl's chin, "I promise you that."

*

"A room of my own," Brenda whispered after Sarah left her in the room designated as *her* bedroom. She couldn't believe her eyes—the room was bigger than her entire house back in Australia. She moved around the room touching all the furniture, the drapes that covered the windows and finally, the bed. On the flight to London, she and Sarah had stayed in hotels where she had a bed to sleep in but nothing like what she saw in this room. A canopy covered the bed and she wondered if it was to keep spiders from sliding down and getting on the bed. She really didn't care what the reason was—she loved it all.

Going to the window, she pulled back a drape and looked out at a courtyard where a man and woman sat around a small table. They were drinking something out of small cups and reading what she knew was a newspaper. Brenda watched in fascination as Sarah joined them and they immediately got up and gave her a hug—no one ever hugged Brenda. The threesome stood talking and she saw Sarah point to the house and wave. Self conscious at being caught looking at them, she immediately stepped back and let the drape fall across the window. She began shaking, waiting for what she knew would be a beating.

There was a knock on the door and Brenda cowered in a corner, waiting for the inevitable beating she knew she deserved. When she heard the door open, she closed her eyes and covered her face. "Please don't hit me. I'm right sorry for spying on you," she said as her body trembled.

In an instant, Sarah was kneeling down by the quivering girl. When she reached out to touch her shoulder, the girl shrunk away. "I'm not going to hit you, Brenda. I would never do that to you." The girl looked up, revealing a tear stained face. "I want you to come down and meet my mother and father, who arrived home an hour ago…they are waiting to meet you," she said in a soft voice. "Come with me. Please."

Brenda had trusted Sarah enough to leave her home and travel thousands of mile away. The novelty of it all had thrilled her and she really didn't consider what it all meant—getting out of the hell hole that was her home was the driving force behind her being in London. As she searched Sarah's face, she only saw… *What?* She couldn't remember anyone ever looking at her the way Sarah did. Her father only ever looked at her with contempt and anger and her mum's face only showed emptiness. Sarah's eyes were far different—they were kind. *Yes, I can trust her.* She stood and wiped her eyes and nose with the back of her hand that she promptly rubbed against her shirt.

"Do I look all right?"

Sarah smiled. "You look perfect."

*

As they approached the plane that Brenda would learn to fly, she said, "I have no way of paying for the lessons you give me, Sarah."

Sarah patted her new friend's back. "I have thought of that and have an offer for you."

Brenda's eyebrows rose almost to her hairline. "What?"

"If you agree to help out around here," she said, pointing to the hangar with the plane, "I will give you lessons plus a small amount of money to use as you would like."

With tears threatening, Brenda looked away. "I have never worked for money, only eggs and milk."

Sarah heard the trembling of her friend's voice and pulled her in for a hug. "Now you will, Brenda, and you can spend it on whatever you like."

Another thing Brenda was not use to—the intimate contact with another person—when her father touched her, it was to beat or molest her. Sarah, on the other hand, would often hug her or touch her. At first she would shy away, not understanding why anyone would treat her in such a way. But, as she became accustom to the gestures, she found she quite enjoyed the feeling. "How can I repay you?"

"It is not a free ride I am giving you, Brenda. I will work you hard and expect nothing less than your best."

"I won't let you down…I promise."

*

As she sped down the runway for her first lesson, Brenda felt her stomach lurch and as the plane lifted off the tarmac, she was certain she was going to throw up. But once she took to the sky, she forgot everything else as she automatically flew, following Sarah's every word exactly. When the tires touched the ground in her landing, she felt a sense of sadness—she wanted to be soaring above the world again.

"Well," Sarah said as she met Brenda when she jumped off the plane's wing. "What did you think?"

"Bonzer! When can I go again?"

Sarah laughed and put her arm around her friend. "First we need to make sure we take care of the plane and everything is put away. I will show you how it is done and then I will expect you to do the job yourself after that."

"No worries," Brenda said. "I will make you proud."

After that, it was clear that Brenda took to flying like she's always been airborne. In no time, she had mastered all aspects of flying and after fifty hours of Sarah training her, she flew the plane alone for the first time. When she landed, Sarah was waiting for her.

"You did it, Brenda. I am so proud of you." They took a few more steps before Sarah stopped. "I've been thinking of teaching people to fly and would like you to help me do that. What do you think?"

Overwhelmed, with tears flowing freely, Brenda looked at her friend. "What about Edward? Won't he want to help you?"

Sarah shrugged. "Yes, after we got engaged, that was our plan."

"Why are you asking me then?"

"With all this talk of war, he joined the RAF and will be going to India in a few weeks."

Brenda now understood why her friend had seemed distant over the last month. Sarah's engagement to Edward Graham, a man she had known for years, was not a surprise. Sarah's mother would often tell Brenda how pleased she was to see her daughter so happy. It wasn't until the last few weeks that the joy that seemed to shine constantly in Sarah's eyes had faded some.

"I'm so sorry, Sarah."

With a quick smile, Sarah said, "Don't be. He is honor bound to help our country if we go to war," she paused, "as are all the King's subjects."

Brenda digested the information before looking at Sarah—her friend's eyes belied her words. In an unfamiliar gesture, she pulled Sarah into a warm embrace. She whispered, "No one has ever asked me what I think about anything until I met you, Sarah." She began to speak again but nothing would come out of her mouth. When she finally spoke, she said, "I…that would be ripper, Sarah."

Sarah hugged Brenda closer then took a step back. "I think we will make a great team. With all this talk of war and with so many of the lads wanting to learn to fly…I am confident that we will be very busy. Are you up for that?"

"I reckon so." Brenda's tear streaked face filled with a smile. "Thank you." She tentatively searched Sarah's face and saw sincerity. "When do we start?"

"First we will get your pilot's license," Sarah said, patting Brenda's back. "Then we start. Who knows what the future holds for us, Brenda."

Chapter Five

May 1940
White Waltham, England

Meg O'Brien stood against a wall and looked around at the people gathered in a briefing room. It wasn't unlike the place where she helped her uncle train the Royal Air Force pilots. Her eyes rested on a group of men who looked nothing like the strapping young lads at Attlebridge Station where she'd lived for the last five months. To her eyes, they all had some sort of deformity—one man had a patch over one eye, another was missing an arm, and one walked with a visible limp.

In another area stood about twenty women and she scanned them, playing a game she had played at Attlebridge—size up the competition. The one person who stood out was a tall woman with hair the color of straw. *She has to be American. No one else would dare have that color.* As she kept her eyes on the woman, she noticed her hands kept touching a slightly taller woman next to her. It amused Meg to see the second woman continually move away from the blonde's gestures. Her eyes then turned to the rest of the group. As far as she could tell everyone else had dark hair but she couldn't be certain since the blonde was so outstanding that she had a hard time seeing much else. *One thing is for sure, I'm the only redhead.* It was easy for her to spot the Brits for they were all together like a mother's knitting group—she counted ten. *They will have the edge if it comes down to between one of them and me.* She had heard that they were trying to recruit some flying ace from Chile and surmised that the light brown skinned woman was that person. *The field is narrowing.* She finally pushed off the wall and walked toward the group of women.

*

Jo Laughlin swatted Midge Reister's hand away for the umpteenth time and finally walked away from her. As she walked out into an unoccupied area, she saw a woman with a sleek body and dark red hair coming toward her.

"Hello," Jo drawled.

"Good day ta you," the redhead said in a distinctive brogue. "You're a Yank, aren't you?"

Jo chuckled. "And, you're Irish."

"That I am." She stuck her hand out. "Meg O'Brien."

"Pleased to meet you, Meg. I'm Jo Laughlin." Jo looked back at the circle of women then back to Meg. "Any idea what happens next?"

"My guess would be ta test us on how well we fly."

"Yeah, that's sort of what I thought would happen too."

"I've spent the last five months getting in as many hours as I can…I hear they are only taking ten of us."

"What about the men? What's up with them? They all look like the last men I'd call pilots."

It was Meg's turn to chuckle. "As long as they can demonstrate their flyin' abilities, they will be accepted."

Jo looked over the group of men and counted heads. "In that case, it means the women's chances for acceptance aren't very good."

"From what I've heard, they will be selectin' ten women for an all female ferry pool." She nodded in the direction of the men. "The newspapers have dubbed them *Ancient Tattered Airmen.*"

Jo's shoulders relaxed. "Thanks, I was worried I came all this way for nothing."

"I think your blonde friend is trying ta get your attention," Meg pointed out.

It was hard to do, but Jo prevented herself from rolling her eyes. "Is she?" she said in a bland tone.

"Are you two here together?"

Jo let out a laugh and shook her head. "We come from the same state in America and traveled here together."

"Seems like your friend enjoys the spotlight," Meg commented as she watched the woman interacting with the group surrounding her.

"Why do you say that?" Jo asked as she resisted the desire to turn and look at Midge.

Meg laughed. "Anyone with that color hair is screaming *look at me*." A blush spread up her face. "That and her breasts…she will be a favorite of the lads, I'm sure."

Jo grinned. "You might just be right about that, Meg."

Just as Jo was about to add more about Midge, a man's voice said, "I need everyone's attention."

*

Everyone in the room looked at the man, who was middle aged with wavy gray hair and sporting a moustache. He was dressed in a dark blue uniform with a black tie and a single breasted leather jacket with ATA embroidered on a dark background in the middle of gold wings. The epilate on his shoulders had two wide gold lines with a thinner one in the middle.

"Good morning," the man said with a pleasant British accent. "I am Captain Reginald Wentworth. The activities you will be involved in today and tomorrow will help us determine which of you will go on and become a member of the ATA." His grey eyes scanned all the eager faces looking at him. "We will evaluate you several ways. First, you will get a complete physical examination. Second, you will take a written test before meeting with a staff counselor. Lastly, we will evaluate your individual flying skills."

The captain turned and pointed at red swinging doors. "Through those doors is the canteen where you will partake in your morning meal, lunch, and tea later on." He held up a packet of papers. "On this paper you will find your individual schedules. Some of you will start by flying, others with an exam, or a medical. As I call your name, please come forward and take your packet then adjourn to the canteen. You will see that at nine-hundred hours we will start the procedure." He held up another piece of paper. "In each packet you will find a map with the locations you will need to report to, along with barrack assignments. The barracks are directly in the back of this building and there are floors for both the men and women. You will find your baggage in the rest room of that building."

Jo felt a hand on her shoulder and didn't have to turn around—it was Midge.

Midge whispered close to Jo's ear, "I'll take the top bunk," she cooed as she discretely licked Jo's ear.

"Stop that!" Jo exclaimed as she took several steps away from the woman.

"Who's your pretty, new friend," Midge asked as she raked her eyes over Meg's body. "She looks positively scrumptious."

"You're comments are vulgar, Midge. They don't have a place here so stop it," Jo said in a low voice. "Stop embarrassing yourself." She straightened her shoulders and gave the redhead an apologetic look. "Sorry," she said.

"No problems," Meg said as she nodded toward the man. "He just said your name."

"Thanks." Jo got her packet and stood near the red door, waiting for her new acquaintance to join her. Midge got there first.

"Come on," Midge said, tugging at Jo's sleeve. "I'm starving."

Jo kept her eyes on the pilots still getting their packets. "You go ahead and I'll be right behind you."

Midge's eyes tracked to where Jo was staring and she let out a big sigh. "Get real, Jo, she's way out of your league."

With blazing eyes, Jo spun around, glared at Midge, and then turned her back on the woman. When she saw Meg coming her way, she smiled.

"Are ya waitin' for me, Jo Laughlin?"

"That I am." Jo opened the red door. "After you," she said as her hand swept the air.

Meg entered the canteen then she stopped. "Will your blonde friend be joinin' us then?"

Jo, following close behind, scanned the area. Midge was holding court in the middle of the room. With a sigh of relief, she said, "No."

*

Brenda Hiller sat nervously on a bench outside a physician's office. Back home in Australia she had never seen or heard of a doctor. Although her friend, Sarah, had told her what to expect, she still felt acute apprehension at the thought of a stranger seeing or touching her body. She did, however, like the sensation she felt when Sarah or Sarah's mother hugged her—no one in her life had shown her any sort of affection until she met Sarah.

"It is best if you're not upset," Beverly Maddox said in her southern drawl.

With eyes wide, Brenda stared at the woman. "Crikey, you're an American."

Beverly smiled. "Yes, I am."

"You're the first one I've met," Brenda said as she took in the athletic looking woman. She had deep blue eyes, brown hair, and was an inch or so shorter than Brenda's five seven.

Silence ensued for a few moments until Beverly smiled at the young woman next to her. "Have you been in England long?"

"'bout the better part of a year." Brenda sucked in a deep breath. "I'm a bit nervous about this doctor thing…I've never been before."

With eyebrows knitting, Beverly looked at the girl. "Never?"

Brenda shook her head. "I'd never been further than three miles from the place I was born until I came here."

"Really? This must be quite a change for you." When Beverly saw the girl nod, she added, "No need to be worried about the physical. It will be pretty much a standard kind of thing…height, weight, blood pressure, eye and ear tests, a listen to your heart and lungs, and blood work." She lifted one shoulder. "Probably will take less than fifteen minutes…oh, and they will ask you about your medical history."

"Right, that is what my friend, Sarah, said too." Brenda let a small smile curve her lips. "Still can't help being nervous."

With a tentative touch on Brenda's hand, Beverly asked, "Do you really want to be part of the ATA?" The girl nodded. "They will be evaluating you as to how you react under stress and if you show you are nervous, they will not take you."

"No? What do I need to do?"

"They want you to be cool and calm when you fly and if you are all worked up because of a medical exam, they will think you'd react the same in a plane in a stressful situation."

"Oh," Brenda said with a crestfallen expression.

"What I do is take a deep breath, hold it, and then blow it out through my mouth ten times." She patted the girl's arm. "You'll do just fine."

With a tentative smile, Brenda breathed in deeply and held her breath before blowing the air out her mouth. After she had done that, a few times she smiled at Beverly. "That's bonzer…it works. Thank you."

Just then, the door opened. "Brenda Hiller," a woman in a white uniform said.

*

Midge Reister climbed out of the deHavilland single engine aircraft with a smile plastered across her face. "Thanks, Henry," she said to the evaluator in the back seat. "I'll be seeing you later," she said before heading for a hangar.

"What was it like?" the hazel eyed Bess Potter asked.

With a smile, Midge winked at the woman. "A piece of cake," she said to the smaller, very cute girl. "I just love that British accent…it is soooo cute."

Bess frowned. "I was talking about the flight you just took…how do you think it went?"

Midge wrapped her arm around Bess's shoulders. "It went smashingly."

"You do know that some of the ten places have already been filled, don't you?"

Midge pulled the girl closer before she whispered, "If you stick with me, honey, we'll both be in the running."

Wide-eyed, Bess let out a nervous laugh. "How can you say that? I have heard that some of them have over a thousand hours…I can't compete with that."

"You go out there, Bess, give Henry your best smile then fly like it is second nature. That plane is so simple that it is a breeze to fly." Midge patted Bess's behind. "Now go out there and fly. When you get back, I'll be right here waiting for you."

Bess felt her face heat up and she looked away from Midge. "Ok, I will."

Midge patted the girl's backside. "That's my girl," she said with a grin then watched as Bess walked toward the plane. *Nice ass.* She kept watching Bess until the plane lifted off the ground. She was thinking about the young girl and future prospects for bedding her when she heard a voice from behind her.

"Are they running late?" a soft English voice asked.

When she turned around, Midge saw a tall, slender looking woman. "Well, hello, gorgeous," she purred as she overtly took in the woman's body. "I'm not running anywhere."

Flustered, the woman said, "Are you next?"

"Well, I certainly hope so," Midge said, ogling the woman's breasts. "I've already flown." She held out her hand. "Midge Reister."

The woman gave Midge a curious look then said, "Sarah Faulkner."

"Ah, yes, Sarah Faulkner, the girl who tried to set the record for fastest time to what was it…yes, Sydney, Australia."

Sarah looked at the woman in surprise. "You know about that?"

"Yes, I do. Let me see," Midge held a finger to her lips, "you were dubbed the *flying debutante.*"

As the red color on her face deepened, Sarah shook her head. "They had it all wrong…I am *not* an aristocrat."

Midge grinned. "But daddy is."

"He was given a title for his services to industry in the British Empire. He would not be happy at your inference. He worked hard for the privilege," Sarah said in a firm tone.

"Fair enough." Midge gave the girl's body another overt appraisal before she smiled seductively. "What do you think of everything so far, Sarah? I suppose with all your notoriety, you won't have any problem with being accepted."

Sarah stiffened her back. "I assure you, I have no advantage over anyone. I am here going through every step, just as you are."

Midge held a hand up. "Hold on there, Sarah, I didn't mean to insult you." She moved closer and softened her voice. "I'm in awe of meeting you. What you did was so inspiring to me that I merely meant anyone who can fly all that distance surely won't have any trouble with what we are having thrown at us today."

"Oh," Sarah said as she relaxed her body. "I misinterpreted what you said."

With a grin, Midge held her hand out again. "Friends?"

A smile turned Sarah's lips upward. "Of course." She took the woman's hand and shook it. "Can you tell me how long ago the person before me took off?"

Midge looked at her wristwatch. "It's been about twenty minutes now. I suspect they will be landing any time now."

"Right," Sarah said as her eyes began scanning the sky. "Then I am done for the day."

"Would you like to join me for dinner?"

Sarah frowned. "What?" she asked before her eyes widened. "Oh, you're talking about tea."

"No, I was talking about the evening meal."

With a laugh, Sarah said, "That is tea to me and yes, I will join you, if you don't mind my friend coming too."

"I would never turn down a chance to dine with two beautiful women." When Midge looked down the runway, she said, "Here comes the plane now."

Sarah nodded and readied herself for her final task of the day. As she moved away from the blonde woman, she stopped and said over her shoulder, "I'll see you later then."

"I'm counting on it."

*

Camila Calvo sat at a long table by herself. Although the ATA had actively recruited her to join their ranks, she felt out of place. She knew she could fly with the best of them but having a limited knowledge of the English language made her apprehensive about her decision to come to England. She looked around the dining area and sighed. She missed her family and desperately wanted to talk with her mother.

"May I join you?" an unfamiliar voice asked.

When the dark eyed beauty looked up, she saw someone she hadn't seen before. "Yes," she said.

The woman sat next to Camila and smiled. "I'm Shannon Brannigan, a senior pilot for the ATA. You're Camila, aren't you?"

Camila's eyebrows knitted as she tried to understand what the woman said. "My English," she rotated her hand back and forth, "is no so good."

The ginger-haired woman smiled. "My Spanish is not so good either." Shannon looked up and saw Mara Nasmith, a woman she met earlier standing with a tray in her hands. She waved at the woman to join them.

Mara sat opposite Shannon and Camila. "Thanks for asking me. I hate eating alone."

"Mara, this is Camila Calvo. She came here all the way from Chile."

With her hand extended across the table, Mara said, "Hello, Camila, I'm Mara Nasmith and I'm from Scotland."

All Camila could do was nod—she recognized very few words. "Yes, it is…um…good see you."

It wasn't but a few minutes before Midge and her entourage entered the room and joined Camila, Shannon and Mara. As it was in the morning, the brash Midge was the center of attention and acted more as if she were holding court than sitting down for a meal.

"I had a marvelous day," Midge enthused. "I don't know about the rest of you but I am certain I'll make the cut."

One by one the other women, except for Shannon, echoed Midge's comments, all proclaiming they would all be ATA pilots come the next day.

Shannon listened to the proclamations and smiled. She knew that the fifteen or so women around the table would fill only six of the ten positions since four were already selected. Many of them would face disappointment the next day. The one thing she was certain of—if she had anything to say about it, the blonde would be on the short list tomorrow. *Wish we had more like her*, she thought as she studied the woman. Midge Reister, with her bleach blonde hair, red lipstick, and sensuous body made Shannon tingle all over. She will be mine, there's no doubt about that. Her attention turned to the new arrivals sitting down next to her.

Meg O'Brien was one of the pilots that would be on the list and Shannon would welcome a fellow Irishmen to the ferry pool. The other woman, Jo Laughlin, she knew only from the letter and application she sent to the ATA.

When the woman had been in her group for flying evaluation, Shannon was impressed with her skill as a pilot. *It was the softest landing I've ever felt.* Out of the ten she evaluated, Jo Laughlin was the most qualified but she also knew that Midge seemed to have a special bond with the woman and that wouldn't do. *Not at all.*

"How have you been gettin' along today, Meg?" Shannon asked.

"It's always a good day when I fly," Meg said with a smile. Then she shrugged. "We needed a wee bit more plane to show our skills on, I think."

"I agree," Jo added.

"You be careful of what you wish for, Meg…you might get it, and a whole lot more." Shannon eyed all the women. "You should all understand that this job flyin' for the ATA will be hard, dangerous work. It will be nothin' like you've ever experienced." When she saw some of the worried expressions on the faces around her, she added, "It is not somethin' for the faint of heart. If your name is called tomorrow, make sure you understand what you're lettin' yourselves in for."

*

Early the next day, having eaten breakfast, Midge, with her admirers in tow, headed for the building where they would learn their fate in the ATA. Midge suddenly stopped and everyone had to react quickly so they wouldn't run into each other.

"Look," Midge said nodding toward a vehicle stopped in front of the building they were going.

A man in a dark suit, with a cap on, got out of the vehicle and walked quickly around it to open the right back door. A woman dressed in a light gray suit with a small hat on her head stepped out of the car. After smoothing down her skirt, she proceeded into the building.

"I wonder who she is?" Bess Potter remarked.

"Maybe it is Commander Gower," Mara Nasmith speculated.

"No, that isn't her," Sarah Faulkner said. "I've met her and that isn't her."

Shy wasn't in Midge's vocabulary and she walked up to the man waiting by the vehicle. "Who was that?" she asked.

"Lady Smyth-Armstrong," the man said in a cultured tone before he opened the door and got in.

"Well, la-de-da," Midge said with an exaggerated drawl. "Looks like we're gonna meet British royalty."

Sarah laughed. "Titles like that are handed out all the time by the Crown. It doesn't necessarily mean they have a bloodline to royalty. However, titles are wonderful for making a reservation at the Savoy for tea."

Midge reached the door. "I'll keep that in mind," she said as she prepared to push open the door. "Here we go…get ready, ladies," she added before she pushed on the door and went inside.

Chapter Six

May 1940
ATA Headquarters
White Waltham, England

"Commander," a strong voice said.

"Yes, Leslie," Pauline Gower, commander of the Air Transport Auxiliary for women pilots, said.

"They're all in the briefing area."

"Good. Thank you. Has Commander Clarke arrived?"

"I haven't seen her this morning, Commander. Would you like me to find her?"

"Yes, and have her come to my office before the briefing."

Once Pauline heard the door close, she returned her attention to the file folder holding the current assessment of the new ATA recruits. From the look of it, this new group of women would work out perfectly for the new all-women ferry pool at Hatfield-Ferry Pool No. 5.

A light knock on the door had Pauline looking up. "Come in." When the door opened, she smiled at Dorothy Clarke. "Good morning, Dorothy. Are you ready to meet your new pilots?"

"Ready, but a bit nervous, Commander."

"You will do just fine. You've been in their position and that will be a tremendous help to you as their commander." Pauline pushed back and rose out of her chair. "From what I've just read, you will have a group of exceptional fliers to command." She moved toward the door. "Shall we go meet them?"

"Yes, by all means."

*

"Ladies, if you will all give me your attention, I will read the names of those selected to join the ATA at this time." When all the women looked at the man, he continued. "I am Reginald Applewhite, the group leader of training and I will be announcing those of you who will carry on with the Air Transport Auxiliary."

A hush spread over the group of twenty women, each anxious to know if they would go on or not.

Reginald shuffled several papers then continued. "Please note that if your name is not read, it does not mean you will never have a future with the ATA. Your records will be added to the list of potential recruits and as positions open, you will be contacted to be assessed again." He turned to the woman beside him. "For those that don't know, this is Shannon Brannigan, who is my first officer and she is who you will report to if you have any problems. We have had a relatively easy time integrating women into the ferry pools…but still, some resistance is possible and if problems arise, First Officer Brannigan is whom you will contact. When you hear your name called, please come forward and stand with her. Those left should go to the barracks, collect your belongings, and leave the airfield. A bus is available for transportation, if you do not have any." He lifted a piece of paper and began.

"The selectees for Hatfield Ferry Pool: Faulkner, Hiller, Laughlin, O'Brien, Potter, Calvo, Maddox, Nasmith, Reister, and Lady Smyth-Armstrong." He looked at the group of women standing with the first officer. "Well done, ladies."

The sounds of disappointment flowed throughout the room as the other women stood and began to move out of the room. Many stopped, hugged those that would go forward and whispered congratulations before they exited the building.

Shannon smiled at the group of women, making sure that Midge got her best smile. "We shall go to a different building where you will meet with Commanders Gower and Clarke. Please follow me."

*

Dorothy Clarke watched each of the new recruits who entered the door with her first officer with a critical eye. She had carefully reviewed each resume and qualifications, pleased with the diverse group. She immediately saw the tall blonde woman and smiled inwardly. Her first officer's comments about the woman didn't seem to do her justice. There was no doubt about the woman's striking appearance—her flying qualifications were of most interest and they were excellent. Her eyes then tracked to another tall woman with ebony hair and the lightest blue eyes Dorothy had ever seen. *Jo Laughlin.* She recalled reading the evaluators' comments about the woman. *Strong flier—no fear.*

Weeks earlier she had met with Sarah Faulkner, Millicent Smyth-Armstrong and Camila Calvo and was impressed with them all. Sarah's friend from Australia, Brenda Hiller, was the least qualified of the group and if she hadn't Sarah's support, probably wouldn't have made the cut. But what she lacked in experience, she more than made up for with enthusiasm. *She has the potential to be our best pilot.* Beverly Maddox, the other American, had skills and techniques in her flying that would be valuable to others. She had flown aircraft other than single engine and that gave her a leg up on the other pilots. Her eyes landed on the smallest woman, Bess Potter, from Sussex whose flying skills made up for her lack of height. A strong recommendation from all the evaluators told Dorothy that the lone Scot, Mara Nasmith, would be valuable to her group of pilots.

Overall, Dorothy was impressed with the women who now sat in front of her and the commander. Her eyes met the commander's and she nodded before taking a seat.

Commander Gower smiled at the assembled group. "Good morning, ladies. I am Pauline Gower, the commander of the women's division of the ATA. Welcome and congratulations for being chosen to be part of the ATA's first all women's ferry pool at Hatfield. We are a civilian organization that works in tandem with the RAF.

"The job you are about to partake in is not easy. Your task is to fly numerous planes from factories to airfields. Often the weather conditions will be appalling, with poor visibility. You will not have a radio or navigational instruments and may even, as some of our pilots found out recently, have to land at an air station, which is in the middle of evacuation. Those who criticize our role will use any negative information they can use to call for our division to disband—we cannot and will not give them that ammunition. At times, flights will only be fifty kilometers, while others could be significantly longer. We selected you because you have strong aptitudes for flying and the ability to adapt. Most of the planes you fly will be unfamiliar to you and you will have to rely on each other for information and hints on those aircraft. The RAF is depending on the ATA to bring the planes to airfields. Our job is significant to the war effort and without the pilots of the ATA," she swept her hand over the group, "which you are now a part of, that effort would be much harder.

"You will all start with the rank of second officer—I would point out that this is the same rank given to the men of the ATA—with experience, that rank will increase. At the moment, you will be paid eighty percent of what your male counterparts are receiving." She saw the frowns on the women. "I know that's not fair. I am working to change that so that you will receive the same pay for the same endeavors. We must remember that allowing women to ferry planes is a big step forward. Right now, we are in our infancy. As time passes, I am confident that women pilots will perform all the duties that your male equivalents do now.

"I would now like to introduce the commanding officer of Hatfield Ferry Pool No. 5, Commander Dorothy Clarke."

"Good morning, ladies. As commanding officer of Hatfield Ferry Pool, it is my duty to see that all planes are delivered on time and that all of you work up to your fullest potential. It is perilous times we live in and as women and pilots, we must do our best to see that our RAF pilots are equipped with the most up to date and modern airplanes. As Commander Gower indicated, you will have to rely on each other for information about the planes you fly. In the future, we hope to have training classes. Until that happens, I want you each to keep a note pad with all the information you have on each plane you fly—this will be training for your fellow pilots. Remember, their lives could depend on the accuracy of that information. As Commander Gower said, you will have to cope with variable weather conditions, without the benefit of radios or training on the instruments of the aircraft. Never feel it a failure to turn back in poor weather conditions. That way we will have you alive to fly again.

"The uniform that we will furnish you is similar to mine. You will receive a pleated skirt, slacks, a one piece Sidcot flying suit and quilted liner, a sheepskin leather flying jacket, a blue service tunic with four pockets, a belt with a large brass buckle, a great coat, and a forage cap. It will be up to you to purchase blue shirts, black nylons, black shoes, and a black tie. All those items are readily available here at White Waltham.

"I will take you to purchase the items for your uniform then will deliver you back to the barracks. You will find a package there with your name—this contains the provided uniform. Please change into your uniforms, gather up your belongings, and meet me back here," she looked at her wristwatch, "at half past ten. We will then fill out all the necessary paperwork before we take a short bus ride to Hatfield, where you will begin your training.

"Right now, you are all rated as class two, section one pilots. That means you are qualified to fly advanced single engine airplanes. Those planes include Hurricane, Corsair, Mustang, Typhoon, Tempest, Hellcat, Defiant, and Skua." Dorothy saw a look of bewilderment on some of the faces. "I know you might not be familiar with the names of these planes but you all demonstrated the skills to fly them.

"Once again, I want to welcome you all to the ATA. If you will please all follow me, we shall begin."

Chapter Seven

May 1, 1940
Hatfield Ferry Pool No. 5
Southampton, England

Jo lifted her suitcase and laid it on one of the two twin beds in the room. "I'm actually here," she whispered as she released the catches on her suitcase. As she lifted the top open, she heard someone else enter the room.

"Well, it took a while but I found you, Jo."

With a roll of her eyes, she turned and looked at Midge. "We are not sharing this room," Jo said. "Find one of your admirers and room with her."

Midge pulled her trunk into the room. "You know they don't mean a thing to me, Jo. It's you I love."

With eyes wide, Jo stared at the trunk. "Get that out of my room. I saw enough of it and you on that boat, Midge, so take your things and leave."

With a broad smile, Midge just waved Jo off and began to open her suitcase.

A hand slammed Midge's suitcase closed. "I said, you are *not* rooming with me." Jo fixed her eyes on Midge. "Now take your suitcase and trunk somewhere else."

"Oh, come on, Jo, you know that we are destined to be together, so why are you fighting the inevitable?"

A voice said from the door, "Oh, I'm not meanin' ta interrupt you…but I thought this was my room."

"It is," Jo said, smiling at Meg. "She was just leaving." Once again, she looked at Midge. "Aren't you?"

Midge let out a laugh. "Don't tell me you've fallen for this one," she said, pointing at Meg and leering at her.

In a flash of movement, Midge's trunk sailed out of the room, followed by her suitcase. "Get OUT."

Surrounding the door, were the other pilots who heard the commotion and were gawking at both Jo and Midge.

"She's up for grabs, ladies. Who wants her?"

Midge pushed past Meg and began to leave the room, only to stop and turn around. "This isn't over…not by a long shot, Jo." She turned again and left the room. "I'm rooming with you," Midge said to the petite Bess Potter.

Bess blushed slightly before she picked up Midge's suitcase. "I'm right next door."

Meg shut the door softly and turned to Jo. "She is a wee bit of a troublemaker."

Jo laughed and shook her head. "Nothing *wee* about her. Why I ever came here with her, I'll never know."

"You came because you love flyin', Jo." She gave her new friend a brief pat on the shoulder as she passed her on the way to her bed. "We will be great friends, I am sure of that."

"That we will be." Jo laughed as she looked around the small room. "Can you just imagine what Bess will think once she sees how much room that trunk takes up?" Once Meg was laughing with her, she added, "The room on the steamer was half this size."

"Poor Bess," Meg laughed. "She is so awed by the flash of that woman, she won't be noticin' somethin' like a trunk."

Jo chuckled. "Poor Bess, indeed."

*

After the women of the Hatfield Ferry Pool No. 5 finished training on the various single engine planes, they set about the job of ferrying planes from the nearby factory to various RAF stations that dotted the landscape of Britain. Ferrying the planes was routine and in some cases, downright boring. Those who joined the ATA to see action were sorely disappointed but were spurred on with the talk of more dangerous flights in the future. The talk during down times centered on the war and what was happening with the British troops fighting in France.

"I can't wait to fly into a battle zone," Midge enthused one late afternoon.

"Blimey, that would rot your socks," Brenda said and laughed when the others looked puzzled.

Sarah put her arm around her friend and shook her head. "Give her a break, you'll get used to it soon enough."

In her slow southern drawl, Beverly Maddox said, "You've been watching too many war movies, Midge. Do you really think they will ever let us fly a combat mission?" She shook her head. "They won't even allow us to fly with any weapons or communication, so what makes you think they'd let us do anything but keep flying those trainers and small airplanes?"

Midge moved her hand in a dismissive motion. "I can out fly any man in the RAF. It's ridiculous that they won't let us fight…they are losing out on a lot of talent."

Bess Potter, with her eyes fixed on Midge, sighed. "I think you're right, Midge, we can fly better than most of the men. They should give us a chance."

Jo snorted. "You all can have this discussion, I'm heading to bed." She let her eyes rest on Bess for a moment then left the room. *Bess only said that because she is in love with Midge. Wonder how long before she finds out that Midge isn't a one woman kind of gal. Oh well, not my problem, thank God.* She chuckled softly and continued on to her room.

*

Jo had been attracted to Meg O'Brien from the first moment she saw the beautiful redhead. The icing on the cake for Jo was that she felt an affinity with the Irish woman unlike she had ever felt for anyone before. Meg had a passion for flying that equaled hers. She was intelligent, with a deep understanding of a wide variety of subjects, and she was often funny, with a quirky irreverence for what was happening around them.

Jo's musings stopped when the door opened. She looked up and saw Meg, wrapped in a thick robe, enter the room. "What are you starin' at, Jo?" Meg said as she began rubbing her hair with a white towel.

"Oh, I was just wondering where we will be off to tomorrow."

"In the bath room someone said that somethin' big is happenin' and we might be pulled out of here." Meg shrugged then laughed. "Not thinkin' there's much truth behind it since it was Midge doin' the tellin'"

With a nod, Jo looked away, for she knew too well what was going to happen. Meg would untie her robe before letting it fall so it puddled around her feet. Closing her eyes, Jo could see the taut body with creamy white skin and the medium sized round globes of firm breast with brown rigid nipples. Meg had no modesty when it came to her body. While others in the community bath kept their backs to the wall and bathed quickly, Meg would languish in the water and let out small moans. She often started conversations with whomever else was in the room, seemingly oblivious to the effect her body had on others—especially on Jo.

"Did you enjoy flyin' taday, Jo?" Meg asked.

Looking directly at the naked woman, Jo squelched the slow burn that was starting between her legs. Clearing her throat she said, "Hmm, yeah, I've flown them before…what about you?" She watched the fluid motion of Meg's arms as it lifted a nightgown over her head.

"No, it was a rattlin' the entire time. When I got my assignment, I was hopin' it would be to fly somethin' other than a death trap that took a hit. But the leprechauns were playin' with me taday, so that was my lot." Meg yawned and stretched before crawling under the sheets. "I'll be sayin' goodnight ta you, Jo. Sweet dreams."

Jo slid under her covers and turned out a bedside light. "Good night, Meg." It wasn't long before she heard the soft rhythmic breathing that meant Meg was asleep. Jo folded her fingers together and put them behind her neck as she looked at the ceiling. *I think she's trying to kill me.* She snorted a soft laugh and tried to assuage the need she had—always had—when she was around Meg. It's going nowhere. *Meg has never given me any indication that she thought of me as anything other than a friend.* Yet, she knew that with every day that passed she and Meg were creating a tighter bond. It wasn't so much in what Meg said, but in the way she looked at her that told Jo that maybe, just maybe, there might be a chance of something deeper than friendship.

With her eyes closed, Jo slid her fingers into saturated folds as the vision of a naked Meg floated to her consciousness.

Chapter Eight

Late May 1940
Hatfield Ferry Pool No. 5
Southampton, England

Someone pounded on the doors of all the pilots, followed by the bellowing voice of Shannon Brannigan saying, "Get your gear and be in the ready room in fifteen."

Half awake women scrambled out their doors still adjusting their clothes and bumping into each other

"What's going on?" someone asked.

"I don't hear the sounds of bombs," someone else said.

Soon, blurry eyed pilots yawned and stretched as they assembled in the ready room. Many were speaking in low tones, speculating on what was happening.

When Commander Clarke came into the room and stood at the front of the women, she tapped lightly on a lectern to get their attention.

"Ladies, as you know, the British Expeditionary Force has been battling with French forces against Germany. With the escalation of that battle arena, the RAF is in need of more bombers. Tonight, a bus will take you to the Fairey factory in Manchester and at sunrise, you will fly Fairey Battles to the RAF station at New Romney. The plane is a single engine, closed cockpit, three seat bomber. You will have an opportunity to see inside the cockpit before you leave. Laughlin, you will be team leader." She looked at the group and nodded when no one spoke. "If there are no questions, ladies, the bus awaits you."

"Where's the *Lady*?" Midge asked in a sarcastic tone.

"She's on the bus," Commander Clarke said. "I expect each and every one of you," her eyes bore into Midge, "to follow Miss Laughlin's lead without incident."

*

Each of the ten women occupied her own seat and tried to stretch out and get some sleep before they reached Manchester.

"Has anyone flown this plane before?" asked Midge, who sat behind Jo. When no one answered, she chuckled. "This should be interesting. Not even our fearless group leader knows about this plane."

Jo turned and glared at Midge. "That won't be a problem. I can fly anything they put in front of me."

"Let's see if we can get some sleep. Tomorrow will be a long day," Sarah Faulkner said. She looked across the aisle to her friend Brenda and smiled. The girl shrugged. "It will be ok," Sarah whispered. "No worries."

Brenda nodded then closed her eyes. She struggled to remain asleep as thoughts of flying a three seat bomber scared her. Up until then, she had only ferried training planes with open cockpits. The thought of flying with her head covered made her panic. She recalled the times her father would make her sit under a small table then cover it with a blanket as punishment. *I'm not a no hoper, I can do this...I can.*

At four in the morning, the bus pulled up to the busy airplane factory in Manchester. Scores of male pilots were standing around several planes. Some were inspecting the cockpits, while others were milling around with their hands in their pockets.

"Everyone, follow me," Shannon Brannigan said as she began to depart the bus. Soon all of them were standing around Shannon inside a hangar. "You have about two and a half hours before takeoff." She pointed to a nearby plane. "This is the Fairey Battle that you will fly. Take some time to familiarize yourself with the instruments. If you have questions, go ask one of the flight engineers or one of the other pilots" After pausing, Shannon smiled at the women. "This is our big chance to do more than ferry training planes and I know you will all do us proud. Once you've familiarized yourself with the plane, take some time to get something to eat and rest." She looked at the men standing on the tarmac. "They think they are superior but we know that we can fly as well, if not better. Be back here at zero-six-hundred for a final briefing." The group began to break apart. "Laughlin, I need to see you and, Potter, go check on the weather conditions."

Jo stood next to Shannon and focused on the map that the woman held open. "Once you see this, you will head west," she said as she pointed to what looked like a large town. "You will recognize it best for the massive church building in the center of the city. The airfield is roughly forty kilometers from there to the west."

As Jo studied the map, Bess returned with a worried look on her face. "The ceiling could well be less than four hundred meters."

"What do we know about the air defense we will be flying over?" Jo asked Shannon.

"You shan't have a problem until you get closer to the Channel and that could prove tricky. The air defense in and around London and beyond will be on high alert, especially with the circumstances in France." Shannon turned to Bess. "Is that same cloud cover predicted for the coast?"

Bess nodded. "At the moment it is."

Jo studied the map and the weather statement. "We can consider a more southerly route then come up the coast or we can go behind," she nodded toward the men standing outside of the hangar, "the other planes and see what happens to them."

Shannon laughed. "If you do that, you will be going to the wrong place. They are taking the twin engine bombers elsewhere." She scratched her face then added, "Since you and Reister flew together and are familiar with various hand signals, I want her to be your point. Stay as high up as the clouds will allow."

Jo nodded. "Will do."

*

All ten female pilots gathered around Shannon for their final briefing.

"As you've seen, this bomber is different than anything you have flown over the last two weeks. It is a low wing, cantilever monoplane with a cockpit for three and is equipped with two machine guns, which will be of no use to you. It has a retractable back wheel…who has that information?"

Sarah Faulkner raised her hand and said, "I do."

"Good. Share that information before you take off." When she saw Sarah nod, she continued. "The cloud cover this morning makes it necessary to fly low, making you at greater risk of overly anxious civil air patrols firing on you, and barrage balloons. We hope they will see the planes' markings and identify you as friendly. You will all fly in a tight formation with Laughlin in the lead. Reister will fly as the point. Pay careful attention to what they are doing and you will arrive at your destination in one piece. When you arrive at the air station, there will be a bus to transport you back to Hatfield."

Shannon watched as her ten pilots climbed into the Fairey Battles and contemplated the significance of their mission. They were taking off in bombers, albeit single engine and light weight, but it was a first for the women pilots of the ATA. She had watched them since they arrived at Hatfield and she had to admit that most, if not all, were excellent pilots. If the cloud cover dissipated with the heat of the sun, there would be no problem for an error free delivery of the planes. But, if they experienced friendly fire, which often was the case, they would have to fly blind through the clouds and that scenario could spell disaster. As she saw the last tail disappear from view, she headed to find someone to take her to the train station.

*

The flight was unremarkable and when Jo looked down and saw the church by the river, she checked her compass and banked to the left. The clouds were somewhat lower and she couldn't see any sign that it was going to lift any time soon. She frowned. *The same damn weather I've seen almost every day since I came here. What I wouldn't give for the wide open skies over Texas.* She glanced out the window to her right, seeing that Midge was still on her wing and could only assume that the others were right behind them. When Midge looked in her direction, she gave hand signals for the other pilot to keep a close watch on the skies. By her estimation, they had about twenty-five kilometers to go—what would happen between now and landing was anyone's guess. Just as she thought that, she caught sight of a flash coming off the ground below. "Shit!"

Midge had seen the flash also and guided her airplane higher into the cloud cover, along with the other planes. Before the ten pilots left, they had devised a plan if ground rocket came at them. Each would change their altitude but not their airspeed, thereby keeping in formation. Just as she entered the clouds, Midge saw and heard a rocket explode below her. "At least they aren't very good shots," she said with a chuckle. Her adrenaline was pumping and she gripped the wheel hard to keep herself from coming out of the cloud cover and playing chicken with whomever was on the ground and firing at them. "What the hell," she said as she dropped out of the clouds and waited for the assault. The trick was to watch for the flash from the rocket then make an adjustment so the rockets would miss her plane.

After fifteen minutes of her playing, Midge saw Jo emerge from the clouds and when she looked, she could see the other planes as well. She tipped her wings in greeting and waited for the others to reciprocate—they didn't. "What's their problem?" she wondered as she saw the airfield in the distance. Falling in behind Jo, she slowed her airspeed, allowing for a greater space between the planes for the landings.

One by one, the ten planes landed at New Romney Air Field. Once situated where the ground crew flagman told her to park her plane, Jo got out and with determined steps, walked to where Midge was exiting her plane.

"Just what were you trying to do, Midge? Get us all killed?"

Midge's eyebrows creased. She had a good idea as to what Jo was talking about but wasn't going to let on just yet. "What are you talking about?

That stunt you pulled by flying below the clouds!" Jo screamed.

Still looking perplexed, Midge waited to see what else Jo would say.

"Did it ever occur to you that those rockets could have hit one of the other planes? "

"Give me a break," Midge said with a grin. "They weren't even close. If that's the best defense England has against enemy bombers then this war will be over in no time."

The eight other pilots came up, stood behind Jo, and glared at Midge.

Jo moved so she was standing toe to toe with Midge and flexed her jaw for a few moments before she spoke again. "What you did was reckless. You endangered all of us and for what…some kind of thrill?" She reigned in her anger and said through gritted teeth, "If you can't take this job seriously then maybe you should resign and go back home. We can't afford to have an out of control pilot like you. Our lives depend on each other, which is something you just don't get."

Midge looked over Jo's shoulder and saw all her fellow pilots glaring at her—even her lover, Bess.

"Do you have any idea what you've done to us all, Midge?" Sarah Faulkner asked in anger. "The visibility was almost zero in those clouds, which was bad enough, but to hear explosions all around was horrible on everyone's nerves." She pushed past Jo and got into Midge's personal space. "If it were up to me, you'd be packing your bags." Her finger poked the woman's chest. "Don't you ever pull something like that again."

"I have two babies at home that need their mother. What we do is dangerous enough without some crazy American, who is one of our own, trying to get us killed," Millicent Smyth-Armstrong said in a cool clipped tone. "I don't appreciate the liberties you took with my life."

"Well, aren't we all prim and proper, Lady Smyth-Armstrong, would you like to sit down for tea?" Midge said sarcastically. "You've got your head so far up your ass that you have no idea what a *commoner* like me thinks or feels."

"Social status has nothing to do with this," Millicent said as she stepped closer to Midge. "What you did was wrong and you need to apologize for your actions and hope that you are still with the ATA tomorrow."

After taking in a deep breath and moving a step back from the angry woman, Midge said, "Ok, I'm sorry. I should have thought about what might happen to everyone else. You really weren't in any danger…but I am sorry if what I did scared you." Her eyes took in all the others, who were just staring at her with malevolence in their eyes. *They are such a bunch of idiots. They all need to lighten up and have fun.*

"That's not the point," Sarah countered. "You endangered all of us."

"I got it, Sarah, and I said I was sorry. What more do you want from me?"

"Personally, I'd like to see your bum heading out the door." Sarah advanced on Midge. "Don't you ever do that again." With a shake of her head and an angry glare, Sarah turned away.

Everyone stood in silence until Beverly Maddox cleared her throat and said, "I don't know about the rest of you but I'm starving. Let's find out where we can get something to eat and relax before the bus arrives."

*

Meg sat at a round table with the other Hatfield pilots, listening to them talk about home and flying. Sarah was sitting next to her and Meg couldn't help overhearing the conversation between Sarah and Brenda, who also sat next to her.

She saw Sarah nudged Brenda with her shoulder and say, "You did it! I'm proud of you."

With a discreet look, she saw Brenda push a strand of her curly black hair back before she turned to look at Sarah. "I was so frightened."

"I know you were, Brenda, but you got through it."

"Yes, I did." She smiled warmly at her friend. "I kept telling myself that it was so much better than scooping up cow and chicken shit."

Sarah laughed. "You've come a long way, my friend." She put her arm around Brenda's shoulders and gave her a hug. "If you could fly through those clouds with explosions all around and make it in one piece, you can do anything."

As Meg listened to Sarah and Brenda, she heard tender emotion in their voices as they spoke to each other. Her thoughts turned immediately to her roommate, Jo. *Is that how we sound?* Her eyes looked once again at the two women to her right. *It must be nice to be such good friends.*

A loud roar of laughter made Meg look across the table. She really didn't need to look for there was no doubt that it was Midge's laugh. Bess, attached to her like a limpet, seemed to be hanging on her every word. To Meg, the stunt that Midge pulled earlier was foolhardy and unreasonably stupid.

As she looked at Jo, she could see she was still seething over the earlier incident. An invisible smile played around her lips as she recalled what transpired just before the urgent need to ferry the planes.

She and Jo had been discussing different ways to assess a plane's downfalls without endangering their lives. For several minutes, she watched Jo's expressive face fill with a sensation that was becoming common place to her. The only word that would come close to what she thought those feelings were was *passion*. But she knew it was something deeper than that, for she felt a longing and a profound need to keep watching those eyes, those lips, and the enchanting face that invariably always made her smile. When Jo looked at her with her quirky lopsided smile, she felt her heart begin to beat faster.

"What?" Jo asked with her eyebrows knitting.

"Twas nothin', Jo. I was just wonderin' how you know so much about flying," she answered knowing it was a bald faced lie. "Did ya learn all this from your da?"

Once again she fell into the magic that was Jo's voice and demeanor. It wasn't the first time the feelings monopolized her thoughts and body but it was the most intense. She remembered spying on her brothers and listening to them talk about girls and sex—it made her blush. Never had she so much as kissed someone, yet somehow she thought that the feelings she experienced when around Jo involved something very private and very intense.

She had long known that she was different from the other girls in her village whose only purpose in life was to have a husband and children. The thought of being with someone in that role always repulsed her—until Jo came into her life. From the moment she first saw Jo Laughlin, Meg couldn't stop staring at the woman. Her heart raced and she felt the same stirrings as when she first took flight.

The banging on the door squelched all feelings, as both she and Jo hurriedly put on their flying suits and rushed to join the others

Lost in her thoughts, she didn't notice that Jo had gotten up until she felt warm breath against her ear. "I'm going to take a look around this airfield, care to join me?" Jo's soft voice whispered.

Meg turned and smiled. "Sure, let's go."

*

Once outside, both Meg and Jo noticed that there seemed to be more activity than they'd seen on other airfields. A steady flow of ATA flown aircraft were landing then being directed to where they had parked their planes earlier.

"There must be close to a hundred planes parked over there," Jo said as she scanned the lineup. "Take a look at that big bomber."

"That's the Handley Page Hampton. They were at Attlebridge Station when I worked there with my uncle. It's a twin engine, medium bomber and all the pilots really seem to like flying them." She nudged Jo in the side. "Do you think we'll ever be able ta fly anythin' other than single engine planes?"

"I heard that as the war escalates, they won't have a choice but to let us fly the bigger airplanes."

They continued walking and inspecting the various planes until Meg stopped. "What are you going ta do about Midge?" When Jo said nothing, she added, "I can tell by the look on your face that you're still annoyed. Are ya goin' to tell the commander?"

Jo shook her head. "I don't see how I can't. Eventually she'll get wind of what happened and if I don't tell her, it will look like I'm trying to cover it up. But, she's a first rate pilot and we need her."

"Her shenanigans put us all at risk." Meg hesitated then added, "I'm not real keen on the British royals and their titles, but she shouldn't have spoken ta Lady Millicent that way."

"I know…she wants to see more action."

"Then she should join the RAF."

Jo laughed. "I doubt the Germans would know what hit them if she did."

*

With an opportunity to get Midge alone, Millicent took the woman by the arm and led her out of the building. "I

134

want to speak with you and you will listen to what I have to say without interruption.

Midge tried to wrestle her arm away but Millicent's grip was too strong. "Let go of me!" With her fingers, she tried to dislodge those holding her arm—they squeezed harder.

"I have no idea how you do things in America but in England you don't ever speak to a Lady in such a rude tone." She kept hold of Midge's arm. "There is no doubt that once Commanders Clarke and Gower hear of your escapade today, you will no longer be part of the ATA."

"You don't know that," Midge countered.

Millicent held up one finger and narrowed her eyes. "This is your one chance to stay in the ATA, so you would be well advised to listen and not speak." Midge began to speak and Millicent held up her finger again. "If I walk away, you *will* be deported. The choice is yours, Miss Reister."

"You can't do that."

"Yes, I can and I will." She watched as Midge opened her mouth, closed it, opened it again and then said nothing.

"Good, I see you are listening now." Millicent let go of the arm she was holding and said, "I will see to it that you will only get a reprimand for what you did today. But…there are conditions."

"And they are?"

"You stop what you are doing with Bess. She is an innocent that you have taken advantage of."

"I didn't force her," Midge said in her defense.

"In addition, you will not pull anyone else into your wicked, perverted web. If you feel the need for someone in your bed, find yourself a prostitute."

Midge's eyes glared at Millicent. "You can't make me do that."

Millicent smiled. "Obviously, you have no idea about the power of the British aristocracy. Even if the commanders only reprimand you, I can and I will see that you are deported."

"I don't believe you, so thanks but no thanks." Midge began to turn away when Millicent grabbed her arm once again.

The Lady smiled again and her soft voice said, "This is your only opportunity to stay in the ATA and in Great Britain. Think long and hard about your decision, Miss Reister, for your fate is in my hands." With that, Millicent turned and walked away.

Bess came up to Midge. "What was that all about?"

Midge's eyes diverted from watching Millicent's back to the young girl standing close to her. "She said she was going to get me deported. She can't do that, can she?"

"Yes, she can. Lady Smyth-Armstrong's husband is a Member of Parliament and has much power in the government." Bess rubbed her hand up and down Midge's back. "She is not someone you want to have as an enemy."

Midge stepped away from Bess. "What do you think the commanders will do to me?"

"They don't have a choice, Midge. They will relieve you from duty."

Chapter Nine

Late May 1940
Hatfield Ferry Pool No. 5
Southampton, England

Dorothy Clarke sat at her desk studying the blonde American who sat across from her. The reckless disregard that Midge Reister showed for the mission she flew was unacceptable. In all good conscience, she could not let the infraction go unpunished. The outrage her fellow pilots expressed for the incident demanded the blonde's dismissal from the ATA. She was surprised at Lady Smyth-Armstrong's urging for leniency as she pointed out the excellence of Midge's flying abilities.

"You are a guest in my country, Miss Reister, and as a guest, you are expected to abide by the rules that govern my country. Also, you are a member of the ATA and are expected to adhere to the rules that govern the ATA and that *you* agreed to follow." Dorothy steepled her hands and began tapping the tips of her fingers. "What to do with you, Miss Reister. You have been part of the ATA for a little over a month and already have a most serious infraction lodged against you. What do you have to say for yourself?"

"What I did was stupid and foolish. I unknowingly put my fellow pilots in jeopardy."

"Unknowingly? It never occurred to you that your fellow pilots' lives were in jeopardy while you were carrying out your little escapade?"

Midge looked down at her hands folded in her lap. "I thought that those on the ground firing at us were idiots that had no idea about what they were doing. Not one of the rockets came close to us."

"What if one had hit your plane, or someone else's?"

"I could see that wouldn't happen."

"So you did consider the impact on the others but continued anyway."

Once she lifted her head, Midge looked directly at Commander Clarke. "What I did was wrong and I'm sorry."

"The thing that worries me, Miss Reister, is that once you broke ranks with the other planes, you didn't think of what would happen when their formation came out of the clouds. You were not where you should have been and are very fortunate that one of those planes didn't crash into you."

Midge lowered her eyes and looked at the floor. "I don't know what else to say, Commander."

"What I *should* do is ask for your resignation. But for some unknown reason, Lady Smyth-Armstrong is your champion and her opinion counts a great deal." Dorothy looked at the clock on her desk—it was half past eight. "I will speak with Commander Gower about this incident tomorrow morning. Until we decide what to do about it, you are on restrictive duty and should confine yourself to the barracks. I am very disappointed in you, Miss Reister. Although you are a fine pilot, we cannot tolerate insubordination." She looked at Midge for a long moment. "You are dismissed."

*

Jo fell into her bed as soon as she was in the room. In seconds, her eyes closed as she enjoyed the peace and quiet. She had been awake going on thirty-six hours and was exhausted. The sound of the door opening and shutting softly made her smile—Meg was there.

"I'm exhausted, what about you?" Jo asked with her eyes still closed.

"Twas a long few days. Did you sleep at all on the bus?"

Jo nodded her head. "No, I kept going over what to do about Midge. In the end, Lady Millicent took care of it for me."

"Why did you let her do that?"

When she opened her eyes, she saw Meg standing across the room and felt the now familiar desire. "Um, she asked me if I wanted Midge to go," she gulped down a breath as the woman sat on her bed, "I told her she was a good pilot but what she did was wrong."

"That it was," Meg said, as she too lay on her bed and turned her head to look at Jo.

Jo couldn't tear her eyes away from the green eyes across the room. "She asked if I would mind her handling it and I told her to have at it."

"It is better that way. Lady Millicent has powerful links at the top and everyone looks to her for guidance. That is why your friend Midge should have never spoken to her the way she did." All the time she was talking, her eyes only saw her roommate. "In England, you don't want to make an enemy of someone in the upper classes, especially not one with such illustrious connections."

Jo yawned. "Aren't you tired?"

"Hmm, I am." Meg said as she closed her eyes. When she opened them, she saw that Jo's eyes were fixed on her. The familiar feelings that Jo always elicited in her made her body feel warm and happy. "Jo, do you have someone special back home?"

A deep chuckle emanated from deep in Jo's throat. "You mean like a fella?" she asked, containing the laugh that bubbled in her throat.

Meg felt her cheeks burn and looked away. "Yes."

"No, there is no one special back home. What about you, Meg, do you have someone special waiting for you?"

Meg laughed. "My brother tried to marry me off to a pig farmer."

"He did?"

"Oh, yes, I was thinkin' he wanted me to marry so we could eat somethin' other than mutton."

Jo finally laughed. "He wanted to barter you for pork?"

Both women began to laugh but immediately stopped when there was a soft knock on the door.

"Oh, no," Jo said as she got up. "I can't believe we have to go out again!" Jo exclaimed just before she opened the door. Standing there, she saw a teary Bess Potter. "What's wrong?" she asked softly.

Meg came to the door and pulled Bess inside before she hugged her. "What's happened? Is Midge leaving?"

With shaking sobs, Bess said, "Sh…she's moved out."

"To where?" Jo asked.

"I don't know. Another room somewhere." Bess wiped her nose. "She said she wanted to live alone."

Jo lifted an eyebrow. "Did they dismiss her?"

Bess shook her head. "No, she said she needs a break from me." She buried her head deeper into Meg's shoulder. After a few moments, she raised her head. "What did I do wrong?"

Jo put her arm around Bess's shoulder. "That's how she is…she doesn't stay with anyone that long." Jo sighed. "I'm sorry she did this to you but it is for the best. Midge doesn't know how to care about others. She is only out for herself…she proved that in the skies today."

*

Midge slammed the dresser drawer shut as she put the last of her clothes in it. Leaving Bess had been harder than she anticipated. The girl had clung to her sobbing *please don't leave me* as she gathered her belongings. "God, how I hate clingy women," she muttered as she heaved her trunk on the other bed in the room. She gazed around the room that was exactly like the one she had left. "At least I have more room now."

Still frustrated and angry, Midge plopped herself down on her bed and closed her eyes. She still needed to make the bed and growled—Bess wasn't there to keep the room neat and tidy and do things like making the bed. So lost in her thoughts, she didn't hear the soft knock on the door until it became louder.

Hoping that it was Bess and she could convince the woman to make the bed, Midge pushed off the mattress and went to the door. When she opened it, she was surprised.

"What do *you* want?" Midge spat out.

"That isn't a very nice greeting," First Officer Shannon Brannigan said, as she moved past the blonde and entered the room.

"I didn't invite you into my room," Midge snipped.

"I think after the day you've had, Miss Reister, you would greet a superior more nicely."

Midge reigned in her anger and considered that the woman was there at the behest of the commander. "What do you want?" she asked in a conciliatory tone.

Shannon moved about the room, running her finger over the surfaces. Her eyes rested on the bed. "You forget your sheets and blanket?"

"No," Midge retorted.

With a nod, Shannon sat on the lone, straight backed chair in the room. "You've really gone and done it this time, Miss Reister. You're fortunate that you are not on a steamer back to America." Her eyes fixed on Midge. "What I want to know is why Lady Millicent is so dead set on your staying?"

Midge said nothing.

"Lady Armstrong doesn't seem like your type." Her eyes raked over the blonde's body. "From what I've seen, you like them weak and needy. Is that why you can't get Jo Laughlin in your bed?"

"You don't know what you're talking about," Midge snarled.

Shannon stood up and moved to within inches of Midge. "I know exactly what I'm talking about," she said in a low voice as a finger skimmed the surface of Midge's cheek. "I don't think you'd know how to handle a woman who has a backbone where you're concerned." She took a step closer so that Midge's ample breasts were touching hers.

Midge's body shuddered at the close contact. "Is this some sort of test?" her trembling voice asked.

A lascivious smile crossed the first officer's face before her lips brushed against Midge's full ones. "Oh, Miss Reister, I want so much more than a test from you."

Certain that the woman was sent by Lady Millicent, Midge moved away before her sexual arousal got the best of her. "I don't know what you want, but you will not find it here."

Shannon laughed. "Perhaps not tonight, but mark my words, one of these nights you will succumb and when you do," she overtly stared at Midge's breasts, "you will no longer want weak women."

Midge pointed to the door. "Get out of my room."

The first officer grinned as she opened the door. Over her shoulder she said, "I'll be back."

Midge glared at the closed door, trembling with the arousal demanding satisfaction before she set about making her bed.

*

Over the next week, the pilots of Hatfield Ferry Pool, minus Midge, flew fifty more Fairey Battles to various air stations around England. The weather turned to rain, stranding many of them at RAF stations and airplane factories.

Sarah ran through the rain then grabbed a door handle and pulled it open. She shook out her umbrella before putting it in the stand next to the door. Once she took off her wet outer coat, her eyes searched the large room where other ATA pilots milled around, waiting for the rain to let up. She spotted Brenda curled up at the end of a long leather couch with a man, who appeared to be of small stature sitting close to her with his hand touching her knee. A feeling of anger coursed through her as she hurried to her friend.

As Sarah came close to the couch, she heard the man say, "I love your accent. Want to come to my room…it's just upstairs?" He ran his fingers along Brenda's leg. "I'll show you a really good time."

She didn't need to be a mind reader to know that Brenda was terrified of the man—her friend was as far into the corner of the couch as possible. "Leave her alone," Sarah said in her deepest, most threatening voice. Although the man laughed, Sarah moved to stand in front of him with her hands on her hips. "Did you not hear me?"

Dark eyes seemed to leer at Sarah's body. "This is none of your affair," he said with another laugh. "The pretty lady and I want to be alone."

Sarah's eyes turned to Brenda, who was visibly shaking in terror. "Is that true?"

"No," Brenda whispered.

"You heard her...she isn't interested."

With another laugh, the man began to massage Brenda's knee.

In a flash, Sarah had the man's shirt wrapped in her hand and was pulling him forward. "Are you deaf, little man? She is not interested," she said in a low growl. She twisted the shirt then let go and moved between the man and Brenda. "I do not think your commander will be happy about this." When she saw she had his attention, she said, "I suggest you get up and go away."

"You'll be sorry," the man muttered as he left.

Still shaking, Brenda leaned into Sarah when she sat down. "Thank you," she whimpered.

Sarah put her arm around Brenda's shoulders and hugged her. "What happened?"

"I saw him walk in and something about him reminded me of my father and I just froze. Then, before I knew it, he was sitting next to me and touching me."

"Did you tell him to leave you alone, Brenda?"

The frightened girl shook her head.

In the softest of voices, Sarah said, "You can say *no* to anyone you don't want to touch you." She tightened her arm around Brenda's shoulders. "Your father is not here and cannot hurt you ever again. We have spoken of this before, Brenda. Standing up for yourself will not result in a beating, or worse."

"I know," Brenda cried. "I was so scared."

"Next time, just tell him to go away. You would be so surprised at how easily that works."

Brenda looked around the room with frightened eyes. "When can we get out of here?"

"No time soon. The field is socked in with rain and fog." Changing the subject, Sarah asked, "Want to go get something to eat?"

"Yes, I could eat the ass out of a low flying duck."

Sarah chuckled at the remark. "I take it you're famished."

"Right."

*

At a small table in the dining area, Brenda and Sarah ate their meals in silence. Occasionally Sarah stole a sideways glance at her friend, who still seemed rattled by the earlier encounter.

"How is your meal?" Sarah asked.

Brenda pushed her plate away. "It's ok."

"Would you like me to get you something else?"

With tear filled eyes, Brenda looked at her friend. "The first time I really remember my father beating me was when I was maybe five. One of my brothers had done something and my father blamed me for not paying enough attention." She rubbed her cheek. "He hit me so hard that I remember flying across the room and into a wall. Then he…"

Sarah placed her hand over Brenda's to comfort her and to show she was there for her friend. From the small insights Brenda gave her about her life in Australia, Brenda didn't find the confession of abuse a surprise. From her friend's reaction to the man earlier, she surmised that the cruelty probably went beyond punching to sexual abuse.

"After that, he beat me at least several times a week, screaming at me, telling me what a fuckwit I was." Brenda swiped at the tears that rolled down her cheeks. "I never could do anything right."

"Did he do this to your brothers and sisters too?"

Brenda shook her head. "No, as far as I remember, it was always just me. If they did anything bad, he'd beat me for it."

Sarah had seen Brenda's father in action before she and her friend flew away from Australia—the man certainly had a mean streak. Sarah's heart ached for what Brenda endured during her short lifetime. With her hand on top of her friend's, she smiled and said, "You never have to go through that again, my friend. As long as I'm alive, I will make sure you are safe from your father or anyone else who tries to hurt you."

Brenda's watery eyes looked at the hand covering hers then at Sarah. "Thank you for taking me away from him…but…," she shrugged, "I still live in fear of him."

"He cannot hurt you anymore, Brenda."

"You can't know that."

"He will have to go through me first. I promise you that he will not hurt you ever again." Sarah squeezed Brenda's hand then moved hers away. "Trust me on this."

"I do," Brenda said in a shaky voice before she returned to her meal.

*

Sarah and Brenda returned to the large rest room at the RAF air station near Berkshire, England after their meal. Sitting on a comfortable leather couch, they listened to the chatter of the pilots around them—they wouldn't be flying any time soon. Sarah picked up a newspaper and began reading it while Brenda read a magazine about flying.

While reading a newspaper, Sarah shook her head. "They are losing the planes faster than we can deliver them."

Brenda's gaze turned to her friend. "Crikey, Sarah, what's happening?"

"I am not sure. I did hear someone say something about our troops evacuating to Dunkirk." Sarah's face took on a dark look. "That means we are losing the war," she said softly, feeling the hairs stand up on her neck. "If they have France, my England is next."

"If the rest of the people in England have your courage, Sarah, then they cannot lose."

Sarah shook her head. "I'm not brave...far from it...but I will defend my country with every last breath I have."

Brenda moved closer to her friend and put her arm around her shoulders. "And I will be right there beside you."

Leaning her neck and head against the arm across her shoulders, Sarah whispered, "I know you will be."

With her eyes on her friend's face, that she thought showed worry about an entirely different thing, Brenda pulled Sarah closer. "There's more, isn't there?"

Sarah looked at her friend and gave her a weak smile. "Yes, I'm worried about Edward. The last I heard, he was in India. I fear with all that is happening in France, that is no longer the case." She looked into her friend's eyes. "I just wish I knew where he is and that he is safe."

Brenda's arm tightened as her hand squeezed Sarah's shoulder without speaking, for there was nothing she could say. All she could do was to give her friend the same support that Sarah gave her when she fled Australia.

Chapter Ten

June 1940
Hatfield Ferry Pool No. 5
Southampton, England

For the next month, the ATA pilots spent long hours transporting airplanes to British air stations. Aircraft factories were producing a record number of fighter planes, bombers, and transports. In addition, they often ferried planes that were damaged and in need of repair. The days for the women pilots of Hatfield Ferry Pool were long and seemingly endless.

One night in late June, a disheveled and visibly dazed Midge stumbled into the rest room of the billet where all the women resided.

"Midge," Bess Potter cried out as she hurried to Midge and wrapped her arm around her waist. "Let me help you," she whispered. "What happened to you?"

Once situated on a couch, Midge closed her eyes briefly before she began her story.

"I got a late start flying one of the Bristols to Deenthorpe. All the other pilots left hours before me," she said shakily.

"That's right, you were scheduled last," Millicent Smyth-Armstrong said. "I don't understand why you took off so late…there was a plane for everyone."

Midge looked at Millicent with a mixture of disgust and relief on her face before her expression hardened into a scowl. "That's right, you took off just before me…my *Beau* started rattling, and along with the sound of the carburetor misfiring, I knew I wasn't going to take off any time soon."

"So why didn't you just come back here?" Jo asked, as she joined the widening crowd around Midge.

"Some jerk mechanic told me to wait…that he'd have it fixed in no time." Midge let out a derisive chuckle. "I told him I'd been around airplanes long enough to know that until the plane was thoroughly checked out, I wasn't going to be taking it anywhere. The condescending ass said, *lady, I know what I'm doing.*"

"How long did you have to wait?" Bess asked as she scooted closer to Midge and patted her leg.

"There I was, sitting in that plane and all I can see is this idiot's backside as he was attempting to *fix* my plane. So I climbed out, gave him a few choice words, and headed back to the hangar." Midge stopped and frowned. "I remember noticing all the activity going on around me and wondering why." She shrugged. "Finally a commander for the eighty-fifth squadron asked me what the problem was and once I explained it all to him, he had me in a different plane and I finally took off."

"Were you tryin' ta do some of yer fancy flyin', Midge?" Meg asked.

Midge's eyes narrowed as she glared at the red haired Irish woman. "NO! It was getting dark and I dropped down to fifteen hundred meters…I didn't see the balloon until it was too late."

The room suddenly went quiet as all the women listening to Midge's story gaped at her in disbelief.

"And you lived to tell the story…amazing," Sarah Faulkner finally said. "How?"

"The wing clipped the balloon and not the cable…"

"Luck was on your side," Bess whispered so only Midge could hear.

"…it was touch and go for a while as I lost control and had to fight to regain it. When I did make it to Deenthorpe, the landing gear failed to deploy so I had to land on the belly." Still dazed, Midge blew out a unsteady breath. "In all the years I've been flying, I've never been so glad to get out of a plane as I did then."

"I'm glad you're ok," Jo said, patting the blonde on the shoulder. "I've seen those barrage balloons…had you hit one of the cables…well," Jo shrugged, "your story wouldn't have had a happy ending."

Midge gave her fellow Texan a slight smile. "Thanks." Around the periphery of the group, she saw Shannon Brannigan standing with her arms crossed, staring at her with a grin. It seemed that wherever she went, the first officer was there watching her with a grin. Tearing her eyes away, she looked at the woman who was speaking.

"With all the pitfalls we face each day, it's a wonder we haven't lost more pilots," Lady Millicent said.

All eyes turned to the woman, who the newspapers dubbed *the flying Lady*, as she continued speaking.

Although Millicent's voice barely changed, there was a faint underlying anger in the tone. "All too often we are sent out to fly planes that we have no way of defending and without the ability to communicate with others in the air or on the ground."

The occupants of the room remained quiet.

"I think I will contact Commander Gower and inquire as to why this is," Millicent said softly. "Yes, that is what I shall do." With those words said, she looked directly at Midge. "Good job," she said before turning away and leaving the group.

"I hope she's successful," Jo said before she and Meg left for their room.

Bess was so close and for a moment, she allowed the comfort the woman gave her. Midge's eyes sought out those of the first officer and when she did, she saw raised eyebrows. Convinced that Shannon was a spy for the commander, she pushed away from Bess, stood, and rapidly left the area. When she turned back, she saw the first officer laughing.

*

After entering their room, Meg said, "I'm gettin' a bath," as she gathered the necessary items to take with her. "What about you?" Meg asked with a grin. "You've been takin' yours in the mornin.' You know you could be sleepin' longer if you take one at night."

Jo nodded. "I know but old habits are hard to break."

"I'll be goin' now," Meg said as she left the room

Jo blew out a breath. No way was she going to risk taking a bath with a naked Meg anywhere near the vicinity. "I can't trust myself."

They had shared a room from the first day they arrived in the billet at Hatfield. With each day that passed, Jo found herself being more and more attracted to Meg O'Brien. Meg was not the least bit shy about her body and at night would strip down to nothing before slipping into her nightshirt.

No matter how hard Jo tried to look away, she always found her eyes drifting toward Meg. clothed or not. She had no indication that Meg thought of her in any way other than a roommate and fellow pilot. And she wasn't about to make any move that might make the redhead run from her, screaming that she was a deviant. Her thoughts halted as she heard the door open—her nightly sexual torture was about to begin once more.

"You look like you're miles away, Jo," Meg said as she closed the door.

Jo lifted her eyes and was instantly speechless at the sight of Meg. She could smell the hint of lavender that always filled the room when Meg returned from her bath.

"Are you all right?" Meg asked with a quizzical look before she let her robe fall away from her shoulders.

Instantaneous desire surged through Jo as her eyes took in the naked woman. Forcing her eyes to look away, Meg shook her head. "Nothing really," she said with a shrug. "I guess…I was thinking how unreal this all seems. I've flown for all of my adult life and before that even. Never did I encounter the perils that we face here every day. What happened to Midge today can happen to any of us…and we might not be so lucky."

Meg slipped her nightgown over her head. "I fell in love with airplanes the first moment I saw one in the sky," she smiled, "I couldn't believe my good fortune when I was selected for the ATA…I get ta do what I love full time." She moved closer to Jo. "The danger doesn't scare me as much as the thought of not flyin'."

Digesting the words, Jo looked into the green eyes before she said, "Even if it costs you your life?"

"If I was worryin' about dyin', I never would have takin' up flyin', now would I, Jo."

Jo chuckled. "No, neither would I…," her face became somber, "I've seen planes crash but I didn't let it bother me…knowing someone who actually had it almost happen…it took me by surprise."

"I remember when my Da died. It was the first time death became a reality for me. My uncle Shamus told me that people in my life will die and it was up ta me to keep on livin' for them."

"Sounds like good advice," Jo said as she gathered the things she'd need for a bath. "I'm going to take your advice and take a bath." When she saw a smile cross Meg's face, she started for the door.

As Meg's arm brushed hers as Jo passed by, Meg whispered, "You'll love it."

*

When Bess entered Midge's room, she found the blonde sitting on her bed with her face buried in her hands. She could hear the soft muffled sounds of sobs and went immediately to the woman.

"It's going to be all right, Midge, I promise," Bess said softly as she put her arm around the woman's shoulder.

Midge rolled over and sat up. "What are you doing here?"

I thought you needed some comfort," she whispered.

"Not from you I don't," Midge blurted. "Leave me alone, Bess…haven't I made that abundantly clear to you."

The hurt Midge's cruel words caused was evident on Bess's face. "I just thought…"

"I don't care what you think, just go."

When she heard the door close, Midge closed her eyes. She desperately needed the comfort Bess was offering but knew she couldn't chance letting it happen. She heard a knock on the door and her heart skipped a beat, hoping it would be Bess—this time she wouldn't send the young woman away. When she opened the door, her smile faded.

"What do *you* want?"

Shannon pushed past Midge. "Close the door," she ordered.

"You can't boss me around in my own room," Midge countered, still holding the door open.

With narrowed eyes and a low growl, Shannon said, "Close the door."

It was something Midge heard in the first officer's voice that made her shut the door. "Ok, now what?"

"What was Potter doing in your room with the door closed? You've been warned about that, Miss Reister."

"Nothing happened," Midge ground out as her eyes narrowed. "Why are you doing this?"

"Doing what?" Shannon asked with a grin.

"Hounding me."

"Tell me about the balloon."

"It was so dark I didn't see the balloon in time. I could barely make out the landing strip...then the wheels wouldn't go down...end of story."

"Were you scared?"

"NO! Not me...I'm never afraid of anything."

Shannon looked at the blonde with disbelief.

"Fear has no place in my life!"

Shannon took a step closer to Midge.

"Why are you here?" Midge asked with a growl.

"I thought you might need a shoulder."

"Not from you."

With another two steps, Shannon was standing so close that they were only a breath away. "Maybe you need more than a shoulder," she said as she wrapped her arms around Midge and drew her close.

All anger drained away as Midge melted into the strong arms. "Please stay," she whispered. "I need you to stay."

Shannon stood and while she was dressing, she looked down on the naked Midge and grinned. "Can't say you are the best I've ever had...but it wasn't bad."

Midge's brow furrowed as she sat up and stared at the grinning woman. "You bitch. I wonder what the commander will say once I tell her how you seduced me."

With a boisterous laugh Shannon said, "Do you really think she will believe you, Miss Reister? Your track record speaks for itself."

"Get out," Midge screamed.

Still laughing, Shannon opened the door. "How does it feel to be preyed upon?" she asked before she closed the door behind her.

Later that night, Midge was still fuming. The occurrences of earlier in the day surfaced and she shivered as tears rolled out of her eyes. What the first officer did to her made her angry but that wasn't the cause of her tears. A bubble of truth surfaced—she wasn't fearless.

Chapter Eleven

July 1940
Hatfield Ferry Pool No. 5
Southampton, England

Dawn was just breaking as Meg walked out of the billet into the gray morning of July tenth. It was still early enough that the area was devoid of activity. She smiled when she heard the sound of birds and was, as always on such occasions, reminded of home. It was at times like these, which were few and far between, that she missed the quiet peace of her home and family the most. As she walked in solitude, her thoughts of her life since her arrival at Hatfield played soundlessly in her mind.

She couldn't deny the joy and freedom she felt each time she took to the skies. Even the incident when Midge had put everyone's life in danger had been thrilling, for it made her feel alive. Her biggest surprise—Jo Laughlin. In a short time, her roommate had become not only her friend, but also the one person who made her feel safe. Not that she felt insecure, for she didn't; it was just that Jo had a way of making her feel… *What is it about her that draws me to her?*

The door to the billet squealed, drawing Meg out of her musings. A smile wreathed her lips when she saw Jo walking toward her.

"It is goin' to be a glorious mornin', Jo," she remarked as she drew near Jo.

"Yes, I do believe you're right. Clear skies bring soft landings and that makes for a great day."

Meg cocked her head to one side. "Did you hear that, Jo? It sounds like thunder."

Jo's eyebrows knitted when she too heard the sound, turned her head toward the east, and squinted. "I don't see anything that looks like storm clouds."

Meg laughed. "This is England, Jo. Rain is a part of the everyday life." She took her friend's hand in hers and said, "I'm famished," before she started dragging her roommate toward the dining hall.

*

The two women ate and spoke in hushed tones as what seemed like all the Hatfield personnel entered the dining hall at once. Unlike most days where everyone ate and the noise was relatively quiet, this day brought the sounds of anxious, emotional words.

"What do you think is happenin' now, Jo?" Meg asked just before Brenda, Camila Calvo, and Beverly Maddox sat down at their table.

"Good morning. Did you hear the news?" Brenda asked as she placed her tray on the table.

"Now what would that be, Brenda?" Meg asked around a forkful of eggs.

"The Germans are bombing in France."

Jo eyed the three women now sitting with her and Meg. "That's nothing new. They've been bombing France for months now.

"You don't understand," Beverly said to her fellow American. "They are targeting all our airfields in France, Belgium, and Holland," she said anxiously. "From what I heard, half the Belgian Air Force and nearly all the Dutch airplanes were destroyed."

Realizing the magnitude and effect of her fellow pilot's words, Jo looked astounded. "When did this happen?" she finally managed to say.

"Is happening now," Camila said in broken English. When she saw Beverly nod, she added, "I go to White Waltham."

"Por qué," Sarah asked.

Camila shook her head and smiled at Sarah—she always appreciated it when Sarah spoke to her in her native language. Looking around the table she said, "They say there are too many good pilots here."

Saddened that Camila was leaving, Sarah wanted to know how long her friend would be gone. "Para cuánto tiempo?"

"I think not for long," Camila said in English for the benefit of the others around the table. "I am to train."

Puzzled eyes looked at Camila. "I thought they already had pilots for that," Jo interjected. "Why do they need you?"

The question went unanswered when Commander Clarke entered the dining hall.

Despite her small stature, Commander Clarke filled the room with her presence. "Undoubtedly you have all heard of the bombings of our forces all over northern and western France." Her eyes seemed to fall on each person in the room. "Our mission is now more critical than ever. We will be on a very intense cycle of delivering planes from here on. I will brief the pilots further, in," she consulted her wrist watch, "fifteen minutes." The Commander nodded before she turned and left the dining hall.

Midge seemingly appeared out of nowhere and plopped down in an empty chair. "Has it occurred to any of you that we might have to face a Messerschmitt without any way of defending ourselves?"

Jo eyed the blonde woman she had known for several years. "I thought you were ready to take on anything and everything. Midge, what's changed?"

With her face scrunched in an angry scowl Midge bit out, "Are you insinuating that I am afraid, Jo? If you are, you'd better take it back right now. I'm scared of nothing and am looking forward to out-maneuvering any attempt they make against me."

From behind Midge someone said, "Unless they are in British airspace, we won't have to worry about that."

All eyes at the table turned toward Lady Millicent, who always looked elegant, even in her Sidcot flying suit. "The commander sent me to tell everyone not to be late."

Everyone at the table took hurried bites before the sound of their chairs scraping across the linoleum indicated that they were leaving.

*

Dorothy Clarke stood at the lectern at the front of the briefing room waiting for the assembled pilots, mechanics, administrative personnel, and ground crew to quiet down. As soon as all eyes were on her she said, "Three weeks ago Prime Minister Churchill spoke to the House of Commons of the *Battle of Britain*. That battle is now upon us," she said in the softest of words. From early reports, many Fairy Battle bombers are destroyed or in need of repair. Our factories are gearing up for the increased production of Hurricanes, Mosquitoes, Tiger Moths, and Spitfires," she paused for a moment to look at her notes, "the Prime Minister also asked of us to brace ourselves to our duties so that in the end it will be said that *this was our finest hour*.

"The road ahead of us is daunting and if you ever doubted your worth to the RAF, know that because of what we do, our combat pilots will have the finest of aircraft to carry out their mission. The task before us will require sacrifice and commitment to the cause. If we fail, so will Britain fail. It is our task to be that vital link between the factories and the fighter pilots. *We* will *not* fail…we *will* succeed."

A low murmur circulated around the room, grew in volume until one woman, Bess Potter, stood, and began to clap.

The commander looked at the pilots before her as a sense of pride filled her. They were *her* pilots…her *female* pilots. She knew they would rise to the call and outperform all other ATA pilots. With a hand held up with the palm out, she waited for everyone to retake their seats. Once she did, she clapped and then said, "It is you who should be honored. I am proud of each one of you, for you have demonstrated daily your commitment to the RAF with professionalism and courage. I will not pretend that what you are about to undertake will be easy. It will be fraught with danger, not only from the Luftwaffe but also from our own overzealous and terrified Civil Air Guard. I am lobbying for you to fly fully functional planes so you can, if need be, defend yourselves. We are not there yet. I will, as I always do, caution you not to take chances, for your lives are more important than an airplane.

"Pilots, you will find your assignments posted in your billet. The other personnel please note that you will all be working on a twenty-four hour schedule. For those of you that have roommates, we have rooms set aside for you to sleep in if changing of schedules makes it a problem for you." A full smile laced with regret crossed Dorothy's face. "The battle is upon us—this *will* be *our* finest hour.

As everyone stood, they all shook their heads in acknowledgement and agreement.

Dorothy watched as the door closed on the last pilot. As proud as she was of each one, there was a sense of foreboding for what they were about to face. Her eyes scanned the report dispatched to her early that morning—the situation was grim.

Chapter Twelve

August 1940
Hatfield Ferry Pool No. 5
Southampton, England

In the early morning hours of August fifteenth, the sounds of explosions rattled the billet. Everyone who was there scrambled out of bed and hurried to the windows to see what was happening. Orange and red flashes filled the sky and in the distance, they could see what looked like a building on fire. Sirens were blaring and they could see those they knew scrambling across the tarmac for what was the lone air raid shelter.

Looking up, Meg saw clearly marked German planes dropping bombs, which she surmised were going to bomb the airfield. A hand on her shoulder had her turning to see Jo holding out her robe.

"Here, put this on. We need to take shelter," she said as the air screamed with the sound of explosions from the bombs hitting targets. Jo grabbed Meg's arm and began pulling her toward the door.

"We won't make it ta the shelter," Meg cried as she cast the robe aside.

"There's a basement to this building. We can make that."

The two women flew down the darken stairs to the pitch black cellar, where they huddled as the impact of the bombs shook the building. They knew that if a bomb found its way to the building, they would be buried alive.

Meg swore she heard the whiz of the bomb that she knew landed on or near the billet. She burrowed her face into Jo's shoulder and whimpered.

"It's going to be ok," Jo whispered as she pulled Meg closer.

In those moments of uncertainty and fear, as their lives hung in the balance, Jo and Meg clung to each other as they would a lifeline. As another bomb landed so close that dust from the rafters fell on them, their lips met in the sweetest of kisses. Neither woman moved as they rested in the safety of each other's arms.

The time between hearing the last of the explosions and when they felt it was safe to leave the cellar was unclear. What was clear, their relationship had taken a turn toward something more intimate and time would tell if it was something very special or not.

Jo held Meg's hand as she guided them up the darkened stairway and pushed open the door that would lead them to the front of the billet. Just before they walked out the door, Jo leaned in and kissed Meg's lips.

"Don't," Meg said as she moved away.

Confused eyes looked at the Irish woman. "But…"

Meg's fingers went to Jo's lips. "What happened down there," she looked back down the dark staircase, "was out of fear of dyin', Jo, it cannot happen again."

"I'm so sorry, Meg. I didn't mean to upset you. I only wanted…"

"No more, Jo."

Jo shrugged. The subject was closed and, in all likelihood, would not be spoken of again. Her heart fell. Just as Jo was about to offer another apology, she saw several of the women heading toward them. Hurriedly she said, "Please, forgive me," she whispered.

Meg whispered, "Nothin' ta forgive," just as the others arrived at the billet.

*

Commander Clarke stood on the tarmac with her hand resting on her hips as she surveyed the damage from the attack. She was surprised to see that only a few of the buildings had minimal damage. The tarmac had extensive damage and she could see gaping holes dotting the surface.

"How does it look, Commander?" Lady Armstrong asked.

"Better than I hoped for," Dorothy replied as her eyes continued to survey the area. "I believe they were probably trying to damage the de Havilland factory and we got the fall out." She gestured to the runway. "We will have to find an alternative place to take off."

Millicent frowned. "I'm shocked our buildings are still standing—it did sound like the bombs were exploding right outside the door."

"I agree…it was a rather frightening experience. I fear it is one that will become commonplace as the days and months go by."

Soon all the members of the Ferry Pool had gathered on the tarmac around their commander. Dorothy took the opportunity to comment on how they should conduct themselves when the next attack occurred.

"Since we are in close proximity to the de Havilland factory, we will probably see this sort of attack again. If an attack occurs at night, you must, at the first sound of the sirens, turn out all lights. You should get in the habit now of closing your blackout curtains at all times. Our air raid shelter has the capacity to hold everyone, so don't do anything foolish like staying in your billet room."

"What about the cellar where Jo and Meg stayed…can't we use that?" Bess asked.

"Only as a last resort. That place was not built to withstand bombing." She looked at Jo and Meg. "You two were lucky there wasn't a direct hit. We'd be digging out your bodies."

Jo and Meg both nodded in understanding.

*

Over the next several weeks, the pilots of Hatfield Ferry Pool continued their grueling task of making sure that they delivered Mosquito and Tiger Moth airplanes to airfields throughout the United Kingdom.

It was not uncommon for them to arrive at an airfield only to find that it no longer existed—the Luftwaffe seemed bent on destroying not only airfields, but aircraft factories as well. The skies over England were fraught with danger in spite of the constant patrolling of the RAF.

Two weeks after the initial air invasion of England, Commander Clarke stood in front of her pilots with a grim expression.

"Ladies, I want to commend all of you on the excellent job you've done over the last weeks. I know that several of you had a harrowing time delivering battered airplanes back to the factories. Yet every one of you has continued to do your jobs without complaint and for that, I am very proud of all of you.

"A positive note, our RAF pilots are proving that they are superior pilots to those in the Luftwaffe." Dorothy waited for the low mummer that spread between her pilots to stop before she continued. "This by no means should indicate that this war will be over soon for I fear it will not. Right now, we are in a battle to save our country and our way of life. Know that each and every one of you is contributing to making that happen."

Changing topics, Dorothy held up a piece of paper. "Here are your assignments for today. You will find that the number of deliveries has increased. It will be another long day, ladies." As each pilot rose out of their chair, Dorothy looked them over before shaking her head. When Jo and Sarah came up to her to get their assignments, the commander said, "Be in my office in fifteen minutes."

*

Sarah and Jo entered the outer office of Commander Clarke and sat in empty chairs.

"Any idea what this is about?" Jo asked.

"Not a clue. I got a look at Brenda's flights for today…if we have the same type of schedule, we need to get started or we will be flying in the dark."

"You know…" Jo began just as the door to the commander's office opened.

"Ladies, will you please join me." It wasn't a question.

Entering the room, Jo and Sarah saw another occupant. A man in a uniform with black wavy hair stood by a window with his back to the others. The three stars on his shoulders told both women that he was an Air Marshall.

The Commander motioned to several chairs. "Please, take a seat, ladies." Once Jo and Sarah sat, Commander Clarke surprised them by not sitting at her desk but in the chairs with them. Clearing her throat she said, "I am certain you are wondering why I asked you to be here." Both women nodded. "That will become clear but first I need to get to know more about you."

"Certainly," Sarah said. "What would you like to know?"

"Direct and to the point, I like that." Dorothy smiled. "Miss Faulkner, I understand that you are fluent in several languages. Would you please tell me what those languages are?"

"Certainly, Commander. I am fluent in Spanish and French and have a good understanding of German, although I do not speak it well."

"I see," the commander said with a nod. "Miss Laughlin, you are by all accounts the finest pilot we have at Hatfield and I believe that would apply to the entire ATA."

"Thank you, Commander," Jo said as she eyed the man at the window who had yet to face them.

The Commander turned to face Sarah. "I attended your exhibition of photographs from the various parts of the world you were in while making your attempt at the record from London to Sydney. I was impressed with the way you captured the variations of light, especially on the faces of the people."

Sarah's cheeks flushed. "Thank you…that seems like a lifetime ago."

Dorothy raised her eyebrows then shrugged. "Yes, it does seem that way, does it not?" she mused, "life has changed so much in such a short span of time." She turned and looked at Jo. "Have you always been so fearless while flying? I know you were a barnstormer…is that why you are such an excellent pilot?" she smiled warmly, "along with being a natural leader?"

It was Jo's turn to be speechless. "My daddy taught me to fly and the one lesson he drilled into my head was that no matter what, if I kept a clear mind and concentrated on what was happening, I would always come out ahead," she shrugged. "He was right," she whispered.

"That brings me to why I asked both of you here."

The man at the window turned to face them. He was a tall, slender man, with thick black hair and moustache to match.

"This is Air Marshall Warren, who works in conjunction with his Royal Highness's Intelligence Core."

In a deep rich baritone, the man said, "Ladies, I have a proposition for you…"

Chapter Thirteen

Late September 1940
Hatfield Ferry Pool No. 5
Southampton, England

The Luftwaffe's Blitz of England began in the first week of September and that ratcheted up the ATA's ferrying responsibilities even more. For the women of the Hatfield Ferry Pool, the days were long and often extended into the night. Both military and industrial centers were continually bombed often, wiping out entire sections of cities. High explosive bombs fell on London, causing a high number of fatalities and the destruction of not only airfields, but also munitions and tank factories. Often the pilots of the ATA would arrive at the coordinates of an airfield or airplane manufacturer only to find the structures destroyed or in such a state of disrepair that landing was impossible.

At the end of each day, the women pilots of Hatfield Ferry Pool would count their numbers then wait for those not yet there to arrive. The anxiety of war arrived squarely on their shoulders, making every delivered plane extremely important to the war effort. Without their courage and fearlessness, the RAF would not have the necessary planes to fight the Luftwaffe in the air.

*

"Sarah, where have you been? We've all been back for hours." Brenda asked her friend.

Sarah put a weary head against the door she had just closed. "It has been a really long day. Jo and I had to fly Fairey Battles up to Yorkshire then we transported two beat up Vickers back."

Brenda frowned. "Did you run into trouble? I've made that flight…didn't take that long."

Pushing herself off the door, Sarah walked past her friend and patted her on the shoulder. "It was complicated, to say the least. Those Vickers had more holes in them than metal," she blew out a breath, "It took all my skills and strength just to stay airborne. I was thankful that I could look out the windscreen and see Jo. There were a couple of times that the plane shook so badly I thought it would come apart."

"Crikey, Sarah, why didn't you just put down?"

Without looking at her friend, Sarah said, "We tried to…"

Brenda was at her roommate's side and put an arm around her shoulders. "What happened, Sarah?"

Sarah's body shook. "It was awful," she whispered as she swiped at the tears threatening to fall. "I couldn't get any altitude and Jo was flying low with me when right in front of us, one Messerschmitt came out of the clouds, followed by two more." She closed her eyes and drew in a calming breath. "I didn't know if they saw us or not and when I looked at Jo, she gave me the signal to land. There was an airfield ahead of us…I could see it. Then the sky erupted in smoke and I could hear explosions all around me. I couldn't see Jo…or the Germans," she shrugged, "I've flown all over the world by myself, faced more than my share of scary moments but nothing compared to how I felt at that moment. When I looked again I could see Jo and she signaled for me to follow her and I did…"

"Want me to make you a cup of tea?" Brenda asked before she hugged Sarah. "I'm so glad you made it, Sarah, I don't know what I would do if you weren't around."

Sarah returned the hug. "Thank you, a cup of tea would be lovely."

"First, tell me how you managed to avoid the Germans?"

"They weren't interested in us...they were after the airfield...in the space of minutes there was nothing left of the airfield or the bomber factory." Sarah shook her head. "I've never seen such decimation. If I hadn't seen the airfield earlier, I never would have known one was there."

Brenda gave her friend one last hug. "I'll go for that tea."

As she heard the door shut, Sarah closed her eyes, thankful to be alive. Now she was more determined than ever to do everything she could to help her country survive.

*

Jo was about to open the door to the room she shared with Meg, when she heard what she thought was the sound of someone crying. Knitting her eyebrows, she gently and quietly opened the door. Her eyes traveled to Meg, curled in her bed with her hands over her face. Ever since the kiss in the basement, Meg had been distant and cool toward Jo. Any physical contact was limited to a brush as they passed each other. As she stood quietly, she was in a quandary as to what to do—go to her friend in comfort or remain at a distance.

With tears streaming down her face, Meg sat up and looked at Jo.

Without further thought, Jo moved toward Meg, sat on the bed, and pulled the woman close. "Meg," she said. "What's wrong?" Jo continued to hold her friend as she whispered words of support, while gently smoothing Meg's hair with her hand kissing Meg's head every so often. "What's happened?"

"He's gone," Meg cried.

For a moment, Jo wondered who *he* was. Over the last month, they hadn't seen much of each other and because of their frosty relationship it was possible that Meg had found a man she cared for. The thought made her stomach knot so she shook away the thought. "Who's gone, Meg? Where did he go?"

"Shamus, my uncle…was killed."

"How…when?"

"Three days ago in an air raid," she sobbed.

The horrific images of the demolished airfield she and Sarah had seen that day flashed in her mind. She remembered the bodies lying on what used to be the tarmac.

"When he heard the sirens he and others got in planes and took off ta fight the attackin' planes." Meg's voice lowered and she whispered, "He was shot down…he never had a chance…he loved ta fly…he wasn't a soldier."

Jo kept Meg close to her as she continued to whisper words of comfort as Meg wept for her uncle. When she felt Meg relax somewhat, she asked, "Are you going home?"

Meg pulled back and her teary eyes looked at Jo in question. "Now why would I go doin' such a thing?"

"For the funeral. Are you going back to Ireland for the funeral?"

"Know what Shamus would say ta me about that, Jo?"

"No."

"He'd say, *"just because someone dies doesn't mean the war no longer exists. There will be time for grievin' when the fightin' is over."* She pushed away from Jo's embrace. "That's what I'm going ta do," she announced as she stood up. "Now tell me, Jo, where have you been all day?"

Jo felt the loss of contact and sucked in a breath—status quo was once again in effect. "Sarah and I ran into a bit of trouble…"

Chapter Fourteen

October 1940
Hatfield Ferry Pool No. 5
Southampton, England

It was so early in the morning that the sun was just peeking over the horizon, as the pilots of Hatfield sat in the briefing room. When Commander Clarke walked into the room, all chatter ceased.

"Good morning, ladies. There has been a change to the way the ATA pilots will ferry planes. For the last months, aerial attacks have become common place. The Luftwaffe has destroyed or rendered useless many of our airfields and aircraft factories."

A mummer coursed through the women.

"It is vital that we ferry the planes as soon as they are manufactured to camouflaged maintenance units where armaments, radios, and the like will be installed. This means our job is doubled, for we now must fly the aircraft from the factory to the MU and then to a designated airfield. The airstrips at the MUs are limited so expect short, bumpy landings. I advise you do three point landings."

A collective groan filled the room.

"To maximize your ferrying time, we have authorized the use of the *Annie* to taxi you to your next assignment. As you know, the *Annie*…Avro Anson…is unsuitable and underpowered as a bomber. No longer will you have to return via land routes for the *Annie* has the capability of transporting up to eight pilots. Some of the *Annies* will be equipped with rear guns to thwart attacks." Dorothy's eyes looked at the women in front of her. "Questions?"

"You said that the MU will outfit the planes. Does that mean we will be able to use the radios and the armaments if we need to," Midge asked.

The commander shook her head. "No. The frequency of the radios will not be set until delivered. As for armaments, nothing has changed; ammunition will not be loaded on the planes you ferry."

Midge, still standing, asked, "Are the locations of the camouflaged MUs on our maps?"

"You will need to commit those coordinates to memory. Any notations about them are forbidden for we cannot afford for that information to fall into the enemy's hands." Dorothy looked for anyone else with a question and when she found none, she said, "We have a job to do, ladies. Let's get to it."

*

As usual, Jo and Sarah, after spending time with the commander, exited from the briefing room.

"Do you have the coordinates?" Jo asked.

"Yes."

Jo's eyes scanned the area and saw that the other pilots were climbing into the planes to be ferried. "Ours is not out yet," she commented.

"We are the lucky ones, Jo. We get to have guns with ammunition and a functioning radio. I wonder what the others would say if they knew."

After considering the comment, Jo said, "We aren't any safer with them. Not having them made all my senses be at the ready. I think I'd rather rely on my skills than a gun that I do not know how to use."

Sarah nodded.

They continued toward the hangar that contained their modified Fairey Battle. The lightweight bomber, no longer weighed down with bombs, was sleek and to both Sarah and Jo, it was much more maneuverable than those they had previously flown. Just as the last plane took off, the maintenance crew pushed their plane out of the hangar.

Jo ran her fingers through her hair before she began her climb into the plane and the pilot's seat. Sarah was right behind her, carrying a bag that held her special equipment.

"All set?" Jo asked.

"Yes. Our heading should be east by southeast until we reach the Channel."

Jo pushed the throttle and the plane began its journey to the end of the runway. In a matter of minutes, the plane was airborne, heading southeast.

*

The Fariey Battle climbed into the clouds and stayed there until they had crossed the English Channel and were over southern France.

"Time to get into position," Jo said to Sarah. "I make the ETA in five minutes."

Sarah stood and moved to the modified bomber bay that held a high resolution camera, specially made for aerial surveillance. Flattening her body, she adjusted the focus then waited for Jo to tell her they had arrived.

Another improvement to the plane was radar. Jo scanned the screen—they were alone—she guided the craft out of the clouds. "Sarah, the target should be below us in a hundred meters."

The earth below passed by as Sarah looked through the lens, waiting patiently. Then she saw trucks, tanks, soldiers, howitzers, and other cannons moving northward. Her finger pressed the button and the camera sprung to life, snapping frame after frame in rapid succession. When she felt the plane bank right, she lifted her finger.

"Trouble?" Sarah asked.

"Got two coming in fast," Jo said as the plane began its climb to the clouds. Her eyes constantly shifted from the radar screen to the clouds that seemed so far away.

Sarah scrambled to the specially fitted gun and took aim at the approaching Messerschmitts. She fired at the first plane, smiled, and watched its smoky retreat. When she realized the second plane was almost on top of them, she chastised herself for not paying attention. Her finger automatically depressed the trigger and streams of bullets hurled through the sky to the plane. To her dismay, the other pilot took evasive maneuvers and began firing at them. She heard the ping of a round hitting the plane just as they disappeared into the clouds.

Jo banked the plane toward the east before heading due west. Although the clouds gave them some protection, she knew they weren't out of danger by a long shot. Somewhere in the clouds, a German pilot flying a Messerschmitt was hunting them.

*

As the specially equipped plane taxied to the hangar, both Jo and Sarah allowed their shoulders to relax.

"That was a close one," Jo said as they got out of the plane.

"Yes, it was but we made it, didn't we?"

They continued in silence as they strolled toward the barracks. Jo stopped in her tracks. "I thought it was exhilarating. It was the same thrill I felt when I was barnstorming."

Sarah laughed. "I thought I was the only one who felt that way. Did you see that plane go down after I hit it?"

"Nice piece of shooting. I did see the pilot's parachute."

"Me too…that is why I didn't get a good bead on the second plane…I won't let that happen again."

"We make a really good team, Sarah."

Sarah put her hand on Jo's arm. "Yes, we do. You have the flying skills and I have the photography skills."

Jo shrugged. "You are as good, if not better, than me at flying, Sarah. I could probably press the button on the camera," she laughed, "Think I could get the pictures they want?"

Sarah laughed too. "Yes. There is no secret to pressing the button." Mirth left her eyes. "I never dreamt that the pictures I exhibited would lead to helping the war effort."

With her hand resting on her stomach, Jo heard it rumble. "I'm famished."

"So am I," Sarah said as they altered their course for the dining hall.

Chapter Fifteen

Early December 1940
Hatfield Ferry Pool No. 5
Southampton, England

Jo entered the barracks and immediately saw Meg standing among a group of women that Midge was entertaining with stories of her barnstorming days. Jo wasn't interested for she'd heard it all before and once the green eyes snared her, she saw nothing else. Her feet glided across the floor until she was standing next to Meg.

"How was your day?" Meg whispered.

"Long. I'm hungry, what about you?"

"I didn't know when you'd be comin' back so I've already had supper, Jo."

Jo frowned.

"Don't be lookin' so glum now, Jo. I'll join you…maybe have a bit of dessert."

With a bright smile, Jo winked. "You do have a sweet tooth, don't you, Meg?" She grabbed Meg's hand and said, "Come on, my stomach is eating my backbone."

Meg laughed. "What an odd expression," she said, then her eyes brightened and she let out a hearty laugh. "Oh, now I understand."

Jo looked at the woman who sat across from her. It had been many months since the kissing incident and she and Meg had slowly returned to their easy friendship of earlier months. She looked at Meg and smiled. "Tell me about your day."

"Would you believe I delivered Spitfires all day? The *Annie* we were usin' ta taxi us from base ta base took ten of us at once. I was feelin' like I was back at home with all my brothers."

"You didn't like being up close and personal?"

"Now you're actin' foolish, Jo. *Annie* does good ta hold eight but ten is a wee bit too many."

Jo's expression turned serious. "How are you doing, Meg? I feel like we are ships that pass in the night but never see each other."

Meg reached out and gently ran her fingertips over Jo's hand. "You look so tired," she whispered. "What's causin' you ta be so tired now, Jo?"

Jo relished the fingers touching hers and closed her eyes. She longed to tell Meg about what she and Sarah were doing instead of ferrying planes—she could not. "Can we just go back to our room and close the door and shut out the world until the blasted sirens go off again?"

"I'm thinkin' that a nice hot bath and a cup of tea is what you are needin'." Meg stood up and held her hand out to Jo. "Come along and let me take care of you."

*

Meg stood on the other side of the door to the bath area trying to collect her thoughts. For months, she put the kiss she shared with Jo out of her mind—at least tried to. Early on, while flying, she'd often find her fingers touching her lips as she remembered the warmth of Jo's lips on hers. The harder she tried to deny her feelings, the more they seemed to intensify. Once she stopped fighting them, she and Jo regained the easy camaraderie they enjoyed before the kiss.

Often, when Jo had not returned to the barracks, Meg would sit by the window watching for her plane. The room they shared was lonely without her there to share a laugh or a hug. She liked hugging and being hugged by Jo. The feeling of strong arms around her, created wonderful sensations that were both pleasurable and frustrating. Blowing out a breath, her knuckles rapped lightly on the door, and her hand reached out for the knob.

*

Goose bumps spread over Jo's skin as she stepped out of the warm, tin bathtub. She could still see the want in Meg's eyes as Meg had undressed her then held her hand as she got into the tub. For the months following the kissing incident, they had been doing a dance of seduction, skirting the edges but never fully revealing what they felt. A rap on the door and the sound of Meg's voice made the goose bumps multiply.

"Are ya turnin' into a prune, Jo?" the voice on the other side of the door asked.

Jo's eyes darted around the room, looking for a towel only to realize that there was none. "Um, no, but I need a towel."

The door opened partially and Meg slipped inside the room, closing the door behind her. ""I've brought you a towel and a robe," she said with a smile before approaching Jo. "Here, dry yourself off. I put your robe over the heater and it is warm."

With quick, precise movements, Jo toweled off then slipped into her robe with eyes averted. "Thanks, that feels really good."

Meg took the towel and moved closer. "It is really cold out in the hallway," she said as she began to rub Jo's hair. "Christmas is comin' in two days and you can't be sick now, can you?"

The warmth of the robe added to Jo's already overheated libido. She briefly closed her eyes before her hands cupped Meg's face. Leaning forward, her lips hovered over Meg's before gently kissing them. When she felt no resistance, she wrapped her arms around Meg and deepened the kiss.

Meg pulled back. "Why are ya doin' that again, Jo?" Not waiting for an answer, she instinctively wrapped her arms around Jo and sighed. "I… know not what ta do…I've never felt this way before now."

Jo drew in a deep breath to settle her out of control emotions. Hearing Meg's tentative word made her realize that how she handled Meg's questions would affect their fledgling relationship. "From the first moment I saw you, Meg, I've wanted to kiss you," she whispered.

Meg moved her head so she could see Jo's face. With green eyes searching she asked, "Was it as you imagined? I have never been kissed like that before." She averted her eyes. "No one has ever kissed me," she added softly.

Jo tipped Meg's chin so she could see her face. "You, my dear, are an excellent kisser," she said before capturing Meg's lips again.

A knock on the door had the two women stepping apart. "I guess someone else is wantin' to use the tub."

Jo smiled and took Meg's hand and felt her hand tremble when the knock at the door became more persistent. "Can you give me five more minutes?" she hollered.

"Don't take any longer than that, Jo," the voice said. "And don't use all the hot water."

Shaking her head, Jo grinned. "Of all people, it has to be Midge." She opened the door slowly and looked around. "No one is out there, let's go." She took Meg's hand and led her to their room.

Once inside, Meg began busying herself with the task of getting ready for bed. All the while, she avoided Jo's eyes.

For her part, Jo flopped down on her bed and just watched a clearly nervous Meg. When she undressed and had put on her nightgown, Jo asked, "Are you doing that on purpose?"

"Doin' what?" Meg asked, still avoiding Jo's eyes.

For months, Jo's eyes had taken in Meg's body—sleek, with small but firm breasts and the triangle of red hair that astounded her. "Take my breath away," Jo said in what was almost a growl.

Meg looked down at her nightgown. "Is that what you think I'm tryin' ta do now, Jo?"

A slow smile crept around Jo's lips as she stood up and stepped closer to Meg. "After kissing you in the bath room, I want to kiss you more and the thought of you so near takes my breath away, Meg…it always has."

"What am I ta do, Jo? I know not of these feelings I am havin'." She shrugged. "The thoughts whirlin' around in my head frighten me…you frighten me." She took a step back. "I've never felt my body react the way it did when we kissed…that scares me, Jo."

Jo went to Meg and pulled her close. For several minutes, she relished the feeling of being so close to the woman. "We have time, Meg," she whispered into red hair. "When the time is right, you will know. I want you to know that I have fallen in love with you," she paused as the rightness of the words astounded her, "I've never said that to anyone before." She pulled back so she could see Meg's face. "I love you."

"Oh, Jo, I…" Meg stopped as the wail of an air raid siren split the air. Without thinking, both women dressed rapidly before hurrying toward the shelter across from their barracks.

As they ran, they could hear the drone of plane engines overhead and just made it to the shelter as the first bombs fell. Powerful explosions rocked the shelter, which was jammed full with at least twice its capacity. For five hours, most of the members of the Hatfield Ferry Pool, packed tightly in the shelter, listened as they heard the scream of dropping bombs, followed by the sound of massive explosions, one after another.

*

Cold night air hit each person who emerged from the bomb shelter after the *all clear* sounded. One by one, they shivered as they looked to the south where the sky glowed in reds and yellows. In the distance, they could hear the sound of more explosions. Each knew that in spite of the fact that it was officially Christmas Eve, no one would be singing carols or eating the traditional holiday fare. Massive fires filled the entire horizon with a red yellow haze—war was raging all around them.

The women of the ATA clustered in the rest room of their barracks as their commander spoke.

"Ladies, I know that those who live nearby," she looked at Sarah and Lady Millicent, "were hoping to spend a few hours with their family tomorrow. I also know of the plans you made for a Christmas celebration here in the barracks. Unfortunately, tomorrow will be just like any other day for us. There are planes that we need to deliver to the airfields so our pilots are equipped to meet the enemy head on." Dorothy turned to leave, before turning back. "Merry Christmas to you all."

From the back of the room, a crystal clear voice sang *Silent Night*. Soon all the women, including their commander, joined in the singing as each acknowledged their commitment to the war effort. Once done, they all gave each other hugs of comfort and camaraderie as they wished each other *Merry Christmas,* knowing that this would most likely be the only time they would be together as a group.

*

The chill of the night had Jo and Meg hugging each other closely, as they and others stood on the barrack's roof looking at the burning horizon. All around them, they could see an orange glow.

"This is a terrible night," Meg whispered as she snuggled closer to Jo.

"Let's go back inside," Jo whispered back. "There is nothing we can do here."

When the door to their room closed, Meg turned to Jo and pulled her in for a hug. "I can't believe all that destruction. I've seen it all from the sky but nothing like what we witnessed tonight."

Jo wrapped her arms around Meg, cherishing the moment with her. "It seems like ages since we met and started down this road," she said. "All I ever wanted to do was fly."

Meg nestled into Jo's shoulder. "Me too. I remember when my uncle," her voice caught, "took me up for the first time…it was like I'd found heaven, Jo."

"Did you ever think…"

"What?"

Jo shook her head before she kissed the top of Meg's head. "I never considered what war was like when I came here. I just wanted to fly. Now, there is this destruction all around us and it is not a far stretch to think we will see even more before the war ends." She pulled her arms tighter around Meg. "Yet, in spite of everything that has happened, I still just want to fly."

Meg gave Jo a squeeze. "I cannot wait for the mornin' ta climb into a plane…any plane…and soar above it all."

She looked into Jo's eyes. "I wanted to tell you earlier that I love you, Jo, and I really liked kissin' you." She shrugged. "I don't know if I can be givin' you more than that."

Jo lightly kissed Meg's lips then pulled away. "There is no hurry, Meg. We will take it slow until the time is right for us both."

For several minutes, they remained in each other's embrace. "Will you hold me while I sleep, Jo?"

"Yes, I'd love to."

Chapter Sixteen

Christmas
December 1940
Hatfield Ferry Pool No. 5
Southampton, England

Meg woke but kept her eyes closed as she recalled the night before and the emotions and feelings that Jo made in her body. She listened and heard nothing—Jo was not there. As she slowly opened her eyes, she recognized an eerie silence that seemed to surround her. Usually there was the drone of plane engines as they took off or landed, along with the sounds of the nearby airfield that always permeated the air. She closed her eyes, concentrated on sounds, and frowned when she heard none.

With one fluid motion, she was out of the bed—Jo's bed—and stretched her arms and her body. A smile filled her face as she once again recalled what transpired the night before. Just as she was putting on her robe, Jo entered the room.

"Merry Christmas," Jo said as she hugged Meg close.

With a sigh of contentment, Meg wrapped her arms around Jo. "Merry Christmas. Tis hard ta believe that I won't be with me family today," she said with a hint of sadness.

Jo kissed Meg tenderly before she pulled back. "War makes life as we knew it seem distant."

Meg grinned. "I do have somethin' for you."

"You do? Meg, I have nothing for you."

After another lingering kiss, Meg took Jo's hand and led her to the trunk situated at the end of her bed. Crouching, she opened the top and extracted a small package before she rose and faced her roommate. "I found this when I went ta Connel two months ago and wanted to get it for you."

Jo took the small package when Meg offered it to her, untied the twine, and carefully unwrapped the brown paper wrapping. When she saw the small, green, metal shamrock, she smiled. "Meg, this is lovely. Thank you so much."

"You can keep it with you and you'll have the luck of the Irish wherever you go."

Jo dug in a buttoned pocket in her Sidcot flying suit and pulled something out. Her hand then opened to reveal a rabbit's foot. "When I was about to take my first solo flight my dad gave me this. I want you to have it, Meg. He said as long as I carried it, I would always return safe." She shrugged and extended her hand out to Meg.

Tentatively, Meg touched the object and immediately felt the softness of the fur. "No, Jo, I cannot take this from you," she said as she closed Jo's fingers over the rabbit's foot. "Your father meant it for you."

Jo opened her hand. "I want you to have it, Meg…it will keep you safe," she shrugged, "I never want to lose you. Please, take it."

The fur tickled her hand as she took the object from Jo's hand. "I'm only takin' this because you want me ta…but I worry that you won't have your luck with you in the sky."

Jo held up the shamrock. "I have this to keep me safe and it is from you, which makes it all the more powerful."

"Then I'll be thankin' you every time I take off and land, Jo, knowin' that you too are safe."

With strong arms around Meg, Jo kissed her soundly before looking into her eyes. "You gave me the greatest gift of all when you told me you loved me last night, Meg. I have never been happier."

For several minutes they lingered in each other's embrace until Meg said, "I wish we could stay like this all day and celebrate Christmas together."

"Me too. I'm off to Southhampton. What about you?"

"Atlebridge."

"We are off in different directions again." Jo kissed the top of Meg's head before releasing her. "I was outside earlier and the fires to the south are still burning. There will be no Christmas celebrations there; only bucket brigades."

There was a knock on the door.

"That will be Sarah…it is time for me to leave."

Meg kissed Jo tenderly then stepped backward. "Come back safe ta me, Jo."

With a grin, Jo said, "I will, and you do the same." She then opened the door. "Are you ready to go, Sarah?" she asked as she walked out of the room.

Meg watched the door close before walking to the window for a last glimpse of Jo before her day, too, began. She noticed the quietness that surrounded her. "How odd." She thought of Jo's lips that had just kissed her and smiled. She loved Jo and that was a big step for her to admit. "Can I ever really *love* her in every way?" She felt her body tingle with that thought and smiled at the warm feelings coursing through her body. After one last look out the window, she got ready for the day ahead.

*

For the three days following Christmas, bombing by the Luftwaffe was nonexistent. The ferry pilots used the lull to deliver airplanes in record numbers.

Sarah Falkner opened the door to the room she and Brenda shared and smiled at her friend. "How many flights did you make?"

"I lost count after six…I went from here to an MU near Portsmouth, hopped on *Annie,* came back here then off to Portsmouth again." Brenda looked at her friend. "You look stuffed, Sarah. Did you have a shocker of a day?"

Sarah thought she'd heard all of Brenda's slang words but *shocker* was a new one to her. "Translate, please," she said with a grin.

Right, was your day bad?"

With a nod, Sarah gave her friend a thoughtful look. "Not bad, just long." Not wanting to add any other details, she said, "Don't you think it strange that the bombings have halted?"

"Crikey, Sarah, don't say that so loud."

Sarah laughed. "Don't want them to be reminded, do we?" She ran her fingers through her hair. "I wish we could say that they've given up but I know that's not true." Sarah's eyes went immediately to the floor so Brenda wouldn't know she had spoken out of turn. "I mean…surely they are regrouping somewhere."

Brenda gave her friend a thoughtful look. "Back home, there was this dingo. Well, it looked like a dingo to me…not that I ever saw one…anyway, the dingo would prowl in the woods as I walked to the farm, growling the whole time. I would always carry a big stick in case he attacked. Then one day he wasn't around and the next day was the same. After a week, I figured the bloke was gone and I no longer carried the stick. A few days later, I was walking home and he appeared out of nowhere in the middle of the road with the fur up on his back growling and showing his teeth. I was right scared since all I had was a milk pail and a basket with eggs. I knew if I ran, he'd get me, so I stood there staring at him and growled back."

"What happened, Brenda? Obviously he didn't kill you."

"Right, after what seemed like forever he ran off and I thought *good, he's gone now and won't bother me again.*"

Sarah looked at her friend and saw there was more to the story and Brenda was struggling to tell the rest. "What happened after that?" she asked softly.

"The next day a bloke down the road shot the *dingo* after it attacked and killed the man's baby daughter." Dark blue eyes sought out Sarah's face. "The Germans are like that animal and will prey on the weaker powers."

"Yes, they've already done that. My country stands alone, for all others have been lost."

"If I hadn't let my guard down, maybe I could have done something to keep that beast from killing that baby." With determination evident on her face, she said, "We can never underestimate the Germans for if we do, the cause we fight for will be lost."

Sarah considered the words and knew the truth behind them. She had seen the buildup of troops, tanks, and planes along the coastline of France. It would only be a matter of time before they would unleash their fury once again. Her beloved country would have to stand and fight if it was to survive. In a small way, she hoped that what she and Jo were doing would help sway the tide to victory.

"Sarah?"

Light blue eyes lifted. "Yes."

"We will not let them win."

Chapter Seventeen

Late December 1940
Hatfield Ferry Pool No. 5
Southampton, England

On the night of December 29th, the Germans returned and pummeled London in an unrelenting succession of fire bombs and high explosive bombs that landed in the city and its port with alarming accuracy. From the roof tops of buildings at Hatfield Air Station, pilots, mechanics, and other personnel watched as the horror unfolded.

The women of the ATA stood on the roof of their barracks, watching and listening to the cacophony of blast after blast as they watched in horror of what seemed to be the annihilation of London. It was only a little more than thirty-two kilometers to London but they could still hear the whir of the bombs as they made their way downward before exploding.

On the horizon, London appeared to be one massive ball of fire that lit the night skies, allowing them to see the Messerschmitts and the rapid deployment of bombs. Behind them, they could hear the sounds of RAF planes taking off to meet the Germans head on, as the wail of sirens filled the air. For the moment, the focus was on London and they felt safe until a voice yelled, "Get off that roof and into the shelter."

"Any idiot can see they aren't interested in us," Midge grumbled as she crossed the tarmac to the shelter. "Who wants to sit in that dark hole for who knows how long, especially with those smelly mechanics?"

"You will do as you're told Miss Reister," an authoritative voice said from the back of the line.

"Yes, ma'am. Sorry, ma'am," Midge said sarcastically as she eyed Shannon Brannigan.

As the women filed into the air raid shelter, Midge grumbled and continued in the same vein while everyone else sat down.

"Give it a break, Midge," someone said from the front of tunnel, squelching the moaning.

"I don't care where we are as long as I have your shoulder to lie on, Jo," Meg whispered.

Taking advantage of the dim light, Jo turned her head and kissed the top of Meg's head. "Nor do I." Breathing in the deep rich scent that was uniquely Meg's, Jo moved her head so it rested on Meg's and closed her eyes—it would be a long night.

Brenda spoke softly to Sarah and a few others, relating another story of her life when she worked at the farm in Australia…

"There was this bloke who always showed up at Claude McGuire's farm at exactly twelve o'clock every Tuesday. This went on for about five years. I always knew it was Tuesday because Claude would grumble even more than he already did. You might be asking why Claude put up with it," Brenda laughed, "the man was the reverend of Claude's church.

"One Tuesday he didn't come and Claude smiled the whole afternoon…even sent me home with two tins of milk and an extra lot of eggs. After three weeks, the reverend came round again and this time Claude asked him why he hadn't been there the previous weeks. The man laid his hand on old Claude's shoulder and said, *I found someone who needed saving more than you.* So Claude asked why he was there and the reverend said he was wrong—no one needed more saving than Claude."

"What happened next?" Sarah asked.

"Well, Claude threw a dummy spit and told the man to get off his land."

"That's a new one, Brenda," Sarah said with a slight laugh.

She shrugged and smiled. "He was really angry."

"The reverend said, *there are some people in this world that hold the lives of others in their hands. Although they do wrong, I am certain they don't always realize the affect they have on other lives. Sometimes it takes an intervention to show them the way.*

"Anyway, I remember seeing the hate and anger in Claude's face as he hollered; *I don't need a damned intervention.*"

"Did he come back?" Bess Potter asked.

Brenda slowly moved her head back and forth. "Three days later, the reverend was walking on the road and was hit by a car and died." She laughed. "I think Claude thought that no one else from the church would bother him again...he was wrong. The next Tuesday a different reverend appeared for the noon meal.

Sarah looked at her friend thoughtfully. "So no matter who you take out of a situation, someone else will be there to fill it. Is that right?"

"Yeah, Claude was going to be saved, whether he liked it or not."

At that moment, Midge stood up and walked to the entrance of the shelter. "I'm getting out of here...any fool can hear that they aren't bombing here."

"You will not leave, Miss Reister," Lady Millicent said as she blocked Midge's forward movement.

"Who do you think you are giving me orders, High and Mighty Lady? You think just because you have some fancy high falutin' title and friends in high places, that you can order others around…well, I'm here to tell you, you can't. Now get out of my way before I make you." As she started forward, she felt a hand on her arm, stopping her motion. When she turned, she saw Jo standing next to her.

Leaning in and whispering, Jo said, "You're embarrassing yourself. Go back and sit with the rest of us."

Midge yanked her arm but was unable to dislodge Jo's grip.

"Go sit back down," Jo said in a measured voice. "You are accomplishing nothing but giving yourself and all Americans a bad name."

Once Midge relented, Jo turned to Lady Millicent. "She can be a real pain in the ass but she does have a good heart…in there somewhere…I think."

Millicent smiled. "I do not judge you by her actions, Miss Laughlin. I'm getting a tad claustrophobic myself and I really don't see why we are in here, but orders are orders."

"Yes, I agree. Without order, we will dissolve into chaos and that is no way to fight a war."

"I am reminded of Sir Winston Churchill's words about so many owing so few for this conflict we are facing. Tonight I witnessed the destruction of my beloved London and fear for the safety of my family. Everything in me wants to find a vehicle and make my way to my home and my children. But right now, I am needed here and the children are with their father and he will keep them safe."

Jo saw the stoic woman tremble and instinctively moved to embrace her. At first, Millicent stiffened before she leaned into Jo's body and sought the solace of human comfort. After a few minutes, she backed away and refused to look Jo in the eyes.

"Thank you," she whispered before sitting back down.

"You're welcome. Often help and understanding comes from people you least expect it from."

Soft brown eyes sought out Jo's face. "Of all the people we deal with each day, you, Miss Laughlin, are the one whom I would trust with my life."

"Thank you," Jo said as she retreated to Meg's side.

"What was that all about?" Meg asked.

Jo grinned. "It was Midge being Midge, trying to go up against Lady Millicent." She chuckled. "You'd think she'd figure out by now that she hasn't a chance."

"Not a chance of her understandin' somethin' like that."

An hour later the *all clear* sounded. As they filed out of the shelter, they looked to the south and saw the horizon glowing high into the night sky.

*

Just as Christmas was a somber affair, New Year's Eve was no different. The ATA pilots, along with the RAF personnel of Hatfield Air Station, met in an empty hangar. Someone brought several bottles of champagne and someone else provided beer. It was a low key affair and although someone played a saxophone, there were no sounds of celebration.

When the clock struck midnight, a low cheer filled the hangar as each participant turned to those closest and clung to them. From what seemed far away, a melancholy voice sang Auld Lang Syne, reflecting the mood of those in the hangar. The war effort was less than a year old and each had seen more than his or her share of devastation and sorrow. The bombings over the last few days brought home to the British members just how vulnerable their country was. For those who were there from other countries, they too worried. England was now their adopted country and they would do what was needed to defend it. War was a grim proposition, yet despite the destruction and death all around them, they all were determined to fight to the end to defend England and their freedom.

*

The Hatfield Ferry Pool pilots spent New Year's Day delivering planes to air fields at a break neck pace. Whenever the weather and the Germans cooperated, they would take advantage and up their daily quotas of ferrying planes.

Jo entered the room she shared with Meg and was saddened to see her roommate was not there. She had about an hour before she and Sarah would depart on another reconnaissance mission over France. She pulled out fresh clothes, paying particular attention to her warmer flying suit since the nights were very cold, especially at the higher altitudes that their missions required.

"Jo, don't be tellin' me you're goin' out again tonight," Meg said when she opened the door and saw her roommate pulling on her flying suit.

"No choice," she said, refusing to make eye contact. "They want us to test out some sort of gadget that is supposed to make flying at night easier. We are flying nor…not far."

"You haven't had any time for yourself," Meg said as she wrapped her arms around Jo.

Jo leaned into Meg and took solace in the warm, comforting embrace. "I'd like nothing more than to stay right here." The kiss she gave Meg lingered until Jo broke away.

"I don't want you ta go," Meg whispered. "Stay with me tonight."

Once again, Jo was enclosing Meg in a hug. "Can you keep that thought until I get back? This shouldn't take long."

Meg pouted then smiled. "Well, I guess I can, if you promise not ta be too long."

"Promise," Jo said as she grabbed her flight jacket. She shivered slightly. "Believe me, Meg; I don't want to be up there any longer than need be." She gave Meg one last, quick kiss before she left the room.

*

Jo had just gotten to the exit from the barracks when she met up with Sarah.

"You ready?" Sarah asked.

"Yeah, guess so."

"Why so glum?"

"I hate having to keep lying to Meg about what we're doing."

"What we are doing, Jo, is important," Sarah said softly as they neared a hangar. "The information we gather helps keep our lads alive."

"Yeah, I know." Jo shrugged as they approached their airplane. "It's just that…"

Sarah stopped and took hold of Jo's arm. "I know," she said softly. "It is hard to keep secrets from someone that you want to share everything with." Her eyes searched out Jo's eyes. "I know."

Jo nodded. "I'm not sure I understand what you are saying, Sarah."

Sarah's eyes sought out Jo's face as they continued to walk. "I shan't go into it now."

"Yes, you will. I want to know what you meant," Jo demanded.

"Last night, when it was midnight, everyone hugged all those around them. You and Meg clung to each other." Sarah shrugged. "I just thought that…it was very touching."

"In case you've forgotten, Sarah, Meg lost her uncle not too long ago. She did not want to go to the celebration; said she had nothing to celebrate." Jo stopped. "I was comforting her," she narrowed her eyes, "what else did you think it was?"

Sarah began walking and turned toward the hangar. "I just thought it was touching, that is all."

As they reached their plane, Jo gave Sarah a quick nod and said, "Right. The sooner we leave, the sooner we return."

Chapter Eighteen

January 1941
English Channel and Northern France

The night was dark. As the prototype Fairey Barracuda torpedo bomber neared the coast of France, Jo constantly monitored the radar screen. The plane, modified for aerial photography, flew just below the clouds, thereby affording Sarah the opportunity to calibrate the camera that was located where one of the torpedoes would go.

"You done yet?" Jo asked.

Sarah, who was on her belly adjusting the focus of the camera specially modified for night pictures, responded, "Just about…give me one more second." Once satisfied with the settings, Sarah said, "Got it," and felt the aircraft begin to climb. She was just about to sit in her seat when she heard a sound and turned to look at the back of the plane.

"Damn!" Jo exclaimed as she took evasive maneuvers to avoid the Messerschmitt that suddenly popped up on the radar screen. She knew at least one round had hit her plane and searched the dials for any indication of how bad it was. "Shit! Sarah, how close are we to land?" she asked as she struggled to keep the plane level.

"About twenty kilometers."

"…twelve miles, that's doable…we can glide in close. We are going to have to land in the water. Be ready to leave the plane as soon as we touch the water."

"Aren't we close enough to the coast to land there?" Sarah asked as she readied for a crash landing.

"We're leaking fuel," Jo said as she held onto the stick with both hands, with her feet working the rudders. "I'll get us as close as I can then we will have to swim for it." Her eyes rested on the radar and she closed them for a moment after seeing the blip of what could only be the Messerschmitt.

"We've been hit again," Sarah cried as she watched the water she knew was frigid draw closer.

It took all of Jo's flying skills and strength to keep the Barracuda from taking a nosedive into the English Channel. As she saw the water nearing, she cut the engine and pulled back hard so she could make as soft a landing as possible. Mentally, she kicked herself for allowing the hit by not seeing the enemy in time. Keeping the nose of the plane upward, she set it down on the water, glad that her dad insisted she learn how to land without a working engine.

Jo scrambled to open the hatch before moving forward to climb out onto the wing. "Looks like we landed in about three feet of water," she said to Sarah.

Sarah nodded. "Let's take whatever we can," she said as she moved toward the belly of the plane. "I'll get whatever I can from the camera, along with the film."

Once back in the cockpit, Jo began gathering items to take as she did her best to destroy the instrumentation and any item she didn't want in the hands of the Germans. "Don't forget your parachute, Sarah. We can use it for cover."

"Got it, along with binoculars, the first aid kit, and the night vision lenses from the camera." She made her way to the wing and watched as Jo climbed out of the cockpit. "I suppose no one has ever told you how horribly cold and unforgiving the Channel can be in January," she said over her shoulder as she moved to the edge of the wing.

"Of course, you realize that once we get the gear on dry land we need to come back and push the plane out into deeper water."

Sarah nodded. "It's going to be icy cold," she lamented as she lowered herself into the frigid waters of the English Channel. She let out a groan as her lower body felt the water seep into her flying suit and freeze her skin. "C…c…come…on JJJo, it issss de…..lightful…"

"Just like a summer swim," Jo said as she moved forward. "We need to get to shore quickly before the Germans come looking for us."

Moving as fast as they could, both women made it to the shore, deposited their gear, and then were about to plunge their lower bodies into the water again when they saw the choppy waters of the Channel draw their plane further away from land. It didn't take long for the plane to slowly begin to sink. Satisfied that the plane would not be easily discovered, they gathered up their belongings and moved further inland.

The bulkiness of their winter flying suits made the journey all the more arduous and both Jo and Sarah felt their legs protest not only the frigid water temperatures they had been in, but also from the added weight of sopping wet flying suits. The Channel was rolling and a sudden gust of wind that blew stiffly seemed bent on freezing their already icy bodies.

As they slogged forward, Jo grunted, "You underestimated…the water was brutally cold."

"We need to get dry as soon as possible," Sarah huffed.

Through chattering teeth, Jo said, "Won't be soon enough for me."

"We have to assume that the pilot radioed our position to the land troops so we shan't stay here very long."

Mustering all their reserves, the two women hurried along the short sandy beach, across a thick outcropping of small stones, over larger rocks, and up a slight incline before collapsing in the sharp grasses of a sand dune.

Sarah lifted her head above the grass cover and surveyed the area as best she could. Her eyes had adjusted to the dark somewhat and she recognized what she thought was a dirt road. "There's a road, Jo," she whispered.

Jo, too, lifted her head and tried to focus on the area on the other side of the road. Just then she saw the lights of an oncoming vehicle and lowered her head as Sarah did the same.

The vehicle passed by and once again, they both peered out over the grass.

"We need to get across that road and find out what is beyond there," Sarah said as she began to dig into a pocket of her flying suit. "I brought the filters for the camera...we can use them to see what is out there." She passed one to Jo as she began to stand up.

Clutching at Sarah's arm, Jo said, "Not yet. If we are going to do that, we need to have all our energy reserves ready to run. Let's give it another hour or two and then go."

Sarah lay back in the grass. "We can't do that...we'll freeze to death and if that pilot indeed radioed where we went down, it won't be long before they come looking for us."

Jo considered the comment before she nodded her head. "Then it's now or never, Sarah." She rose, as did Sarah.

With a semi crouched walk, both Sarah and Jo made their way slowly to the road. When a vehicle approached, they flattened on their bellies and held their breath. Once the danger passed, they stood and ran as fast as their soggy boots and equally wet clothes, would allow. They found that the other side of the road sloped downward, affording them the ability to keep moving without worrying about who might see them from the road.

"I need to stop for a minute, Jo," Sarah said as she rested her hands on her knees. "I think we are far enough that they won't find us right away."

Jo snorted. "Unless they use dogs," she warned. "We need to keep moving and put as much distance as we can from the coastline."

"Please, give me a minute to catch my breath and see if I can wring any of the water out of my clothes."

After considering where they were and what condition they were in, Jo held the lens filter up to her eyes and scanned the area.

"Can you see what's out there?" asked Sarah, quivering as she took a step closer.

"Yeah, but I don't know exactly what it is I'm seeing."

Sarah held her lens up to one eye. "Spot on, I can see some sort of structure."

"I must be holding mine wrong," Jo said before adding, "is it anything useable?"

Sarah pointed at something. "Do you see that?"

Jo too put a filter up to one then the other eye as she followed the line of Sarah's. "It looks like some sort of broken down structure…probably bombed out."

"It's most likely a shepherd's station. I went on a walking holiday of the French countryside and they are quite common," Sarah whispered as Jo drew closer.

"Shall we see what it is? Maybe we can get out of these clothes and let them dry."

"Right, let's go then."

With careful steps, Jo and Sarah made their way to what they thought was a building. All the while each was consciously looking for any sign of a German patrol. When they were almost to the dilapidated shack, Sarah squealed after the crack of a steel trap pierced the air.

"Sarah, what is it?"

"My foot. I must have stepped on some sort of trap."

Within seconds, Jo was on her knees and fumbling in her emergency sack. She pulled out a flashlight and focused the beam on Sarah's foot. "Does it feel like anything is broken?"

"No, I think my boots kept that from happening," she frowned, "where did you get a torch?"

"It's part of my emergency pack," Jo said handing Sarah the flashlight. "Here, crouch down and hold it close to your foot. Hopefully, if any Germans are about, they won't see the light."

"Any way you can cover your hands?" Sarah asked.

"Yep." Jo pulled her hands up into her sleeve before she grasped either side of the small trap—she wasn't about to have her fingers freeze to the metal. If they had, she would lose her fingers when the spring trap closed. "When you feel it release, you step out of it immediately," Jo instructed as she spread the trap wider. Once Sarah's foot was out of the trap, Jo released the metal, which made a loud snap. "Do you think you can walk?"

With caution, Sarah put some weight on her foot and cringed. "Yes, I can make it…not that far now."

When they arrived at the building, each let out a sigh—the structure looked like a strong wind would cause it to fall down.

"This will have to do," Sarah looked around as Jo's torch lit up the area.

"Over there," Jo pointed a beam of light at one wall that was mostly upright, with a part of the roof collapsed between several timbers.

"Oh, gracious yes, that's perfect" Sarah said. "I've got to get out of these wet clothes and take a look at my ankle." She looked at Jo. "You should too. It would be ironic to survive a plane crash then contract pneumonia and die."

Jo sat on a large stone that had once been part of the wall then opened her emergency pack before releasing her parachute from its confines. "We can use this one over there to keep the wind out and use yours to keep us warm, if that's possible."

"What do you have in the bag?" Sarah asked as she continued to shiver.

"My dad always insisted I always carry a kit in case I was forced to land, so I enhanced the basic kit ATA gives us." She looked up at Sarah. "I've added to the standard issue." She opened the tin case and was happy to find all the contents were dry. She found a chocolate bar and broke it in half. "Until we find something else to eat, we'll need to ration this."

Sarah held up her hand. "No, save it for when we really are hungry."

With a quick shrug, Jo put the chocolate back in the kit. She pulled out what looked like a square of wax, along with a tube that looked like it had once held a cigar. "Let's move over there," she said, pointing a corner of the building. "It looks like the most stable part of the building and once the parachute is in place, we will be completely out of the wind."

With a nod, Sarah limped further into the run down building. "I need to get out of these wet things," she reiterated.

"Let me take care of this first then we'll look at your ankle."

Jo busied herself gathering rocks and lining them in a circle near the corner where Sarah sat. Once satisfied, she put the piece of wax in the center before striking a match and lighting a wick. "This is all the risk for light that we can take now…it won't keep us all that warm but it will be better than nothing." She stripped off her flying suit and angled it so it was reaping the benefits of the small flame.

"Take yours off and maybe it'll dry a little or we can use them as a soggy blanket."

"I'm glad only the bottom part is wet, although some water did creep on up. I think I'd expire if I was completely wet." Sarah struggled but managed to stand. Once she did, she removed her flying suit and handed to Jo. "I'll go see if I can find anything that we can put between us and the cold ground."

Seeing the grimace, Jo said, "No. I already found something. There are some timbers and planks that we can put together to at least keep us off the ground."

"I need to help and do my part. It will be quicker if we work together."

Jo raised her eyebrows. "Ok."

In no time, they erected a makeshift platform to lie on while they slept. They had stripped out of their still soggy flying suits, heavy water logged boots, cold wet socks, along with the trousers that they wore under the flying suit. Jo draped their clothing over a timber, where the wind was blowing the hardest.

Sitting on the platform next to Sarah, Jo said, "Let me have a look at that ankle."

"I'm fine," Sarah bristled. "We can tend to it in the morning. Right now I just want to get warm."

"Me too," Jo whispered. "If we sleep close together we can use each other's body heat and if we fold the parachute enough, that should help to keep us warm too."

"I'm freezing, although I have to admit I do feel some heat from your *fire*."

Jo stretched out then patted the wood. "Come on, I'm freezing too." Once situated, Jo pulled the folded parachute over them."

With chattering teeth, Sarah moved closer to Jo. "At least you are somewhat warm. This reminds me of a time when I was trying for a record between London and

Brussels," Sarah said with a hint of mirth. "My plane ran out of gas and I was forced to land in the middle of nowhere."

"And you had to sleep on the ground snuggled up to another person?"

"No, but it was extremely cold. Have you ever slept in an open cockpit with the wind blowing snow on you?"

"No, can't say that I have."

"Trust me, Jo. This is a whole lot warmer." She moved so that her body and Jo's were touching. "Maybe in the morning our flying suits will be a little drier and we can figure out how to get back home."

Jo draped her arm over Sarah's smaller body. "Home. I wonder if they miss us yet."

Chapter Nineteen

January 1941
Northern Coast of France

The sound of birds chirping first woke Jo. She opened her eyes, assessed the surroundings, and then listened for anything that might tell her they were in danger. Not hearing anything untoward, she disengaged from Sarah's body and stood up before stretching to alleviate the ache from lying on the cold hard wood. When she touched her flying suit, she wasn't surprised that it was still damp.

"Are they dry?" a sleepy voice asked.

"No, but they aren't sopping wet," Jo said as she shivered, after putting her clothes back on. The sound of something snapping beyond the building had Jo protectively covering Sarah with her body.

In silence, neither woman breathed as they listened for any sign that they were in danger. Again, they heard a snap, followed by nothing, as the birds began to chirp once more.

Jo's eyes went to Sarah's. She rolled silently off the woman and held her index finger to her lips. She pointed for Sarah to move into the corner near the still burning wax before she made her way along the wall to where she could look over it without being seen. Peering over the edge, she let out a sigh of relief as she saw a deer lazily chomping on the grass directly on the other side of the wall. Scanning the rest of the area and feeling satisfied that there was no danger, she stood up and walked back to Sarah.

"Just a deer," she said as she scooped up her emergency sack, pulled out the chocolate, and offered some to Sarah. "This will have to do until we can find something else." She eyed Sarah. "How's your foot feeling?"

"Painful."

"Let me look."

Reluctantly, Sarah lifted her foot. "It's just bruised."

Jo's eyes inspected the deeply bruised area above Sarah's toes before they looked up at her fellow pilot. "I don't see any broken skin, which is good. Can you wiggle your toes?"

"They're not broken," Sarah remarked as she moved all five of her toes.

"We should wrap it with the gauze from your first aid kit…it won't give you a lot of support but some is better than none." Once she found the white material, she began wrapping it around Sarah's foot.

After the ministrations to her foot were completed, Sarah donned her still damp flying suit and attempted to pull on an almost dry sock.

Jo heard the yelp and looked at Sarah. "Here let me help with that." She knelt down and gently pulled the sock onto Sarah's foot, followed by a boot. "How does that feel?"

"Not as bad as I thought it would."

"Good."

"Jo?"

"Yes."

"Thank you."

Jo smiled and nodded before she went back to rewrapping her parachute.

"Do you have a compass in that bag of yours?" Sarah asked as she pulled on her other boot and stood up.

Jo rooted around in the bag before she pulled out the issued round, brass escape compass. Holding it in her palm she turned then stopped. "North is that way," she said nodding away from the road."

Sarah pulled out a map she'd taken from the now sunken plane and spread it over the platform they used for a bed. She pointed to an area on the map. "We should be around here. Our last coordinates were forty-nine degrees north and zero degrees east. There's a port here where I suspect there will be numerous German soldiers, so we don't want to go there."

Jo nodded. "I agree. The question then becomes…" Her voice went silent as she heard the distinct sound of vehicles and tanks. "We need to get out of here."

No sooner had Jo spoken than the all too familiar sound of bombs whirling toward the earth filled the air. Explosions rocked the earth as both women gathered all their belongings and moved quickly out of their makeshift residence.

"Over there," Sarah shouted above the din. With the unwrapped parachute trailing her, she disregarded the pain in her foot and ran quickly into a stand of trees.

"Stop," Jo yelled when they were deep into the cover.

"Jo, we can't stay here, it's too dangerous."

"I agree but we need to get your parachute back into its bag before it snags on something and you take a tumble."

Annoyed, Sarah began gathering up the silky material and stuffing it as fast as she could into the bag. "Done. Now let's be on our way."

Jo looked at her compass. "That way," she said pointing off to their left.

Onward they pressed through an increasingly denser thicket of brambles, trees, and ground clutter. Ever moving, they could hear voices in the distance as they slowly picked their way forward, until they came to a complete stop when the thick undergrowth proved to be impenetrable. The voices floating on the wind grew louder—their need to find a way forward became urgent.

"Over there," Jo pointed to an area to their left, "do you see it?"

Sarah followed Jo's finger. "Yes, it looks like some sort of path."

"Probably made by deer," Jo quietly responded as they moved toward what they hoped was a way out.

Just as they came to the narrow path, it became deathly quiet all around them. Then, a cacophony of booms and rat-a-tat-tats surrounded them. They knew that RAF pilots, flying the Spitfires that protected the bombers in the second wave of bombing, were in a dogfight.

Without hesitation, they thrust forward along the path where thorns, small trees, and undergrowth vied to penetrate their flying suits. In the lead Jo pulled her sleeves over her hands as she broke dormant branches and contended with the thorns of wild roses. All the while, eyes ever searching, along with ears listening, were on high alert for anything that spelled danger.

For Sarah, every step her injured right foot took made her grimace in pain. Yet she persevered forward, for the need to survive was far greater than her pain.

The two women picked their way along the narrow path until they came to a small meadow. Staying hidden, they surveyed the area.

Jo pointed and said, "Over there," when she spotted a large stone house, along with a barn, on the other side of the meadow.

Sarah had her binoculars up to her eyes, scanning the buildings for any sign of danger.

"What do you see," Jo whispered.

As she continued her surveillance, Sarah said, "The windows on the house have all the outside shutters closed and the barn door is also closed, with what looks like some sort of lock on the door." Removing the lenses from her eyes, she looked at her companion. "My guess, it is someone's summer home. I see no sign of activity, as the ground surrounding the area seems undisturbed…of course that could change once we get there."

Jo dropped the pack holding her parachute to the ground before sitting on it. "If we try to get there now we will be like sitting ducks."

"I agree," Sarah said as she, too, dropped her parachute pack and sat on it. "When it gets dark we can look at the house again and see if there are any telltale signs of lights on inside."

*

Once dusk arrived and they assured themselves that no one was in the house, two crouched figures made their way across the small meadow. The closer the pilots came to the stone house, the more cold and uninviting it became. They had no choice but to press on as the strong southerly wind carried the sounds of machinery and the whisper of voices that they could only assume were coming from the dirt road they'd left behind.

For a split second, Jo flashed a beam of light on the ground near the closest door on the side of the house. "See anything?" she asked.

"No," Sarah whispered as they drew closer to the door. Once there, her hand rested on the cold metal door knob before she gently turned it, surprised when it opened. Her eyes, now adjusted to the waning daylight, looked at the woman next to her.

With a slight nod, Jo pushed on the door that creaked loudly as it swung open—she held her breath and looked at Sarah. With quiet steps, the two ventured inside the dwelling, immediately glad they were out of the biting wind. Ever so gently, Jo pushed the door shut before she let a beam of light search the area where they stood.

They were standing in the kitchen on thick slabs of rough wood that was the floor. The beam of light made a three hundred and sixty degree scan of the room. To one side there was a heavy looking table that, upon closer inspection, they found was set with a large cloth covering it. Along the wall next to the table was a sideboard that was also covered.

"This is definitely a summer home," Sarah said as she pulled out a chair from the table and collapsed into it. "There are probably candles in one of the drawers," her weary voice said.

"Stay here while I look around," Jo said, unable to see the look on her fellow pilot's face.

Sarah nodded in gratitude as she listened to Jo's footfalls while Jo walked around the room. The rustling of drawers opening and closing kept her attention.

"Ah ha. I've found the candles, along with matches." She pulled open several cupboard doors until she found a small plate. Lighting the candle, she dripped wax on the plate before pressing the bottom of the candle to the melted wax. She lit two more candles and fastened them to other plates. Picking one up, she moved toward Sarah then placed it on the table. "By the look on your face, I can tell your foot hurts. Let me take a look at it."

"No," Sarah blurted, more strongly than she wanted to. Softening her voice she said, "It's fine…I just need to keep off of it for a while."

Jo nodded before she ran a gentle hand along Sarah's cheek. "Let me find the bedrooms and we can get some sleep."

Sarah leaned into the hand that still held the coldness of the outside. "I'll see if I can find any food."

*

Jo moved quietly through the house, opting to use one of the candles instead of running down the flashlight's batteries. She opened each door she came to gently, listening for any sound that might indicate someone else was there. When she came to what she thought was the master bedroom, she sighed in relief when she saw a large, four poster bed that was unmade. Her hand automatically tested the mattress and she smiled at the softness she felt. After rummaging around in a tall, mirror fronted chifforobe, she turned to the smaller armoire where she found pillows, sheets, and a down comforter. Grabbing the comforter, she spread it on the bed before getting the pillows and placing them over the blankets.

She shivered as she entered another bedroom and once finding the same items, she fixed the smaller bed much as she had in the larger room. As she left the room, she felt her body tremble again; she was bone weary and the house was a veritable icebox. Without another thought, she went back into the bedroom, pulled the comforter off the bed, and returned to the master bedroom where she spread the second comforter over the first. Tonight they would sleep together, thereby keeping a bit warmer.

Once she had investigated all the rooms on the second floor, she went down the squeaky, wooden staircase to see what else there was on the first floor. Finding nothing of significance, she headed back to the kitchen and Sarah.

*

Sarah looked up when Jo reentered the kitchen. "Find anything?" she asked as she stood by the sink. "The larder is decent and I found several jars of meat. It is a mystery what it is but at least it will fill our stomachs," she paused and added, "There is also a basement that has other food stuffs."

"I found the master bedroom and made up the bed. We can also change our clothes as the chifforobe in each room has clothes." She moved from her position by the table to stand next to Sarah. "Are those peaches?"

With a smile, Sarah shook her head. "It is meat and peaches for our meal…who could ask for more?"

"Sounds very tasty to me." Jo was standing close enough to feel her companion shiver. "I don't know about you, but the bottom half of my flying suit feels like it is encased in ice."

"Only ice, Jo? Mine is more like a deep freeze." Sarah yawned. "Let's eat then we can change and let everything dry out."

"I think we need to keep watch throughout the night."

"I agree. I can take the first shift."

Jo shook her head. "No, I will."

"I'm perfectly capable of staying awake, Jo," Sarah countered with a hint of indignation in her voice.

"Yes, I know you can, Sarah. It has more to do with your foot. If you are lying down it will help the swelling and pain."

"Who said anything about my foot being swollen," Sarah said quietly.

Jo put her arm around her companion's shoulders. "We've been on the move all day…how can it not be swollen, Sarah? If we have to make a run for it, the condition of your injured foot will make all the difference."

Sarah handed Jo a plate. "Let's eat," she said as she walked over to the table and sat down. It was not the time for pretense, so she pulled out another chair and propped her right leg on it. "You will wake me when it is my turn, right?"

"Yes," Jo said as she took her first hesitant bite of the meat. "Hey, this isn't half bad."

As they sat in companionable silence while they ate, each seemed lost in her own thoughts. When Sarah finished and pushed her plate away, she gave her fellow pilot a serious gaze.

"Are you scared, Jo?" Sarah asked.

For a long moment, Jo contemplated the question. "While I was growing up, my daddy always told me, *when you're scared, you no longer have faith*. I know we will get out of this so the answer to your question is *no*, I'm not scared. What about you, Sarah?"

Ready with an answer, Sarah said, "Flying, as you know, is full of risks. I've flown from London to Brisbane, Australia, and been stuck in snow so deep that I was afraid I'd have to stay until the spring thaw. Through it all, I never felt I was in danger…this is different, Jo…I don't feel safe at the moment."

*

Jo dozed in the kitchen, sitting at the table with her head resting on her fist when something startled her. With her ears on full alert, she cautiously walked toward the door and put her ear to it. She could hear the distant sound of a vehicle's engine. As she listened, the sound got a bit louder and she turned quickly and made a dash for the staircase. Just as she turned the corner, she saw Sarah coming down the stairs.

"Did you hear it too?" Sarah asked with her arms full of their belongings.

"Yes…a truck…maybe a Jeep, not sure." Nodding her head, Jo closed her eyes for a brief moment. "We should have had an exit strategy."

"We can go to the cellar. There's a spot under the stairs where we can hide."

Jo gathered the candles, took one last look at the kitchen, and noticed the chair she was sitting in wasn't in like the rest. Hurrying over to the table, she pushed the chair back in place as she heard the sound of vehicle doors closing. "Damn," she whispered as she scurried across the floor to the opened cellar door. Once she was on the first step, she quietly shut the door as the outside kitchen door was opening.

Once in the cellar, she briefly saw the light from the flashlight and made her way toward it. As she slid beside Sarah there was the distinct sound heavy boots crossing the floor above.

A male voice said, "Hast du jemand gesehen?"

"Nein," another man's voce answered.

"Stell' das ganze Haus auf den Kopf!" the first voice said.

As they heard the sound of many boots on the floor above, Jo whispered, "I wish I knew German."

Sarah leaned close and in a bare whisper said, they want to know if they found anyone and now they are searching the whole house."

Jo lifted an eyebrow before she nodded as she pulled her flying suit over borrowed clothes. "Good thing I have you along," she said in a low voice.

Both women froze in place when they heard the door to the cellar open.

"Hast du eine Taschenlampe?"

"Nein, die ist im Panzer."

"Da unten sind nur Ratten."

The door closed with a decided slam.

"What was that all about?"

"The first guy wanted a torch but it is out in their tank," Sarah frowned, "it didn't sound like a tank to me."

"Me either. Why didn't they come down here?"

"He said there was nothing but rats down here. Now, we wait them out."

Both women slept on and off for what seemed like an inordinate amount of time. Each ventured out of their hiding place to relieve their bladders and on one such trip Sarah returned with another jar of canned peaches.

"Beeil dich. Wir müssen los. Die Bomber sind im Anflug."

Finally, their wait in the cold dank cellar seemed to be ending. They stayed where they were for another hour just to make sure they were alone. Then Jo, with her knife in hand, quietly crept up the stairs and opened the door part way. The kitchen was dark but some light that was streaming in from between the shutters made everything visible. She stepped out on to the wooden floor and froze at the loud squeak the floor made.

"Hendrik, bist du das?"

"Shit," Jo whispered as she crouched near the doorway into the kitchen from the rest of the house. The first thing she saw were highly polished black boots. As the man moved further in, Jo leapt on him, causing him to fall to the ground. In one quick move, she slit the man's throat. She lay on top of the man as she listened for any other sounds—she heard none.

From the top of the basement doorway, Sarah said, "We need to get out of here."

Jo nodded as she pulled the dead man's gun from its holster. Turning to Sarah, she took part of what she was carrying before they both made their way to the door. "What did that guy say?"

"He wondered if it was Hendrick making the noise."

"Then Hendrik must be nearby," Jo said as she put her ear to the door. "We can either find him or wait for him to come our way."

Sarah walked quickly to a cabinet, opened a drawer, and took out a long butcher knife. When she arrived back by Jo's side she said, "I'll go out the front door, you this one."

"Good plan." Jo touched Sarah's arm. "Be careful out there."

"I'll let out a whistle when I get to the door." With a quick nod, Sarah took off for the other door.

After hearing the low whistle, Jo cautiously opened the door and suddenly the bright sunlight blinded her. A man's voice instantly said something in a language she didn't understand and she whipped her head in his direction. She narrowed her eyes to reduce the brightness of the sun and saw a man in a German military uniform pointing a gun at her.

"Hendrik?" she asked hoping to throw the man off enough to have time to take a defensive action.

"Wo bist du denn, Warner?"

"Dead," Jo said, noticing Sarah creeping up behind the man.

"Und du auch!" Sarah purred as the length of the blade went through the left side of the soldier's back.

The soldier's eyes widened as he turned and saw Sarah before he fell to the ground with a thud.

Sarah took the man's gun and motioned to Jo. "We need to get out of here, right now."

With adrenalin pumping through their bodies, both women took off running toward another stand of trees a meter away. Just as they reached cover, they heard the sound of a vehicle coming from behind them and they immediately fell to the ground and flattened their bodies against the earth. Sounds of men shouting from the house traveled to them and they remained where they were until the voices died down.

Crawling on their bellies, Jo and Sarah made their way behind a large boulder before they went into a crouching position. Sarah took out the binoculars, rested them atop their cover, and looked through the lenses at the activity at the house. Jo turned to the wooded area and scoped out a route that would take them away from the soldiers, yet stay on the northwest course she knew they needed to take.

Sarah sat on the ground next to Jo. "I counted two dozen soldiers, three trucks, and a Jeep. They seem to be concentrating their search in the area that would lead back to that road."

"We need to get moving." Jo pointed in the general direction of north. "It looks like we can move along that path and those boulders will give us cover."

"Good thing our flying suits are this dark tan, it will blend in with the background."

"Well, they are warmer now that they are dry. Let's get going and make as much distance as we can between them and us."

Both women turned around at the pop of a gun firing. Sarah was back at the rock with binoculars to her eyes. "They've shot a man…he looks like a local…" Sarah trailed off before she fixed her eyes on her companion. "They think he killed those soldiers…he paid with his life for what we did, Jo."

All Jo could think about was putting as much distance between them and the soldiers as possible. "It's war, Sarah. Do you think for one moment those soldiers would have let us live?"

"No, but that man…"

"What do you want to do? Run over there and tell them you killed their comrade? Do you think you would make it halfway across that field before they shot you?"

Sarah looked away, fighting the sting that hurt the back of her eyes.

"War is hell, Sarah, and right now we are fighting not only to defeat the Germans, but for our lives."

"I know." Sarah began gathering her belongings. "Let's go while we still can."

*

Once they were certain that they were far enough away from the soldiers, the two women sat on the ground. Sarah was the first to crack as the tears and horror she had held back since stabbing the soldier, escaped. "We killed them, Jo," she sobbed. "I took another human being's life. How can I justify that?"

Jo, who fought her own demons once the rush of adrenaline disappeared, let out a strangled cry. "We do what we have to so we can survive." Her body shuddered as she looked down at her hands stained with the soldier's blood. "God, I can't believe that I killed him and it was so easy to do." She looked at Sarah, who had her arms wrapped around her midsection. "We had no choice," she whispered with her trembling voice.

Sarah buried her face in her hands as she relived her emotions as the knife she held sank into the man's body. "I killed a man," she moaned as tears filled her palms. "How can we ever rectify that, Jo? How? I carried a gun with me where ever I flew in the world but all I ever shot at were tin cans. Never did I think I would kill someone."

After swiping her sleeve across her nose, Jo moved closer to her fellow pilot and pulled the hands away from her face. "We are trying to survive and get back home, Sarah," she said in a voice that belied her inner turmoil. "What do you think would have happened if we had just stayed in the house and hid out in the basement?"

"I don't know," Sarah's shaky voice answered.

Jo said in a soft voice, "Eventually we would have been found and either been killed or taken as prisoners." She sucked in a breath. "They would have raped and tortured us before they killed us, Sarah."

"You don't know that."

"I've read enough about other wars to know that is exactly what would happen."

Sarah just looked at her companion.

"Which do you think would be worse, Sarah? Killing to survive or being defiled then murdered at the hands of the enemy?"

Softly crying, Sarah said, "It doesn't make it hurt any less, Jo. I killed him and that will never change."

Jo pulled Sarah into her arms and held her while she cried. "I know," she whispered as she fought the demons that vilified her.

Chapter Twenty

January 1941
Hatfield Ferry Pool No. 5
Southampton, England

"Well, look at you," Midge drawled as she looked at Meg O'Brien, who was coming out of her room. "You can mourn all you want but the fact is…Jo loved me, not you."

Meg narrowed her eyes and glared at the woman who chided her about Jo every chance she got. "Go rot in the deepest pit in hell," she said as she brushed past the woman.

Midge let out a deep laugh. "And I'll be there, right alongside Jo."

Meg stopped in her tracks and turned back to the woman. With balled fingers, she moved closer to Midge as a snarl filled her face. With one quick motion, she punched the woman in the stomach. "You're a pitiful woman, Midge. Jo didn't love you, she hated you…hated everything about you."

As she clutched her stomach, Midge grinned. "You stupid *paddy*, don't you get it? I was in Jo's bed long before she even knew you existed." She let out a maniacal laugh. "She still came to my bed once we got here."

The next thing Midge knew was she was lying on the floor with her jaw aching and her nose bleeding.

"Don't you ever call me that again," Meg growled. "If you're thinkin' I believe any of the rubbish that comes out of your mouth, you are a fool."

Overhearing the exchange, Brenda Hiller sneered at Midge as she stood up. "You're a fuckwit, Midge."

"Oh, please give me a break, Hiller. Everyone knows you are nothing but a backwoods bumpkin who latched on to Sarah so you could run away from home."

Brenda moved so she was toe to toe with Midge with her eyes glaring at the woman. Anger replaced the sorrow heavy in her heart as she flattened her hand before slapping Midge's cheek. "I may be from the backwoods but at least I'm human."

Midge held her hand against her stinging cheek and sneered as she watched the Aussie walk away. "Bitch."

In the bath room, Midge was holding her bloody nose as she attempted to quell the flow. Her eyes turned to the door when she heard it open.

"You just can't keep your mouth shut, can you, Miss Reister?" the first officer asked. She moved so she was in Midge's space. "Obviously, you didn't learn anything from the first lesson I taught you."

"Get the hell away from me!"

After laughing, Shannon said, "Not going to happen. From day one I've made you my priority and as long as you are here making trouble…well, let's just say you don't want to know what I'm capable of."

Midge's brown eyes glared at the woman. "If you think you are scaring me, you are mistaken. You are nothing but a two bit whore."

Shannon nodded and left.

A shiver of fear ran down Midge's back before she returned to stopping her bleeding nose.

*

The day was cloudy and gray, with a distinct chill in the air. Meg had pushed through the doors of the rest room and a cold blast of air immediately assaulted her. Anger was still coursing through her body. "She was doin' nothin' but lyin'. I know Jo couldn't stand her…don't I?"

Bursting out of the door right behind Meg, Brenda called out, "Wait up," as she hurried to catch up to the woman. "Midge is a *drongo* and you shouldn't listen to her."

Meg's eyes finally gave way to tears that always seemed to threaten lately. As they were streaming down her cheeks, she looked at her fellow pilot. "It can't be true…"

With a comforting hand on Meg's shoulder, "Apples, they'll be back, Meg. Don't pay any mind to Midge…we all know she is a no-hoper."

With a perplexed look, Meg's eyebrows creased.

"Right, Sarah isn't here to interpret for me…Midge is a misfit and it'll be all right…Sarah and Jo will be back soon."

"I'd feel it if Jo was de…gone…I can't stand the thought of her out there lost somewhere…or floatin' in the Channel's freezing water."

"She's got Sarah with her, mate, and I know she will fight to stay alive."

Meg looked at the woman next to her and saw the sorrow in her eyes. "I'm sorry, Brenda, I know you are just as worried about Sarah." She looked up as a Spitfire flew over head. "What I don't understand is why they were both flying over the Channel. Jo said they were flyin' north."

Brenda considered the words. "Can't say that Sarah said where she was going that night."

"And I find *that* puzzlin' too…why were they out there flyin' at night doin' tests?"

With a nod, Brenda continued to walk toward the planes. Changing the subject, she asked, "What are you flying today?"

"Only Spitfires," Meg said automatically.

Brenda stopped and put her arm around Meg's shoulders. "It's only been two days, Meg, give the RAF time to find them," Brenda said softly.

Meg snickered, "The RAF is fightin' a war. They haven't the time ta search for two women from the ATA."

*

With a heavy heart, Meg guided her last flight of the day toward Friston, an airfield located on the English Channel. She gazed at her wristwatch, noting that two hours of daylight remained. Recalling that the commander had said something about a plane going down in the Channel, she bypassed the airfield and flew out over the water. "I don't care if I have to go back in the dark or even if I miss a meal…I need to find Jo."

She flew low enough to see the surface of the churning water—the sight made her cringe. "How can anyone survive in that?" she asked as her eyes scanned the water for any sign of Jo.

"Where are you, Jo?"

Suddenly, out of the corner of her eye, she spotted something and she whipped her head around to see what it was. Flying next to her was a plane she knew all too well—a medium class bomber, the Vickers Wellington. The pilot was signaling her to turn back and she reluctantly complied.

The bomber followed her back to the Friston Air Field and landed right after her. When she got out of the plane, the pilot from the bomber was waiting for her.

"What on earth do you think you were doing up there, Second Officer? Have you gone daft?" he asked, getting into Meg's personal space. "The skies are filled with Messerschmitts just waiting to shoot us down."

Meg, not wanting the man to see her unshed tears, looked away.

"What do you have to say for yourself?" he asked again.

Meg took a deep breath, hoping to stave off the tears she knew threatened to come. She looked at the man whose rank was that of a squadron leader. He was taller than she was, with a ruddy complexion and sandy brown hair that peeked out from under his leather helmet. "My…friend…might have gone down in the Channel…I was looking for her."

The man's face softened. "I heard about that," he said over the roar of planes landing and taking off.

Meg could no longer hold back the tears.

"Look, I fly out there all the time…I'll keep my eyes open." He moved closer to Meg and patted her arm. "Don't give up hope,"

Overcome with emotion, Meg could only nod as she leaned into the man's touch. "I'm sorry," she managed to say, knowing that a taxiing Spitfire would drown out her words.

The man nodded before he shouted. "Take care and thank you for the excellent ferrying job you and the others do." He pointed over her shoulder and added, "There's your transportation home."

Meg turned and saw the Avro Anson that everyone in the ATA affectionately called *Annie* taxiing toward her. "Thanks," she said in a moment of relative quiet. "I won't do that again." With those words, she wiped her tears and left the squadron leader to take care of the business he was at the air field to do.

Chapter Twenty-One

January 1941
Northern Coast of France

Jo and Sarah kept up a steady pace as they moved farther away from the German soldiers they'd encountered earlier. The trek wasn't particularly difficult as they climbed low hills and walked along terrain that was nearly flat. As dusk began to fall, the distinct chill that was staved off by their constant movement returned as the sun set.

"We need to find some place to sleep," Sarah said as she scrutinized the area around them. "If we wait much longer, we won't be able to see where to go."

Jo too looked at their surroundings, hoping to find a niche where they could rest out of the breeze that seemed to blow continually. She spotted an outcropping of large boulders and said, "Over there."

Sarah's eyes fixed on the location. "To get there we will have to leave the cover we have," she looked at Jo and added, "Do we take the risk?"

Jo wiped a hand over her face, feeling how cold her skin was. "We haven't seen hide nor hair of anyone in a long time." She shrugged. "It's either there or where we stand."

"Let's go then, while we still have some light."

Twenty minutes later, they were in a natural depression created by three large boulders. Once they adjusted one of the parachutes to block the wind, they settled in, keeping the parachute bags between their rears and the cold ground.

"It is a lot warmer with a dry flying suit," Sarah remarked, sitting shoulder to shoulder with Jo in the narrow space. "Are you hungry?" she asked as she rooted in her bag before pulling out a jar of meat.

Jo's eyes widened. "God, Sarah, my mouth is watering…I'm so glad you thought to bring food."

Once Sarah pried the lid off the jar, dirty fingers dug in repeatedly as they devoured the meat quickly. When it was devoid of the meat, they greedily drank the liquid in the jar.

Jo let out a small belch. "Sorry. Man, was that good. How about a piece of chocolate for dessert?"

For the first time since they took off from Hatfield, Sarah smiled. "That sounds delightful."

Feeling full and satisfied, both women leaned their heads so they were touching and fell into a fitful sleep, where nightmares reigned.

*

It was the click of a rifle cocking that woke Jo. As her eyes lifted, she saw the barrel of a rifle pointed at her. She felt some relief when she noticed that the man did not wear a uniform. All she could see were hands that looked massive, a dark brown felt hat, which she learned when she first arrived in England was call a Fedora, stubbled cheeks, and there was a grim slant to the man's lips.

A deep gravelly voice said, "Qui vous est?"

Sarah's eyes flew open. "Nous entendons vous aucun dommage," she answered.

"Allez, je ne veux pas mal."

Jo listened to the dialogue, desperate to ask Sarah what the man was saying but knowing if she moved, he might shoot her.

Sarah said, "S'il vous plaît nous aider. Notre avion s'est écrasé et nous avons besoin de la nourriture et de l'eau. "

The man's eyes shifted as he looked around nervously. "Venir. Hâte."

"Gather everything you can," Sarah whispered. " Merci beaucoup!"

"What was that all about?" Jo asked as both women hurried behind the man.

"He wanted to know who were and I told him we meant him no harm. He told us to go away, he didn't want trouble and I said our plane was shot down and we needed food and water," Sarah said breathlessly as she tried to keep up with the man's quick pace. "Finally, he said for us to come with him."

When they entered a wooded area, the man came to a stop and turned. Jo eyed him again. He wore a dark jacket with the middle two buttons buttoned, with his massive hands sticking out of too short sleeves. What looked like some sort of sweater stuck out near his face and below the hem of the jacket. The only clothing that wasn't dark was a white shirt peeking out from under the sweater. His trousers, made out of the same material as the jacket, were loose fitting. Dark eyes seemed to appraise her before they turned to Sarah.

"Vous pouvez rester dans l'écurie," he said then added, "Ce n'est pas loin maintenant," before he picked up the brisk pace again.

"Tell me," Jo said as they began trotting to keep up.

"He said we can stay in his barn and it isn't far."

*

As Jo and Sarah entered the small stone barn, their noses immediately smelled the odor of straw that covered the dirt floor. In one stall there was a cow and in the other, a massive horse.

The man pointed to the loft and said, "Là, en haut.."

Sarah said, "S'il vous plaît, la nourriture et l'eau."

With a nod, the man said, "Je reviendrai," before he turned and left them.

"I wish I'd learned a foreign language," Jo said in an irritated tone.

"I doubt you had much use for French in Texas, Jo. I asked him about food and water and he said he'd be back."

Jo unbuttoned her flying suit halfway and looked around the barn. "At least it is warm." She followed Sarah up the rickety wooden ladder to the loft that, for now, would be their home. "I think the main question is will this man sell us out to the Germans?"

Sarah assessed the loft. "I agree." At one end, she saw what looked like a door. "Look at that," she said as she moved toward the area.

"It's what they use to put the bales of straw up here," Jo said. "See that wench? It is used to haul bales of the stuff up here."

Sarah's eyes held a glint to them. "Just who are you calling a wench, Jo?"

Jo couldn't help but laugh. "Certainly not you, my dear Miss Faulkner."

With a serious glance at the area, Sarah asked, "Can we use it for an escape?"

Jo blew out a breath. "If push comes to shove, we can…as long as there are no Germans below us outside."

Sarah wandered back to the middle of the loft as she unbuttoned her flying suit. After pulling her arms out of the sleeves, she sat down on a bale of straw, unzipped her boots, and pulled off her flying suit before wiggling her toes. Serious eyes turned to her companion. "Do you think we will still get out of this alive?"

"Yes, I do." Jo nodded at Sarah's feet. "How is it feeling?"

"It is better," she wiggled her toes again then added, "What if that man brings the Germans?"

"If that happens, we will deal with it, Sarah."

The squeaking of the barn door had both women peering down from their perch with their hands on the guns they had taken from the dead soldiers. The man and a woman entered the barn.

"Bonjour," Sarah called out.

"Nous vous avons apporté une nourriture," the man said, holding up a tray covered with a cloth hiding what lay beneath it.

Jo looked down at the couple, noting that the woman was tall and lean with her hair pulled back into a bun. She wore what looked like a long skirt, protected by a white apron. Not asking for a translation, Jo asked, "They have food for us?" After Sarah gave her a slight nod she said, "Let's go then. I'm starved."

After making their way down the ladder, Sarah said, "Merci Beaucoup."

The man remained stoic but the woman smiled at them. The man moved to the side of the barn and began leading the horses and the cow outside.

"Are you English?" the tall woman asked in halting English.

"Yes, ma'am," Jo said in a slow drawl.

The woman's eyebrows creased. "American?"

"She is American, I am English," Sarah replied.

"Nous n'avons pas beaucoup, mais vous êtes sûrs ici," the woman said.

"Merci," Sarah said with a smile before saying, "She says we are safe here."

Jo too smiled at the woman before taking a deep breath and saying, "Merci."

The woman looked in her husband's direction and with what looked like a satisfied smile, moved toward him.

Once there, she placed the tray on two stacked bales of straw and motioned to the single bales on either side. With her hand gesturing toward the two bales, she said, "Assoyez-vous s'il vous plaît.":

Jo didn't need an interpreter to tell her that the woman invited them to eat.

Sarah said *merci* before she too sat and tugged at the towel covering the food. Sarah clasped her hands to her face. "Oh, my." She looked at the woman and gave her a grateful smile.

The woman said, "Bon appitite," as she and her husband left the barn.

With great enthusiasm, Sarah and Jo devoured the two slabs of ham, a hunk of cheese, a partial loaf of bread, and two glasses of milk.

Sated, Jo leaned back and let out a contented sigh. "I had no idea just how hungry I was," she said as she turned serious eyes on Sarah. "Do you think we're safe here?"

"For the time being." Sarah stood and grasped the tray. "We need to find out where we are and formulate a plan on how we get back home. I'll take this back and see if I can find out at least where we are and the location of the loo."

Jo smiled "Before now, I never thought of sitting on a toilet as a luxury—I have to say, I'm so tired of squatting on the ground."

Sarah gave her fellow pilot a knowing nod before leaving the barn.

*

Jo stretched out on a thick pile of straw with her eyes closed. Until that moment, she hadn't allowed herself to think about Meg—survival uppermost in her mind. "I wonder what you're doing, Meg. Can you feel that I'm still alive?"

Everything she and Sarah had done since their plane crashed into the Channel kept them on high alert, ever vigilant of their surroundings. She knew their journey took them north of Normandy but she had no idea how far they had traveled or how they would get back to England.

"We certainly can't swim there." She shivered as she recalled the freezing water. It wasn't until they were in the barn that she really warmed up. "Perhaps we can find a boat." For a few moments, she considered the possibility, before dismissing it—they'd be like sitting ducks. "If we could find an airfield, we could steal a plane." That idea appealed to her and she began to devise a plan on how to make that happen. Not long into her thought process, she realized that with German markings, any plane they stole would be shot down..

Jo's ears picked up as she heard the unmistakable sound of a vehicle coming to rest outside near the barn. She quickly gathered all their belongings and moved behind several bales of the straw. Concentrating on sounds, she heard doors open and close, along with voices that she couldn't quite discern. Her thoughts turned to Sarah and she moved out of her hiding spot and quickly moved down the ladder, and held the gun out as she went toward the barn door. Just as she was about to push open the door, she heard Sarah's voice speaking rapidly on the other side. As she listened, she heard another voice, female, speaking in soft tones in French.

I cannot leave Sarah out there alone, she thought as she pushed open the door holding the gun at her side. The day was much as it had been before they entered the barn a few hours earlier—bright and a bit cool. Once her eyes adjusted she saw a medium size woman with black hair dressed in a gray suit. Sarah was standing close to the woman in what Jo could see was a relaxed pose.

The woman looked at Jo and glanced at the revolver in her hand. "Bonjour."

Jo nodded before casting her eyes on Sarah in question.

"C'est mon ami Jo."

Guessing at what Sarah said, Jo stuffed the gun in her pants and moved forward with her hand extended. *Soft* was the word that popped into Jo's mind as she wrapped her hand around the smaller one.

"Bridget is Émilie and Antoine Oyler's daughter. She says she can help us," Sarah said with her eyes fixed on her fellow pilot.

Wary eyes looked at the man, the woman, and their daughter. "How do we know we can trust them, Sarah?"

"We don't wish you harm," Bridget said. "My brother was taken by the Germans six months ago and beaten. He came back to us barely alive. Now he is a broken man who cannot do the basics for himself." Her eyes narrowed. "We have no love for the Germans."

"You speak excellent English," Jo said with suspicion in her voice. "Where is your brother now?"

Bridget's eyes misted. "In the house."

For the benefit of Émilie and Antoine, Sarah asked, "Pouvons-nous rencontrer votre frère?"

"Oui," Émilie said.

"Come, Jo, we are going to meet their son."

*

Just like the stone house Jo and Sarah had stayed in the day before, the Oyler's house seemed cold and dark, in spite of the fire burning in the kitchen fireplace. A massive cook stove sat against one wall with a large round black pipe going up the stone wall. To one side there was a sturdy, dark wooden table with a cloth covering what looked like place settings. A large cupboard that was typically used in rural homes as a larder, stood against a far wall.

When Émilie motioned for them to follow her, Sarah and Jo stood shoulder to shoulder as they went forward into the unknown. For all they knew, a German soldier with a gun in his hand was waiting for them through the doorway. What they saw was the ghost of a man sitting strapped into a chair, with a wobbly head that he was trying to lift.

Sarah moved forward and knelt next to the man. "<u>Mon</u> Dieu, qu'ils vous ont fait?" (what have they done to you?) she whispered. She turned to Émilie and asked, "Quel est son nom?"

"George."

"Jo, come meet George."

With hesitant steps, Jo moved toward her friend and the frail man.

"Don't be afraid," Bridget said as she walked alongside Jo. "He was such a wonderful man, so full of life. I do not see him as he is now, but as he was." As she too knelt in front of her brother, she added, "Join me, Jo."

Jo looked into the soft brown eyes of the man and saw intelligence and pain. "Will you tell him that England will eradicate the Germans from France?"

Bridget smiled, "He understands English."

Jo noticed George's lips move ever so slightly into what she thought was a smile. "No one should have to suffer like you are, George," she whispered as she took the man's hand. "No one," she said again as she let go and stood. "We need to get home…back to England. How do we accomplish that?"

"Come into the kitchen where we can sit and look at a map, so you know where you are."

For the next two hours, Sarah, Jo, and Bridget sat around the table devising a plan to avoid the Germans and help the pilots get back to England.

"This will not be easy," Sarah remarked as she pushed back and stood. "Where is the loo?"

"Fortunately for us, it is located outside at the back of the house."

"Why fortunate?" Jo asked.

"The Germans will not seize our house for their use…they want indoor plumbing."

*

Both women left the house and headed around to the back to relieve their bladders.

"What do you make of it, Sarah?" Jo asked as they walked.

Sarah lifted one shoulder. "Not sure the plan will work."

"Do you trust these people?"

"Do we have a choice?" Sarah asked.

As they reached what was the bathroom, Jo looked out at their surroundings. "We have a choice…we always have choices. It is George who convinced me that we can trust this family."

Sarah pulled the door open. Then we shall put the plan in motion and see where we go."

Chapter Twenty-Two

March 1941
Northern Coast of France

For several days after Jo and Sarah arrived at the Oyler farm, they worked on a plan with Bridget Oyler to get them back to England. After several more days, Bridget finally stood in exasperation and said, "We don't have the knowledge to formulate a plan ourselves. I know you want strict secrecy but my fiancé, Charles Osmont, can help us."

"How?" Jo asked with a hint of suspicion.

"He is part of a group that is trying to mount a resistance to the German's occupation. He has resources and the contacts to make this happen. What we are planning now is fraught with danger and hazards we can't even begin to fathom."

Once the pilots agreed, they met with Charles and began the plan for escape once again. Over the next two months, they revised plans, threw them out, and made new ones as conditions of the war were in a state of constant fluctuation.

Each night, as Jo and Sarah laid down on the straw in the loft, they discussed the events of the day.

"Do you think he can actually come through with what he says he can?" Sarah asked.

Jo shrugged. "Either he does or he doesn't…we have no way of knowing. To me it sounds like he knows what he is talking about but we both know to take it with a grain of salt," she pulled a cover over her, "It all comes down to whether or not we think we can trust him to deliver."

"You're right, Jo, we have no other choice. Right now, Charles Osmont is our only ticket home."

"I can't wait to get there," Jo said wistfully.

"Me too," Sarah added before she closed her eyes and fell into a deep sleep.

*

Jo helped Antoine dig a trench, which he said was necessary for when the British invade France. An actual bomb had never fallen near them but he had seen plenty of planes flying in the skies overhead and felt it was only a matter of time before the war came to his doorstep. Jo enjoyed the manual labor, for she knew by the nature of digging, her muscles would gain strength—she would need every ounce of muscle to accomplish their escape.

It was with a heavy heart that Jo helped dig the last meter of the trench. For the majority of her waking hours that weren't spent on the escape plan, her mind, and heart, were only on Meg. The dreams of the woman she hoped one day would be her lover kept her thoughts of going back to Meg positive. She recalled what Meg had said to her on New Year's Eve. *When you have no dreams, Jo, you have no life. For it is our dreams that keep us going, that give our lives purpose and meaning. Promise me you will never forget to dream.* The words resonated through her consciousness and she knew the truth behind them as she pushed the shovel into the hard ground. "I will never stop dreaming, Meg. I promised you that and I always keep my promises," she whispered.

With that thought, Jo began to dig with more determination. She couldn't wait until Sarah returned.

*

Because she spoke fluent French, Sarah accompanied Charles on several trips to scout out where the escape would take place. Both she and Jo were surprised to find out they had traveled about twenty-five kilometers in their trek away from the plane wreckage. Oyler's farm was about twelve kilometers west of Rouen, France, the city where Joan of Arc burned at the stake. The city had a large port but after she and Charles visited the area, they realized that German soldiers filled the town, making an escape from there nearly impossible. No, they needed to find an area where they could make a surreptitious departure.

Both she and Jo were growing weary of constantly hiding and living in fear of discovery. They had been away from Hatfield for almost three months and she was certain that by now, all hope of them returning was lost.

Sarah watched the scenery go by but did not see it. Her thoughts were on her family and friends, who thought she had died in a plane crash. How she wanted to reach out and somehow get a message to her parents and her fiancé, letting them know she was still alive. Sarah's thoughts turned to Brenda, the girl she helped escape from a life of abuse over a year earlier. Her friend had blossomed into a beautiful woman both inside and out. She smiled as she recalled some of the outlandish phrases the girl would use and how it was up to her to tell the other pilots what Brenda meant. *How I miss her.*

The smell of salt water brought Sarah out of her thoughts of home as she looked around. "Where are we?"

This is La Havre, a large port on the English Channel," Charles explained. "We will go further north along the coast to Sainte-Adresse, which is less of a port and more of a sailing city." He pointed to the water. "We have someone with a fishing boat there and that is who we will visit. I expect he will agree to take you and your friend across the Channel in his fishing boat."

"What if he doesn't?" Sarah asked softly.

"Then we will find another way, Sarah. Please trust me on this."

Sarah gave the man a half hearted nod as she returned her gaze to the landscape outside the window. When the small car made its way through the city of Sainte-Adresse, Sarah smiled. It was charming, not unlike many hamlets and towns in England. She saw a pier dotted with fishing boats and numerous sailboats moored out in the bay. Even the small number of German soldiers who strolled down the streets couldn't detract from the appeal of the city.

Five minutes later, both Charles and Sarah sat in a café, sipping tea as if they had not a care in the world. A man in a red, heavily ribbed sweater took a seat at their table and nodded to them both. Sarah knew that in France it was common for other people to occupy an unused seat when a café was crowded. She nodded at the man, who immediately began reading his newspaper.

Sarah looked at the headlines of the paper and translated the words. *The War Rages On—Sweeping German Victories Send A Message To The British.* Her heart broke, as she feared for her country. *Are the headline right? Is the war now going that badly?*

She had been on enough of this type of trip with Charles to know that the man wasn't sitting there by accident. His ruddy complexion and red, chapped hands told her that he was most likely the fisherman who would take Jo and her to England. She listened intently to the conversation the man and Charles engaged in. Picking up several key words, she realized that the man would indeed risk taking them across the Channel.

She let out a sigh of relief as she and Charles stood up to leave.

"Vous avez oublié" the man said, handing Charles the paper.

"Merci," Charles replied as he tucked the paper between his arm and chest.

Once in Charles's vehicle, he engaged the engine and sped away. "Open the paper," he said to Sarah.

Once opened, Sarah asked, "What now?"

"Go to page ten."

When she opened the page, all she saw was bunch of letters scribbled in the crossword puzzle."

"Tell me what you see."

"All that is here is part of a crossword puzzle finished."

"Good, when we get back to the Oyler's farm, I will decode the message and we will know when and where you will leave France for England.

Sarah felt a surge of happiness with the prospect of knowing she and Jo would be home soon.

*

The moonless night was so dark that none of the three people crouched on the sandy beach could see anything but a distant light that seemed to be blinking on and off. Behind them, in the city of Sainte-Adresse, blackout curtains hid all lights, as they had for the last eight months.

"It's so dark…how can we find the fishing boat?" Jo asked over the din of the rolling English Channel.

"We go toward that blinking light," Charles responded.

All ears picked up as they heard the distinct sound of a vehicle on the road above them.

"Run," Charles cried as he saw a beam of light search the sandy beach.

As fast as their legs could take them, all three ran toward the blinking light. Just as they reached a pier, they heard shouts of *Halt* followed by cracks of guns firing.

Sarah fell onto the soft sand and Jo immediately went to her.

"Help me carry her to the boat," Jo cried as she began picking her friend up.

More shouts and bullets competed for attention with the roar of the churning Channel.

Charles stood over the two women. "There is not time. We must go now."

"Not without Sarah we don't," Jo screamed.

The light the Germans were shining on the beach could not reach as far as the pier—unfortunately, their bullets could.

Charles grabbed Jo's arm. "If you don't go now, you won't go at all and you will be caught," he pleaded.

"Not without Sarah," Jo reiterated.

"Go, Jo," Sarah cried. "Go home and tell my parents that I love them."

"No," Jo screamed. "Either we both go or we both stay and take our chances with the Germans."

Sarah reached out and grabbed the front of Jo's jacket. "Go without me, Jo. One of us needs to make it home, and I can't go now," she said between deep heavy breaths.

Voices were growing louder as Jo gathered Sarah in her arms, stood, and began walking blindly down the narrow pier. The blinking light had stopped when the spotlight fell on the beach and Jo knew the gamble she was taking with all their lives by going forward. Charles was nipping at her heels, covering her back as they reached the end of the pier and the fishing boat waiting for them.

"Hurry," Charles ordered as they stepped down onto the flooring of the fishing boat.

The fisherman pushed off from the dock before using oars to move them further away from the pier. It wasn't until they were well into the Channel that the fisherman cranked up the engines to move the boat faster toward its destination.

As the searching light began to fade along with the voices, Jo looked down at her friend still in her arms. "We're going to make it, Sarah. Just over thirty kilometers to go, so hold on for a little longer and we will be home." She sat down on a bench and hugged Sarah close to her—the darkness prevented her from seeing the red stain creeping further across the jacket Jo wore.

Chapter Twenty-Three

March 1941
Portsmouth, England

The fishing boat bumped into a sandy shoreline and Jo felt her heartbeat increase. They had made it. They were back on English soil. "We've made it, Sarah," she whispered to the lifeless woman in her arms. "We are finally home." Her eyes searched out Charles and when she saw him, she asked, "Where are we?"

A conversation in French went between Charles and the fisherman before he said, "Southsea."

Jo closed her eyes, knowing that less than a few kilometers away in Portsmouth there was a Royal Naval Base. Sarah opened her eyes and whispered, "Home."

Charles and the fisherman secured the boat before moving toward the women to help them disembark. Just as they were about to take Sarah out of Jo's arms, a dozen or so, heavily armed soldiers were pointing rifles at them.

"Don't move," a male voice ordered as a strong beam of light focused on Charles and the fisherman. "State your business."

Confused by the words, the fisherman looked to Charles who squinted into the light. "We mean no harm," he said.

"State your business," the voice ordered again.

Jo carefully stood up, still clutching Sarah to her and slowly made her way to the bow of the boat. "I am Second Officer Jo Laughlin of the ATA. Another pilot and I were shot down last January and these men are helping us get back home."

The beam of light fell on Jo as she stood near Charles. "Are you American?" the voice asked.

"Yes, my friend here," she nodded at the woman in her arms, "is British."

The beam of light rested on Sarah.

"What is wrong with her?" the voice asked.

"She was shot by German soldiers…she needs urgent medical attention," Jo answered. "Please, we need to get her help or she will die."

Once again the light was on Jo.

"Are you injured?"

Jo looked down at where the light focused. Her jacket was full of blood—Sarah's blood. "No," she whispered as the magnitude of what had happened to Sarah fell heavy on her shoulders. "Please," she pleaded, "my friend desperately needs medical attention."

In the darkness, sounds came from the beach as several soldiers scrambled onto the boat and moved toward Jo and Sarah. When they lifted the woman out of Jo's arms, Sarah let out a loud moan.

"Please be careful," Jo said before big hands encircled both her arms.

"Come with us, Second Officer," a voice next to Jo said.

"I want to go with her."

"Once we verify who you are, we will take you to her."

"No," Jo adamantly said. A beam of light focused on her face.

"The choice is not yours, Miss. You will go with us."

Jo watched as soldiers carrying Sarah's body moved away and out of sight. She stared after her for a long moment then whispered, "I'll be right behind you," as she was taken away from the shore Behind her, she heard an authoritative voice tell Charles and the fisherman to come with them.

*

Jo sat in a well lit room located on what she knew was the Portsmouth Naval Base. A man in a naval uniform with sandy blonde, wavy hair and a ghost of a mustache looked at Jo with a speculative eye.

"You say you belong with the ATA, Miss Laughlin." It wasn't a question.

"Yes, I joined the ATA a year ago."

"You are American?"

"Yes."

"Tell me how you and the other pilot," he looked at his notes, "Sarah Faulkner, came to be in France."

"I am not at liberty to tell you that," Jo said.

Lieutenant Commander Hall looked at the woman across from him and narrowed his eyes. *"Can't,* or *won't?"*

"Look, if you call Hatfield Ferry Pool No. 5 and speak with Commander Clarke, she will give you all the information you need. *I* am not free to tell you why we were in that area."

"Very well then," he said before his chair scraped against the floor and he stood. Without another word, he left the room.

When he returned, he looked at Jo with a raised eyebrow. "Commander Clarke confirmed that a woman by your name does indeed belong to the ATA." His eyes scanned the seated woman's face. "From her description, you appear to be that woman."

"What about my friend? Where is she?"

"She is in hospital. I will have someone escort you there."

Jo felt a sense of relief begin at her shoulders then travel down her body. "Thank you." She stood up and glared at the man. "Am I free to go?"

"As I said, Second Officer, someone will accompany you to the hospital. For the time being, I do not think it is prudent to allow you to go anywhere on the base without an escort."

Jo felt her temper flare. "What is wrong with you? For the last several months, my friend and I have been in France, hiding from the Germans. Now that we are back on English soil, you are treating me like the enemy," she growled. "I assure you, I am not."

The Commander glowered at Jo. "Until I have visual confirmation that you are who you say you are, Miss Laughlin, you will always be in the company of a security guard. If you were indeed in France, as you say you were, I don't need to remind you that we are at war. Perhaps the Germans caught the pilots and you are spies...we have to check all eventualities."

Jo matched the man's intense gaze. "I am well aware of the fact that we are at war, Commander. My friend is lying in the hospital, most likely fighting for her life, after the enemy shot her," she shook her head, "so don't you go lecturing me about being at war, for I have seen it firsthand."

The commander walked to the door, signaled to the guard in the hallway, and said, "Escort this woman to the hospital, and make sure she sees the woman we brought there earlier."

Anxious to see Sarah, Jo stood up and without another word, joined the guard.

*

With shaky hands, Jo grasped the cold, lifeless hand of Sarah. "We've fought so hard to get to this point, Sarah, so please don't give up now." As Jo looked at Sarah's face, she saw how white she looked—as if all the blood had drained out of her.

Her eyes traveled to the jacket of Antoine Oyler's that she wore. The man had insisted she take it with her and she was certain that whatever else he had in the way of an outer covering was not as warm. The kindness that the Oyler family extended her and Sarah was touching. She feared for them and for Charles and the fisherman. She never did learn his name. "I have to make that right…the people here cannot incarcerate them."

Weary from being awake for more than twenty-four hours, Jo pulled a chair up alongside Sarah's hospital bed and took a cold hand in hers. "Draw your strength from me, Sarah." She yawned and laid her head on the bed. "We…*I* need you to stay alive," she whispered before her eyes closed and she fell into a fitful sleep.

How long she slept, Jo did not know but the distinct and constant rapping on the door had her lifting her head as the door opened. Standing immediately, she said, "Commander Clarke."

A bright smile wreathed the commander's lips as she saw the standing pilot until her eyes turned to the hospital bed and the other, very pale pilot. "Miss Laughlin, it's true. You both are alive," she said in amazement.

Jo cast her gaze on Sarah and saw that her chest was still rising and falling before she returned her attention to the commander. "We had quite a time," she whispered.

A genuinely concerned voice asked, "How is Sarah doing?"

"She hasn't regained consciousness for," she searched for the clock on the wall, "a long time now. Time doesn't seem to make sense anymore…so much has happened."

Commander Clarke gave Jo a critical look. "Have you slept or eaten since you got here?"

Jo shook her head.

"By the looks of you, Miss Laughlin, I'd say you are in need of a hot bath, clean clothes, and a soft bed."

A brief smile crossed Jo's face. "I haven't had a proper bath in almost three months. The clothes I am wearing were given to me by what seemed to be a poor farm family." Her eyes lifted to the commander. "I don't know how I can ever repay them for their generosity and help." Her eyes widened. "The two Frenchmen who helped us to get here…don't let them imprison them…they did nothing wrong…they helped us."

The commander moved further into the room until she was standing next to her pilot. "That has already been taken care of," she said softly. "I've arranged for a room in a billet for you to stay in until you feel strong enough to go back to Hatfield."

For the briefest of moments, Jo closed her eyes as she thought of Meg. "Is everyone still there?"

The Commander nodded. "When we heard that you and Sarah went down everyone cried but continued to do their jobs. I met with them all this morning. The smiles that have been missing from their faces returned." She let out a small laugh. "They were all trying to have deliveries down this way so they could come and see you both."

"I can't go back until I know Sarah is going to recover," she stated. "We went through a lot together and I owe that to her."

"Yes, I understand that, but you must remember that we are still at war and I will need you back at the job of ferrying soon."

"Right now, I am too tired to think of that. Once Sarah is awake, I will return to Hatfield."

"Excellent. Now, let's get you to that billet room and into a hot bath."

Jo took one last look at the still Sarah and gently patted her hand. "Clean clothes too," she said as she followed the commander out the door.

"Of course."

*

As Jo removed her bloodied clothes, she stopped and reached into a pocket inside the jacket. She pulled out the stone the woman gave her on the streamer and the shamrock Meg gave her for Christmas. Often over the last months, she would reach in her pocket and finger the items. As she recalled what each meant, she hoped that they would help in keeping her and Sarah safe. Now, as they rested in her palm, she smiled—they did indeed keep her safe.

Jo emerged from the room holding the tin bathtub and walked slowly down the hallway to the room assigned to her. The feel of the hot water over her body was wonderful, as was using real toilet paper. In the past, she hadn't appreciated the simple things in life but now she saw everything with new eyes. She opened the door to her room and looked at the inviting bed as she yawned. "I could sleep for days," she murmured as the robe she wore dropped to the floor. Pulling back the tightly tucked in sheets, her naked body slid between them.

"Oh," she moaned, not even noticing the scratchy starched sheets—she was in heaven. It didn't take long for her to fall into what would be another night of a sporadic sleep that never let her rest completely .Dreams that came and went were a mix of Jo running to find safety, to her being held safe in Meg's arms. At some point, Jo let her eyes open and she swore she saw Meg lying naked beside her. She wrapped her arms around the woman, feeling loved as she drifted back to sleep.

After being on alert for two straight months Jo's hearing tuned into anything out of the ordinary. Her fingers searched for a gun she could not find as she heard the sound of a door creaking open. Haunted eyes jerked open, as she was desperate to find the gun that had been her constant companion ever since she killed the German soldier.

"Who's there?" she asked in her most menacing voice.

"Why darlin', I was in the neighborhood and thought I'd pay you a visit."

Jo closed her eyes and tamped down the anger she was feeling. "Midge, what are you doing here? I didn't think snakes came out in the cold."

"Well, that's a fine how-do-you-do. I come all this way to see how you're doin' and you insult me. Do you have any idea how devastated I was when we thought you were dead?"

"I'm not buying into your bull, Midge. This is the first chance I've had to really sleep in months so I would appreciate it if you would crawl back under the rock you slithered out from."

Midge stayed rooted in place until there was a soft knock on the door. She opened it and her mouth opened, then shut. "Commander, how nice to see you."

"Exactly what are you doing here, Miss Reister?"

"I…I had to deliver a plane at Hawkinge and thought I'd stop by to see how my old friend is doing."

Dorothy Clarke eyed the tall, brash woman who, if she wasn't an excellent pilot, would not be part of her ATA ferry pool. "How did you get here, Miss Reister?"

"Train."

"How many planes are you scheduled to deliver today, Miss Reister?"

"Five."

"Then I'd suggest you get busy doing just that."

Midge looked at Jo and glared at the commander before she opened the door.

"One moment, Miss Reister."

Midge glared.

"When you return to Hatfield, please see First Officer Brannigan."

With a shrug, Midge scowled and closed the door behind her.

"Thank you," Jo said softly. "I'd get up but I don't have any clothes to wear."

Dorothy smiled. "That is exactly why I am here," she held up a small suitcase, "Your roommate put some of your clothes in here for you."

The thought of Meg packing a bag for her caused a big smile to grace her face. "Thank you and please thank Meg for me." Jo's brow creased. "She kept all my things? Surely after all this time they would be thrown out."

"Miss O'Brien insisted that you were not dead and you would be back, so she kept everything and asked to not have another roommate since you'd be back." Dorothy smiled fondly at the memory. "In all these months, her faith has never faltered."

Choked with emotion, Jo sucked in a deep breath to calm herself. "Have you heard anything about Sarah?"

"I'm on my way there now. Shall I wait for you to go with me?"

"Yes, please. It won't take long to get ready."

The Commander nodded. "I shall wait for you in the rest room."

Once the door closed, Jo practically leapt out of bed before she grabbed the small suitcase and held it close. Meg never gave up hope she thought as she placed the suitcase on the bed. When she opened it she saw an envelope with her name on it. A shaking hand picked up the envelope and carefully opened in. A tear coursed down her cheek as she recognized Meg's distinctive writing style.

My Dearest Jo,

You're back! I always knew that you were not lost or dead...I knew you'd come back to me. I didn't pack much for I hope you will be back in my arms soon. The Commander explained about Sarah and your need to stay with her. All I could do when she told me that was smile, for it is so like you to do that.

Unfortunately, Midge procured the only ferry that was going toward Portsmouth but know that the next one that comes up I will take and there will be no stopping me from seeing you. Know that I love you, Jo, and you are always in my heart.

Love,

Meg

Jo could not stop the flow of tears that rolled out of her eyes and down her cheeks. "I love you too, Meg. I always have," she whispered as she carefully put the letter back in the envelope before quickly dressing.

*

When Jo opened the door to Sarah's room, she was disappointed to see the woman lying so still in the bed. A nurse was in the room, busily doing her routine to ensure that the patient was on the mend.

"How is she today?" The Commander asked the petite woman who was shaking a thermometer.

"I've just come on," the nurse said. "From her chart I see that there isn't any change from when she arrived." She jotted something on a piece of paper held by a clip board.

"The doctor should be in soon and he can give you a better assessment. If you'll both please step out, I need to give her a quick bath.

Once the nurse left Sarah's room, Jo and Dorothy stood on either side of her bed.

With the back of her fingers, Jo stroked Sarah's face. "I've always liked Sarah," she began. "At first, I thought she was some spoiled rich girl with an expensive hobby." Her eyes lifted to look at the commander. "But I found out that isn't the case…she is a very brave and strong woman. Never once did she complain or refuse to go on." Jo sucked in a deep breath. "We both killed over there…she saved my life when it was in danger. In spite of watching as an innocent paid with his life for our kills, she pressed on with dignity and courage." Jo looked back to Sarah's face and for a long moment remained quiet. She finally said, "Grace, dignity, and a fierce desire to succeed…I know…she isn't spoiled…I trusted her with my life and she did not fail me."

"I have known Sarah and her parents for a number of years," Dorothy smiled, "she was always strong and confident, with a mind of her own. Spoiled, perhaps to some degree, but she knew what she wanted out of life and would, at times, throw caution to the wind and plunge headlong into whatever she was doing."

"She can't die," Jo whispered. "We can't let her die.

Both women turned and looked at the door as it opened. A smallish man with short cropped brunette hair, wearing a gray shirt, dark trousers held up with suspenders, and a bow tie walked into the room. "Commander," he said as he neared the bed.

"I need an update on her condition, Doctor Higgins."

The doctor looked at Jo and smiled. "Are you the one who was with her when she was shot?"

Jo nodded.

"Fine job of keeping pressure on her wound."

With a frown, Jo said, "I don't understand."

"Miss Faulkner was shot in the back. The bullet ricocheted off her spine and found its way through her gut, causing a great deal of damage before it exited her body. Had you not put pressure on the wound, she would have bled to death."

Jo's forehead furrowed. "All I did was hold her close to my body…she was shivering."

"That action saved her life."

"What is her prognosis?" the commander asked.

"She lost a lot of blood…that we've replaced. We also repaired the damage to her intestines and heavily sedated her so her body could rest as it initially heals. The next forty-eight hours are critical. The bullet perforated her large intestine and that let a great deal of waste expel to other parts of her body. Right now, the greatest danger is infection, which we are fighting with antibiotics. A short time ago, we gave her something that should counteract the sedatives and bring her back to consciousness." The doctor's eyes fixed on Sarah. "You should know that preliminary tests show there may be damage to her spinal cord."

"What does that mean?" Jo asked.

Brown eyes captured Jo's light blue ones. "She may have paralysis in at least one of her legs."

Jo looked at her friend then back to the doctor. "But that is not certain, is it?"

"No," Doctor Higgins replied. "She first needs to regain consciousness."

As if on cue, Sarah let out a small moan and opened her eyes. After she shook her head as if shaking off the drugs, her eyes fixed on Jo before looking at Commander Clarke. She opened her mouth but nothing came out. Trying once again, she whispered, "We made it."

Jo took Sarah's hand in hers. "Yes, we made it, Sarah. We are safe now."

Sarah's eyes grew wide. "What about Charles and Henri?" she asked.

"They are fine," the commander answered, fixing each pilot with a stern warning from her eyes.

Silence ensued as the doctor examined Sarah. When he was done, he said, "Would you like something to eat?"

A face filled with worry looked at him. "Have my parents been notified?"

The doctor shrugged, "I don't know." He hesitated for a moment then said, "I will have someone bring you breakfast."

Once the doctor left the room, the commander said, "I have notified your parents and they are on their way."

Sarah let out an audible sigh of relief.

Jo pinned the commander with her gaze. "Where are the men that helped us?" she demanded.

Unfazed by the harsh tone, Commander Clarke said, "I believe that they are with British Intelligence."

Jo frowned. "Why? They did nothing but help us get back here. They are *not* the enemy."

"No, I know they are not. Just know that they are in good hands and it is hoped that they can help fight the war from within France."

"How?" Sarah asked.

For a long moment, the commander remained silent. "I cannot say any more on this subject."

"Can I at least see them to thank them for helping us?" Jo asked.

"That is impossible."

*

Sarah's eyes brightened as she saw her mother and father, accompanied by her fiancé, Edward Blankenship, enter her room. Her mother, with arms outstretched, walked quickly to her daughter with tears streaming down her cheeks.

"Oh, Sarah," the older woman cried, "I couldn't believe it when they said you were gone and now look, you are back."

Sarah hugged her mother close and felt bereft when she pulled away. Her eyes then cast on her father who also had tears in his eyes.

"I never believed it for a moment, even at the memorial service I said *no, she isn't gone.* The happiest day of my life was when Dorothy called and told us you were alive and in Portsmouth."

The closeness of her father told Sarah just how happy he was. When he moved aside, she saw Edward, the man she was to marry, lean heavily on a cane as he moved to the side of her hospital bed. "Oh, Edward, what has happened to you?" she asked, seeing the haunted look in the eyes of the man she loved.

"A bit of bad luck, I'm afraid. I was hit and had to crash land."

Sarah shivered, understanding the look in his eyes and wondering if she had the same look. "It is a terrifying experience," she whispered.

Edward leaned in and kissed Sarah's cheek. "Yes, a life altering experience," he said as he pulled away.

"Brenda was such a dear through all this," Elizabeth Faulkner interjected. "She came to visit us every chance she got. I was always buoyed by the letters she wrote too."

"How is she?" Sarah asked as she eyed Edward carefully.

"The last I heard, she was over the moon that you were back."

Sarah smiled. "Yes, that would be like her."

An awkward silence filled the room.

"Darling," Michael, Sarah's father, said. "Is there anything we can get you? Anything you need?"

"Yes," Elizabeth said. "Something to read?"

Sarah gave them a weak smile. "Would you mind if I spoke with Edward for a few minutes?"

"No, no, not at all. Come, darling," Elizabeth said. "Let's find a nice cup of tea."

Once her parents had left, Sarah patted the bed. "Come sit with me."

Edward reluctantly made his way to the bed but didn't sit. "I...don't know what to say, Sarah." He stalled for time. "You know what I thought when they said you had crashed and were dead?"

"No, please tell me," Sarah said, not knowing where her fiancé was going.

"I thought how lucky you were."

Sarah's eyes widened. "Why would you think such a thing, Edward?"

"Because you wouldn't have to live with reliving it every night," he sobbed. "I can't get the bloody plane doing a nosedive out of my head, Sarah."

Sarah held out her arms. "Come here."

Edward refused to move. "I can't...not now...give me time, Sarah...please, give me time." He looked at her and shook his head. "I don't think I can marry you, Sarah."

"Give yourself time, Edward...give us time," Sarah said trying to quell the panic she was feeling. "Please, Edward talk to me."

Edward shook his head and Sarah watched as the man she promised her heart to, turn and quickly leave the room—she couldn't shake a feeling of foreboding. Within seconds the door opened again and she looked, hoping to see Edward again. Instead, Jo was standing there and all Sarah could do was cry.

Rushing to Sarah's side, Jo bent down and gently hugged her friend. "What is wrong, Sarah?"

Chapter Twenty-Four

March 1941
Hatfield Ferry Pool No. 5
Southampton, England

Once *Annie* had landed and Midge disembarked, she headed for the office to get her next assignment. Before she reached the door, First Officer Shannon Brannigan stopped her.

"Where are you goin', Miss Reister?" Shannon asked.

Midge tried to push past the woman. When she failed she said, "Get out of my way. I need to pick up my new assignment."

"You're not much for taken' notice of rank, are you?"

"Not from the likes of you, I'm not," Midge said as she once again tried to push past the woman.

"Pity that. I do believe, Miss Reister, Commander Clarke ordered you to speak to me when you got back."

Midge stopped and looked into the dark blue eyes that searched her face. "What happened between the commander and me is none of your concern. Now, let me get by so I can get my next assignment."

Shannon laughed and shook her head. "I'm afraid it is the end of the line for you, Miss Reister."

Midge frowned. "What do you mean?" she demanded.

"You are to go to your quarters and stay there until I come to get you. At that time, I will take you to the commander's office, where you will meet with her concerning disciplinary matters." She fixed Midge with a hard gaze. "Do I make myself clear?"

With arms across her chest, Midge scowled at the woman. "You can't make me do that…I am not a British citizen and you can't order me around like that."

With a quick motion, Shannon seized Midge's arm. "That is correct. You are not a British citizen but as long as you are in this country working for the ATA, you *will* submit to the orders your superiors give you. I, Miss Reister, *am* your superior. Now, go to your quarters and wait there for me," Shannon ordered in a low menacing voice.

Something in the tone of the woman's voice told Midge it would be advisable to do as the First Officer said. With a curt nod, she walked toward the billet, wondering if she had finally broke the camel's back.

*

When Shannon knocked on the door, Midge got up from her bed then opened the door.

"Come with me," was all the first officer said.

In what would be termed meek for Midge, she followed her superior yet held her head high, her back straight, and her shoulders squared.

Once they arrived at Commander Clarke's office, Shannon motioned for Midge to take a chair. "Stay here until I come for you," she ordered before she *knocked on the door and disappeared inside.*

Shit, shit, shit, how am I going to get out of this? Midge then smiled, knowing no matter what the situation, she always came out ahead. When the door opened and Shannon's index finger beckoned her in, Midge felt her stomach flip and shook it off. Squaring her shoulders, she stood then entered Commander Clarke's office.

"Please take a seat, Miss Reister," the commander said.

With a glare at the First Officer, Midge took the seat indicated before her brown eyes fixed on the commander. "Why am I here?" she asked. "You told us that the ferrying of planes was essential, so why am I here and not doing that?"

Dorothy looked at the woman across from her and shook her head. "I hardly think you are in a position to ask me anything, Miss Reister. Yes, ferrying planes is vital, but it is equally vital that the pilots who ferry those planes know how to follow orders. If there is not a chain of command that everyone follows, then we shall have anarchy. Which brings us to why you are here, Miss Reister."

Not having heard the commander speak in such a menacing tone before, Midge squirmed in her chair. She opened her mouth to speak but stopped when Commander Clarke held up her hand.

"I am certain you have a considerable amount to say, Miss Reister, but now is not the time." Dorothy opened a folder and looked at the contents. "Since you have been here, Miss Reister, you have disobeyed orders fifteen times. I chose to overlook most of them for you are an excellent pilot and the ATA needs pilots of your caliber."

Midge let a cocky smile cross her face.

"If I were you, Miss Reister, I wouldn't be so quick to smile. The ATA needs pilots that are proficient in flying but also have the skills to follow orders that they are given. You have repeatedly demonstrated your lack of respect for the chain of command." Gray eyes fixed on the blonde pilot and held her gaze for a moment. "I should have suspended you late last May when you pulled that stunt that made the ground defenses fire on you and your fellow pilots. For some reason, Lady Smyth-Armstrong thought you were worth defending." The Commander shook her head. "I should have gone with my instincts in that matter."

"Listen…" Midge began before the commander held up her hand and shook her head.

Her gaze went to her First Officer then back to Midge. "There is nothing you can say at this point that will change my decision. You will go with First Officer Brannigan to your quarters where you will collect all your personal items and pack them for your trip back to America.'

Midge was on her feet. "You can't do that!"

"Sit down," ordered Dorothy. When she saw the pilot retake her seat she said, "I can, and have done that." She took an official document and held it out to Midge. "Here is the order for your deportation, Miss Reister. Once you have collected your belongs, you will be taken to the United States Embassy, where you will remain until such time as arrangements can be made to send you back to the United States."

Defiant, Midge raised her voice and said, "*No*, I won't go and you can't make me! You need me…I'm the best pilot you've got."

"I will *not* discuss this further with you, Miss Reister. My decision *will not* be revoked. You may be a good pilot but you are a detriment to the ATA. Your actions have jeopardized your fellow pilots, along with countless others." The Commander stood. "That is all, Miss Reister, you are dismissed."

Midge was about to speak when Shannon grabbed her arm and whispered, "You should quit while you are ahead, Miss Reister."

Midge yanked to free her arm and the grip tightened. "Let go of me!"

"There is nothing you can do. Just come along with me quietly and keep your dignity, Miss Reister."

"Never," cried Midge.

Shannon stopped and gave Midge a stern look. "Is this how you want the others to see you?" she said, pointing to two security guards waiting outside the door. "The choice is yours, Miss Reister.

Midge nodded and began to walk back to the barracks with her head held high and her heart heavy with shame.

*

Jo entered the rest room of the women's barracks and wasn't surprised to find no one there. It was, after all, the middle of the day and despite what she and Sarah went through, the war still raged. Planes still needed ferrying and it was the mission of the ferry pool to provide that support. Just as she was about to go up the stairs, someone from behind her said, "Welcome back, mate."

"Brenda," Jo said softly as she turned and took the woman in her arms, giving her a tight hug.

With eyes filled with happiness, Brenda said, "Is Sarah here too?"

Jo wrapped her fingers loosely around Brenda's forearm and gently guided her back into the rest room. Once they were sitting on a large leather sofa, Jo took Brenda's hand in hers. "Did anyone tell you that Sarah was injured?"

A hand went immediately to her mouth, as Brenda let out a low cry. "Yes, but the commander wouldn't tell me how bad. Please tell me what happened?"

"She was shot while we were escaping from France. She's in the Naval Base hospital in Portsmouth."

"Will she be ok?" Brenda asked softly.

"She is mending." Jo hesitated. "They think she might be paralyzed or have some sort of impairment to her legs."

Brenda sobbed quietly, taking in large gulps of air ever so often. "Can I visit her?"

"Yes, I think she would love to see you, Brenda."

The younger woman stood immediately. "I will have to find the commander and arrange to go to Sarah.

"Wait," Jo said, grabbing Brenda's wrist. "There's more."

"Oh, I don't like the sound of that."

"You do know that her fiancé was shot down and injured, don't you?"

"Of course, he was at her memorial service."

Jo rubbed a hand over her face. "Apparently, he is in a bad place and told Sarah he no longer wanted to marry her."

"He was right devastated at the service." Brenda frowned. "Why would he say such a thing?"

"He didn't say but Sarah's father spoke to him and found out it had something to do with his injury and him not being able to have kids."

"My poor friend," Brenda whispered. "She was there for me. Now I must try to do the same for her …I need to see the commander immediately." She looked at Jo.

"Go," she said patting Brenda's shoulder. "You will be just what she needs to heal."

Tear filled eyes looked at the American. "She saved me."

As Jo watched Brenda walk away she whispered, "She saved me too."

*

As she pushed open the door to the room she shared with Meg, Jo's breath caught when she saw the woman she loved sitting on a bed. "You're here," she cried as she rushed into Meg's arms. Jo held Meg tightly, never wanting to miss the feeling of Meg's body against hers again.

"I knew you'd come back ta me," Meg whispered as she breathed in the smell that was uniquely Jo.

Their kiss was long and slow as they melted into each other.

"I love you, Meg."

"As I love you, dear sweet, Jo. I never let go of my faith that you'd be comin' back ta me."

The tears and the anxiety that Jo had shoved into the background so she could be strong and survive, came flooding out as Meg held Jo in her arms. Her sobs seemed never ending, just as Meg's comfort was.

"I was so scared," sobbed Jo. "Everywhere we turned there was danger." She sucked in a breath. "I killed a man, Meg. I didn't even stop to acknowledge what I'd done…we had to keep moving…keep hiding…keep trying to outwit the Germans."

"Shh, sweet Jo, you're safe now." Meg kissed Jo's head as she cradled the woman she loved close to her. "I've got you. No need to fight it anymore. Just let it all out, darlin'."

For the first time in many months, Jo felt safe and loved yet her tears continued unabated.

There was a soft knock on the door but it went unheeded as Meg continued to embrace Jo with her love. Now was Jo's time and there was no way she'd let anyone intrude on that. "I've got you, my love," she whispered as Jo let a new series of tears fall.

Over the next several hours, Jo sat on Meg's bed surrounded by loving arms that held her safe from the outside world. In the late hours of the day, Jo let out a sigh and whispered, "Please never leave me," to Meg.

The reply, a kiss, which lingered as it built in intensity. Soon lips tasted each other as Meg and Jo renewed the deep abiding bond they had.

As her heart rate slowed and she was able to catch her breath, Meg snuggled up to Jo. "Never leave me again, Jo," Meg whispered into an ear. "I love you so much that when you were gone my body hurt, craving your touch. I never knew such a feelin'" She kissed Jo's lips before she pulled back and looked deep into her eyes. "What happened to you, my love?"

"I love you so much, Meg." She lifted her head. "I just want to hold you and feel your body next to mine. Can we talk about it later?"

"Yes."

For several hours, they lay entangled in each other's arms rejoicing at being together. Jo held Meg as she stared at the ceiling, lost in feelings she did not understand. The sights and sounds of her time in France haunted her dreams and all her waking hours. The joy and safety that Meg instilled in her could only assuage those images for a short time. A tear escaped from the corner of her eye and she willed herself not to let any more fall. She knew she needed to put the events of the last several months behind her— how to do that was the question.

Chapter Twenty-Five

March 1941
Royal Naval Hospital Haslar
Portsmouth, England

Brenda pushed through the doors of the Royal Naval Hospital in Portsmouth and walked directly to the first person she saw in white. "Can you help me?" she asked of a stout woman dressed in white who sat behind a desk.

"Certainly, my dear."

"I'm looking for my friend, Sarah Faulkner."

The woman smiled at Brenda before she ran her finger down a paper. "Yes, here she is. Take the lift to the second floor and ask the nurse there to show you to her room."

"Thank you," Brenda said as she hurried to catch a waiting lift. Once on the upper floor she went to a tall desk and inquired about Sarah.

"This is her room," a blonde nurse said as she pushed the door open. "Please don't stay long. She needs her rest."

Brenda nodded and walked into the darkened room. A dim light was on over the head of the bed and she gulped when she saw Sarah's profile. Soon she was standing next to the bed, watching her friend's chest rise and fall with each breath.

"Don't just stand there gawking, Brenda. Come give me a hug."

With a bright smile filling her face, Brenda complied by bending over and gently engulfing Sarah in her arms. "I'm so glad to see you, Sarah. Crikey, two days ago I never imagined I'd see you again."

Sarah patted the bed. "Please sit and tell me what you've been doing since I've been gone."

Brenda sat on the edge of the bed and looked earnestly into Sarah's eyes—she saw pain. "My life since New Year's is bog standard next to what you went through."

Sarah laughed and held her side. "I've missed you, Brenda. What exactly is *bog standard*."

Brenda shrugged as she felt her face heat up. "Nothing special."

For a few seconds Sarah closed her eyes before blowing out a long breath. "I was terrified most of the time." She refused to make eye contact with her friend. "Jo was magnificent and so positive that we would get out of there in one piece..." she gestured at her body, "I'm still in one piece, but damaged."

"Your coming back answered every prayer I said each day...losing you left a big hole in my life, Sarah. Your parents asked me to stand with the family at your memorial service." She swiped at a tear she promised herself she'd not let fall. "Your mum and dad asked if I'd come stay with them when I had time off." A slight smile wreathed her lips as she lifted one shoulder. "I didn't have the heart to tell them we didn't get time off."

In a soft voice, Sarah said, "They just kept hugging me when they were here. They had to go back home for a day to take care of a family matter but should be back here later today...," she paused. "Edward was here too...he's not doing so well."

"Why?"Brenda asked as she saw the pain in Sarah's eyes.

"I'm not sure, Brenda...he broke off our engagement."

Brenda leaned over and held Sarah as close as she could. "I'm so sorry to hear that," she whispered. "Jo told me you were shot."

"Yes, we were making our way to a fishing trawler that was going to take us across the Channel. German soldiers came by in a vehicle, flashing a big spotlight across the sand. When they saw us, they began firing." Tears ran down her cheek. "I was just about to step onto the pier when I felt the bullet hit my back…"

Except for the clicking of a wall clock, the room was still as Brenda waited to see if Sarah would say more.

"I wanted Jo to go without me…to be safe…I was injured and knew I would slow her down." Sarah stared at distant corner of the wall. "She wouldn't leave me there and picked me up, held me close and carried me to the waiting boat. I'm not sure what happened after that. All I know was that I felt safe. The next thing I remember is waking up here with the commander and Jo by my bed."

"Oh, Sarah," Brenda cried.

"Wait, there's more."

Brenda nodded.

"The bullet injured my spine," Sarah said in a trembling voice. "I might not ever walk again…or fly." Sobs began wracking Sarah's shoulders. Once her tears subsided, her shaky voice said, "You know…the funny…thing?"

"No."

"Edward said when he heard I was dead, he thought I was lucky." She swiped at a tear. "I didn't understand why he would think that…but now I do."

"How so, Sarah?"

"The terror never leaves," she whispered.

Moving carefully, Brenda leaned in and held her friend close. When the sobs dissipated, she looked in Sarah's face and smiled before she stroked her cheek. "Shh, don't cry, Sarah."

"Look at me, lying here, unable to even go to the bathroom by myself. I don't even know if I will ever fly again."

Brenda ran her hand up and down Sarah's arm in a soothing fashion. "As far as I was concerned, my life was over before it began, then I saw this flying machine come out of the sky. All I knew of living was hard work, beatings, and abuse. It was you, Sarah, who saved me...who showed me that I could have a better life...deserved a better life. Had you not saved me, I probably would be dead, for that was where my life was going." Her fingers gentled over Sarah's hand. "You saved me. Please let me help you get better...help you fly again."

"But, there's nothing more to do. The doctor said, in time, he will know how permanent the damage will be."

"Then let me be here for you, Sarah. Have faith in me, as I had in you."

A smile filled Sarah's face. "While we were on the run, I asked Jo if she was scared. She told me that her father always said *scared is when you no longer have faith*." In a whisper, she added, "I have faith in you, Brenda."

For the next several hours, Brenda and Sarah talked, laughed, and cried. When her parents came into the room, they could see and feel the difference in their daughter— she was buoyant and happy and they knew they had Brenda to thank.

*

Once everyone left, Sarah looked out the window, unable to stop the flow of tears. She had put on a good act for her parents and Brenda but that was all it was—a show. Even now, as tears trickled down her cheeks, the memories haunted her. The feel of the knife going into the soldiers flesh and the gurgling sound of his last breaths preoccupied her every waking hour. When she did sleep, it was often fitful, full of planes crashing, the sound of gunfire filling the air as an innocent man fell, and running, always running. Although her parents' and Brenda's offers to help her were sincere, she knew that they couldn't help her. No one could. "Edward was right…I'd be better off dead."

*

Michael and Elizabeth Faulkner, along with Brenda, stood next to the hospital bed that Sarah had occupied for a month. She had recovered fully from her injuries but walked with a slight limp of her right leg that necessitated the use of a cane. Sarah emerged from the bathroom and smiled at her family. The news that Edward had completely disappeared did not surprise her, for there were times over the last month that she too wanted to run and hide. It was what Jo had shown her more than a week ago that changed her attitude…

The only way Sarah could go on was through the frequent visits that Jo made. She was the only one who understood the demons that now were a part of both their lives. It was Jo who convinced her she would fly again by telling her that there was a reason for the ATA being called *Ancient Tattered Airmen*, and she was part of that illustrious group.

"But what if I can't do it, Jo?"

"The first time I went up after I got back, I thought my stomach was going to rebel against me and I'd have my breakfast all over the cockpit," Jo said with a chuckle. "But once I was airborne and looking out at the vast sky around me," she shrugged, "I knew I was where I belonged."

"But you're whole, Jo," Sarah countered.

With a nod, Jo softly said, "And so are you. Be right back."

Sarah's eyes looked at Jo when she returned then at what she was pushing. "What are you doing?"

"How long has it been since you left this room, Sarah?"

"I haven't been outside of here...I can't walk...don't you remember that?" she asked angrily.

The door opened again and a tall nurse dressed in white came in. "Ready" she inquired.

Jo nodded and together they lifted Sarah out of the bed and into the wheelchair.

"Thank you," Jo said to the nurse before turning her gaze on her visibly upset friend. "It's time you saw something other than these four walls." With that, Jo pushed Sarah out into the brightly lit hallway. "You'll be surprised at what you might find out here."

Sarah kept her arms crossed and a scowl on her face as Jo wheeled her through the various wards. "Why are you doing this?" she finally asked.

"So you can see."

When they arrived in the vestibule where other patients were sitting in wheelchairs, Sarah began to look around. There were about two dozen men sitting in wheelchairs speaking in low tones to one another. Jo pushed Sarah's wheelchair up to a man strapped into a chair with his chin touching his chest. "This is Mark," Jo said.

The man struggled but eventually he lifted his head and smiled.

"Mark is a navigator on one of the big bombers." Jo smiled at the man. "One of the RAF's finest."

The man let out a strangled laugh.

"Can't wait to be back out there, can you, Mark?"

Mark's eyes danced as he tried to speak. "I'm gonna get those bastards," he mumbled.

Jo moved closer to the man before she bent down and gave him a hug. "I'll see you again," she said before going back to Sarah.

Sarah was quiet as the wheelchair journey continued. What she saw horrified her. She remembered how bravely George Oyler faced life. When they got back to her room and after the nurse and Jo lifted her back into bed, she looked at Jo. "How do you know Mark?" she asked softly.

"I was waiting to see you last week and was directed to the vestibule to wait." Her eyes focused on the floor. "What I saw humbled me, Sarah. There were all these men with injuries I had never contemplated. Mark reminded me of George and how he suffered at the hands of the enemy." Her eyes focused on Sarah's light blue eyes. "You said you were not whole, Sarah. How can you say that after seeing what those men have suffered? Many are missing limbs, while others have faces burned beyond recognition. Men like Mark must face the rest of their lives with injury to their brain…that is the horror that war brought to all of them. Don't you dare say you are not whole, Sarah…don't you dare."

Sarah looked away in shame.

"Yes, we have nightmares of all the horror we saw but it is nothing compared to what those men went through." Her fingers gently grasped Sarah's chin and turned her face so she could see the woman's eyes. "Before I saw those men, I felt like a shell of who I was."

"I know how that feels."

"Yes, I know you do." Jo smiled warmly. "I went back to Hatfield eager to see Meg…eager to tell her how I truly felt about her. I told her all about what happened to us, thinking it would make the dreams go away—it didn't. Even in the safety of her arms, I felt alone and scared."

Sarah clutched Jo's hand and held it close to her heart.

"It wasn't until I saw those brave men that I realized just how lucky I was. Somehow it made what we went through seem so inconsequential."

"Have the nightmares stopped, Jo?"

Jo shook her head. "No, not entirely. When I wake up in a cold sweat and terrified, I think of them and again realize just how lucky I am."

Sarah contemplated Jo's words as she remembered the men in the vestibule. "You know, as I looked at all those wounded men in the eyes, I saw the same thing—hope."

"Yes, and pride in their country."

"Thank you, Jo."

Sarah had visited the vestibule several times a day since Jo had taken her there. For hours she sat with Mark reading Alexandre Dumas's *The Count of Monte Cristo*. As the days went by, other injured men wheeled next to her, engrossed in the story. By the time she read, *"...human wisdom is summed up in two words— wait and hope,* and closed the book for the last time, the group around her had grown to thirty.

"Tomorrow I must leave you all," she told the group of injured soldiers. "I wish I could continue to visit every day but I need to go back and do my job."

A well of sighs filled the room.

"Each one of you have buoyed my spirits and made me realize that not going forward is not an option. It is to you, the brave soldiers who have given your all for our England, that I dedicate my life." After hugs and goodbyes, Sarah returned to her room and for the first time since the plane crash, knew that there was no higher calling than that of helping her country defeat tyranny.

Now, Sarah looked at her parents and dear friend, Brenda, who were there to take her back to her childhood home. They were all looking at her expectantly and she loathed bursting the bubble of happiness that was in her parents' faces but she knew she must. She had no other choice but to resume her duties with the ATA.

Chapter Twenty-Six

April 1941
Hatfield Ferry Pool No. 5
Southampton, England

Two Spitfires, flown by Second Officers Hiller and Laughlin, landed with the squeal of their tires as the breaks were applied, before they taxied toward a hangar. Five minutes later, the transport plane, affectionately known as *Annie*, touched down on the same tarmac. Once it came to a stop and the door opened, the occupants of the plane disembarked.

Jo and Brenda, waiting at the bottom of the stairway, both grinned when Sarah appeared in the doorway. They waved and watched as Sarah made her way to them with the aid of two men. Once on the ground, Sarah was engulfed in the arms of her waiting friend.

"It's bonzer to have you back, mate," Brenda said as Sarah hugged her back.

Sarah looked at Brenda and smiled. "It's good to be back. " Her attention turned to Jo, who was standing off to the side."Hello," she said with a smile. "Thanks for the escort."

Jo moved toward the woman who shared harrowing times and memories that neither would forget. The bond they shared of mutual memories would last beyond the war and, most probably, throughout their lives.

Sarah took in a deep breath before she leaned on her cane and began to walk toward their barracks. "I've missed this place," she whispered as she moved along at a slow pace.

"And we all missed you, Sarah," Brenda said as she put her arm into the crook of Sarah's arm. "Just lean on me…I won't let you fall."

Sarah smiled at her friend. "I know you won't." She watched Jo, who was walking ahead of them, and wondered if the time would ever come when she felt safe again…if either of them would ever feel safe. Life, she now knew, was fleeting and in the blink of an eye, it could end without warning. The face of the German soldier she killed always haunted her. She could see the grimace on his dead face and not for the first time, wonder what his last thoughts were and if he had a family that would miss him. She knew without a doubt, that had she not stabbed the man, he would have killed Jo. She did the right thing but the self loathing she felt did not disappear.

"You all right?" Brenda asked when she felt Sarah shiver.

"Yes. I can't wait to sink into a nice warm bath and soak all the grime of the last months away again."

Brenda, not buying Sarah's words, eyed her friend. "That is something I can do for you, mate."

With a weak smile, Sarah looked at her friend. "I can always count on you, Brenda. Why is Jo in such a hurry?"

Not looking at Sarah, Brenda said, "Don't know," as they reached the door and she swung it open.

With her mouth open, Sarah gaped at her fellow pilots who, gathered in the rest room, were smiling at her. A large sign reading, *Welcome Back Sarah* stretched across a doorway. Her hand went to her mouth as tears escaped her eyes. She was back, back among her fellow pilots, who all welcomed her home. Her eyes found Jo, who was standing with Meg, and smiled a *thank you.*

The first person to approach Sarah was Commander Clarke, who smiled at her and held out her hand. "It is good to have you back, Miss Faulkner. Thank you for your service to the Crown. Your tenacity and bravery is what brought you back to us."

Sarah let go of the commander's hand and nodded. "I had a lot of time to think while in hospital and I don't think I was brave, as much as I was determined not to die."

"Bravery comes in all forms, Miss Faulkner." The commander's eyes swept the room "Everyone here, in one way or another, is brave every day, for it is the love of county that drives us onward in our fight to save England."

Sarah closed her eyes and nodded. "Yes," she said.

"I had best let the others greet you before we need to get back to the business of war. Are you ready to resume ferrying?"

"Yes, I can't wait."

"Good, check the roster tomorrow for your assignments. You can take the rest of today to sort things out here." The commander smiled and moved away from Sarah as one by one, the other pilots, mechanics, and ground crew, came up to Sarah and shook her hand, hugged her, or did both.

"Ladies and gentlemen, our short respite from the war is over and we must get back to our duties," the commander announced and everyone began filing out of the rest room.

Only Jo and Sarah remained as they stood in close contact, speaking in soft tones.

"Are you ok?" Jo asked.

"Yes, for the most part," Sarah answered. "The nightmares still haunt me but not as much as they did."

Jo hugged Sarah and whispered, "Whoever said *time heals* didn't know what they were talking about."

Sarah let out a breath and wrapped her arms around Jo. "I have to believe that *is* right or I won't be able to go on, Jo. If we lose hope, then all is lost and we die."

"I will always be here for you, Sarah."

"Only you and I share the bond of what happened to us, Jo." She released her friend and took a step back."I need to get back to flying…I need to take my life back and continue to do my job to help fight for freedom from the Germans. We saw what they did to George Oyler and all those brave men in hospital and that cannot continue," she noted with sadness in her voice.

For several minutes, Jo considered Sarah's words. "I know others will be tested much as we were, if not more so, Sarah, and not all will survive. Perhaps one day, when the war is over, we can go back to France and thank the Oyler's, Charles, and the fisherman who brought us to safety."

"I would like that." Sarah patted her friend's arm. "For now, we must make sure that the RAF pilots have the planes to fight the enemy." Sarah looked into Jo's eyes. "How did you feel when you first went up after you returned?"

Jo smiled. "At first, I was nervous when I went up by myself." She let out a chuckle that originated low in her throat. "As the plane left the ground, all my worry disappeared as I realized there was nothing more exhilarating as being one with the sky." With a quick nod, she said, "Get that bath, Sarah." A serene look crossed Jo's face. "When I got back here, it was the best bath I ever took. I will get back to flying and tomorrow, my friend, you will take to the sky again."

*

Sarah woke with a smile on her face as she stretched. Perhaps it was being back at Hatfield or the safety she felt around Brenda that shut out the nightmares that had plagued her for so long.

"Wake up and get ready to fly, Sarah," Brenda said. "You don't want everyone to think you're a no-hoper, do you?"

Sarah laughed. "How I've missed you, Brenda. Please enlighten me as to what a *no-hoper* is."

"Umm, you know, like you aren't up for the job…umm…incompetent."

"Well, I certainly don't want anyone to think that."

"Then get your arse going so we can have a bite to eat before we fly."

With her hand flat and at her brow, Sarah gave her friend a crisp salute. "It won't take me long…I've been waiting for this for months.

*

The chatter around the table at breakfast made Sarah smile—it was as she remembered.

Bess Potter, who sat across from Sarah, smiled before she asked, "Did the Navy flyers give you any hints while you were at Portsmouth?"

"Are you kidding? They never let me see anything but the hospital."

"I flew a Hawker Hurricane the other day," Lady Armstrong said.

"The modified version?" Jo asked.

"Yes. It was an interesting flight."

"How so?" asked Meg.

"It was fully fitted. When I delivered it, one of the pilots said that it was the plane he preferred to fly."

"How did it handle…any problems?" Jo asked.

"I didn't have a problem."

"A plane we ferry without a problem? Surely you are joking," Sarah said with a chuckle.

Everyone around the table laughed as the volume of the chatter increased.

"Crikey!" exclaimed Brenda. "Do you see what time it is? We'd better get our assignments if we don't want to end up like Midge."

Chairs were hurriedly pushed back as they all stood up and quickly made their way out of the dining hall.

"What happened to Midge?" Sarah asked Jo as they crossed the tarmac.

"Deported."

Sarah stopped and grabbed Jo's arm wrapping her fingers around it. "Deported…why…when?"

"After she pulled the stunt of coming to the hospital in Portsmouth to see me instead of coming directly back here, the commander confined her to quarters until she was sent to the embassy, where she spent a week before taking a steamer back to the States."

"Are you ok with that?" Sarah asked as the neared their destination.

"Midge was trouble when I first met her…your country is better off without her."

*

With her day's ferrying schedule in hand, Sarah made her way to a Spitfire she was flying to Black Isle in Scotland. She welcomed the longer flight for it would give her more time to fly. Her stomach did a flip as she thought about flying solo again and as she neared the plane, it was in full revolt.

She did her usual inspection of the exterior of the plane and thought, "I shouldn't have eaten breakfast." Once she climbed into the cockpit, her eyes did a visual of the instruments before she started the plane.

Sarah pulled back and the Spitfire lifted toward the sky. As her plane soared into the atmosphere, she rejoiced in the freedom it afforded her. Up there among the clouds, safe in the cocoon of metal, all that had happened to her disappeared, as she became one with the plane, secure in the knowledge that she was a survivor.

Epilogue

World War II raged on for the next four years, culminating with the German forces surrendering in May of 1945. The ATA Museum indicates that the pilots of the ATA flew a total of 415,000 hours and delivered over 309,000 aircraft of 130 types. By the end of the war, the ATA had 650 pilots, with 110 of them being women. Over one hundred ATA pilots were lost, fifteen of whom were women.

In 1943, the British government was the first to recognize equal pay for equal work and began paying the women of the ATA the same as their male counterparts.

With the end of the war, the ATA completed its mission and disbanded, leaving few opportunities for female pilots to find jobs. Yet, the small band of fearless female pilots continued to grow and, just as they had made inroads in aviation history, they continued their march forward. It is perhaps through their courageous efforts and dedication that women throughout the world have the recognition of being capable pilots.

About the Author

Erin O'Reilly resides in the Texas Hill Country on Lake LBJ. Erin has previously lived in various cities around the world. When not enjoying the lake, she owns and runs a small computer consulting business. A lifelong bird watcher, Erin also likes to cook, sew, read, and do various crafts in her spare time. Erin belongs to the Sapphic Readers, which is a lesbian book club in Austin, Texas.

First challenged by a friend to write a story, Erin has since written numerous online and publish works. Her story Deception was a GCLS Finalist in 2008. That book also garnered the Sapphic Readers Award in 2009. Story creation involving strong characters always seems to dictate the story and invade her mind at all hours. It always amazes her when the characters she is developing suddenly take on a life of their own and lead the story down a completely different path. If the characters make an impact on the storyline, the story is better for it since they are the ones who tell their story.

E-Books, Limited First Edition Print, Print, Free e-books

Visit our website for more publications available online.

www.affinityebooks.com

Published by Affinity E-Book Press NZ Ltd

Canterbury, New Zealand

Registered company 2517228